The Talking Hills

Contents

Capper Fireside Library

*F*eaturing
the most popular novels previously
published in *Capper's* magazine, as well as
original novels by favorite *Capper's* authors, the
Capper Fireside Library presents the best of fiction in
quality softcover editions for the family library. Born out of
the great popularity of *Capper's* serialized fiction, this
series is for readers of all ages who love a good
story. So curl up in a comfortable chair,
flip the page, and let the storyteller
whisk you away into the world
of this novel from the
*Capper Fireside
Library.*

————————◆————————

Published by Capper Press
1503 SW 42nd, Topeka, Kansas 66609

Cover Illustration: Bruce Bealmear
Editor: Samantha Adams
Assistant to the Editor: Pat Thompson

ISBN 0-941678-46-6
First printing, October 1994
Printed and bound in the United States of America

————————◆————————

For more information about Capper Press titles,
or to place an order, please call:
(Toll-free) 1-800-678-5779

The Talking Hills

LETHA BOYER

A sequel to *Of These Contented Hills*

CAPPER PRESS
Topeka, Kansas

CHAPTER ONE

Country Hospitality

I had fallen asleep on the sofa again. I woke to the feel of Davy's hand brushing the hair back from my face.

"You gonna sleep all day?" he chided, his voice gentle.

I stretched lazily and snuggled deeper into the quilt. "What time is it?" I asked drowsily.

"Almost five o'clock."

"Five o'clock!" I exclaimed, becoming wider awake. "My goodness! I've been asleep for three hours."

"Closer to four. That sayin', eatin' for two, does it apply to sleepin', too?"

"Evidently. At least for me. There were so many things I needed to do today, too."

"They'll wait. Guess what? I jist come from Mom's an' she's some perturbed. Miz Baxter stopped by an' told Mom that she heard we was goin' to have twins."

"What?"

He nodded, a quirky grin on his face. "Said Miz Adams told her an' Miz Wilson told her. Mom wanted to know why she was th' last one to know."

I groaned. "I know how that rumor started. Mrs. Wilson stopped by school yesterday. In the course of our conversation, I mentioned that my mother is a twin. That's all it takes around here."

"It's prob'ly all over th' countryside by now."

"Oh well, there's lots worse things they could be saying. I should get up. You're probably getting hungry."

"Mom's invited us over to eat with her. She's fixin' fried rabbit an' gravy. Sure did smell good. Want to go?"

I shivered, listening to the wind howl around the cabin. "You want me to go out in that, in my condition?" I protested.

"Do you good to get a little fresh air an' exercise."

"I get plenty of fresh air and exercise walking to and from school five days a week. Is it still snowing?"

"Nope, but th' wind's blowin' th' snow around so much, you can't much tell th' difference. Can't hardly see your hand in front of your face. It's gettin' colder, too."

"What a change. Last week it was spring."

"March is like that. It's like a woman. Don't know what to expect from it from one day to the next."

"Thanks a lot. I love you, too."

"Want to go?"

"I don't think so."

"It ain't so bad if you're not out in it too long. Dad's been out in it for two days now."

"He has?"

"He went huntin' yesterday an' ain't come back yet."

"Aren't you worried about him?"

"No. He's used to it, an' he's got places he knows to go." Davy got up and went to the stove, opening the door to add a couple of pieces of wood. "I'm thinkin' Mom's a little lonely, though," he added.

"She does spend a lot of time alone. I feel guilty that I haven't been over to see her for so long, but I've been so busy and tired all the time."

"You ain't busy now, an' you shouldn't be tired after layin' on that sofa all afternoon. Besides, I'm hungry, an' that rabbit a sizzlin' in th' skillet sure did smell appetizin'."

A fresh gust of wind hit the side of the house. The lights flickered and went out, leaving the room in darkness.

"Stay where you are," Davy said. "I'll light th' lamps."

He opened the stove door, using the light cast by the dancing flames to see as he reached up on a high shelf for one of the kerosene lamps. He lit it and set it on a lower shelf, then took down the second lamp and lit it also, setting it on the coffee table in front of the sofa where I lay. He closed the stove door and came back to sit down beside me.

"Now you'll have to go with me over to Mom's," he said with a note of satisfaction, "or else you'll have to cook supper on th' heatin' stove."

"Oh no I won't. There's cold chicken in the refrigerator."

"Cold chicken! A man oughta have a good hot meal in his belly on a cold night like this."

"Your mother spoiled you."

"Guess so. Well, if we're not goin', guess I better go on over an' tell her."

"Oh, all right. If you have to go over there anyhow, I'd just as well go with you. I'm certainly not going to attempt to cook a meal on that wood stove tonight. I'm too lazy."

I pushed the quilt aside and sat up with a little difficulty. I was nearly six months pregnant and beginning to feel heavy and awkward. Davy gave me his hand and helped me to my feet.

"I'm starting to feel pretty hungry myself," I said. "Fried rabbit and gravy, did you say?"

"With mashed taters an' green beans an' corn, an' a big chocolate cake for dessert an' glasses of Jell-O in the window."

I smiled. I remembered glasses of Jell-O in the window from last winter, which I had spent in the older Hilton's home. It was the only time my mother-in-law could fix Jell-O, as they had no refrigeration. It was a great treat.

"It all sounds delicious. Just let me freshen up a bit, then we'll go."

By the time Davy and I stepped into the warmth of his mother's kitchen, I was shivering and my teeth were chattering. Davy helped me off with my boots and set them on the newspapers his mother kept on the floor by the door for just such a purpose. I went and stood close to the wood burning stove, hugging my coat around me.

My mother-in-law, Clemmy, stood before the stove, turning the meat in a large iron skillet. Her plump face was flushed and smiling, her sleeves rolled up above her elbows, a large apron enveloping her. The kitchen was warm and redolent with the meal she was cooking. The lamps cast the outer edges of the room in shadows.

"It's nasty out there," I said.

"Dad not home yet?" Davy asked, coming to stand beside me.

"Ain't seen hide ner hair of him," his mother replied in her placid way.

"You're not worried?" I asked.

"He'll come home when he's good an' ready an' not before."

"I sure would hate to be out in that tonight."

I removed my coat and hung it on one of the large nails behind the stove. Taking the teakettle from the back of the stove, I poured hot water into the shallow enamel pan Clemmy kept on a small table by the door. I cooled the hot water with a dipper of water from the bucket beside it, took up the bar of soap that was in a saucer there and washed my hands. While I dried them on the towel that hung from a nail, Davy began to wash his hands in the same water I had used.

"What can I do?" I asked Clemmy.

"You can mash these taters, soon as I pour th' water off for th' gravy. Jist use th' cream from off th' top of that crock of milk there."

I opened a drawer and took out the potato masher and a large spoon and set to work. "There is one good thing about this weather," I observed. "At least you don't have to carry the milk all the way down to the creek to keep it cool. It's plenty cool here by the window."

"Progress is fine," I continued when no one replied, "but sometimes the simple things are best. I'm thankful for my electric stove and refrigerator, but on a night like this, your kitchen is much more cozy and homey than mine, Clemmy. Besides, the electricity went off while I was asleep on the sofa, so it would have been cold chicken and sliced bread and butter for us tonight if you hadn't invited us over. Thank you."

I went over and gave her a hug. I was extremely fond of my mother-in-law.

I put the cover back on the pan of mashed potatoes and set the table while Clemmy made the gravy. I poured large glasses of milk and set them around, then put the potatoes in a bowl and set them on the table. Clemmy had the oven door open and was taking out a large pan of corn bread. She cut it right there on the oven door, then set the pan on the table. Already there was the usual small bowl of sliced raw onion in the middle of the table. Clemmy served it with the noon and evening meals every day in the wintertime. She said it prevented colds.

The three of us sat down to a meal that to me looked large enough to feed a small army, but I knew that when Clemmy cooked, she always cooked extra. Someone was always dropping in at mealtime, and if they didn't, she used the leftovers for a later meal. The way the wind was rattling the windows, I doubted anyone would be dropping in tonight.

We filled our plates. The food was delicious. When I had cleaned my plate, Clemmy urged more food on me.

"You gotta eat good to have a healthy young'un," she said. "I got some eggs saved up for you. Th' hens ain't a layin' too good yet, but there's enough. You need to be eatin' plenty of eggs an' fresh milk, an' you should eat at least a couple spoonfuls of sorghum molasses ever' day, an' some raisins for iron, an' some peanuts, an' plenty of raw onion, so's you don't take cold."

"Thank you, Clemmy, I'll do that, but I couldn't possibly eat anymore ... well, all right. Just one more small piece of meat and some of the onion."

Davy needed no urging to fill his plate again. I looked at

him with amusement and a little chagrin. His mother would think I wasn't feeding him properly.

With a blast of cold air the door burst open. A snow-covered bearlike figure appeared, followed by two more figures, one of whom seemed to be having trouble staying on his feet. There was a lot of stamping and arm flailing, and for a few minutes there was almost as much snow flying through the air inside as there was outside. I hurriedly rose from my chair and stepped back to avoid the snow shower, thinking ruefully that even in this kind of weather, Mr. Hilton could find some of his cronies to bring home to supper. As usual, one of them was probably drunk.

"Build up that fire there, boy," Mr. Hilton was gasping. "Found these here folks in th' ditch, near froze, mule down; don't know if his leg's broke or not."

Davy and his mother rose at once. Clemmy opened the oven door and pulled a chair close. She helped one of the bent figures into the chair, and I saw that it was a woman. She was shaking with a severe chill, and her teeth were chattering. Davy pulled up another chair and helped the man into it.

Mr. Hilton had removed his cap. Hitting it against his leg to remove the excess snow before he hung it on a nail, he disregarded the mess he was making on the floor. His hair was standing on end, his face was beet red and his eyebrows and eyelashes were encrusted with snow. He shook his head as if to clear his sight and wiped his hand across his face before moving to stand beside the stove.

"What can I do?" I asked helplessly.

"Get th' dishpan down an' put it on th' oven door," Clemmy answered, removing the woman's wet outer clothes. When I had done as she said, she filled the pan with hot water, diluted it with cold water, then took the woman's hands and immersed them in it. The woman cried with pain, but Clemmy held her hands firmly down.

"Put his hands in here, too," Clemmy told Davy. "We don't want them to lose no fingers 'cause of frostbite. Anne, honey, put some more water on th' stove, jist a little bit in two or three pans so's it'll het up faster, then go get two of them quilts off'n th' bed an' bring them in here. We got to get these folks out of them wet clothes an' into somethin' dry."

While Clemmy and Davy and I busied ourselves caring for the visitors, Mr. Hilton helped himself to a piece of meat and came back to stand beside the stove to eat it. He still wore his coat, but he seemed fine, so no one paid any attention to him. Presently, he removed his coat and sat down at the table and filled a plate.

When the man and his wife were both dry and huddled into quilts before the fire, their feet in pans of warm water, Clemmy and Davy held cups of hot coffee to their lips. The woman seemed to have fared a little better than the man. Her teeth chattered against the rim of the cup, but she took it from Clemmy and held it with both hands, sipping the hot liquid gratefully. She looked up at Clemmy, tears coursing slowly down her cheeks.

"I been hearin' a hoot owl a hootin' outside our bedroom winder th' last three nights in a row. That means someone close by is gonna die 'fore too many days. Thought for sure it was gonna be me or Dad here, 'fore your man come along an' rescued us."

"There now," Clemmy said soothingly. "Ever'thin's gonna be all right. You jist sit quiet there a little bit longer while I get th' food het up, then I'll bring you a plate. You can eat your supper a sittin' right here by th' heat of th' stove. Likely you're both near starved after all you been through."

While she heated the food, I made a fresh pot of coffee. Davy brought in more water. He refilled the teakettle, then looked at his father, who was still at the table.

"Where's their mule?" he asked.

"Jist a mile or so up th' road, by that ol' shack on th' corner."

"You think his leg may be broke?"

"Broken," I corrected mentally, but I didn't say it aloud. Davy could use quite good grammar when he chose to, but when he was around his family or any of his cronies, he always slipped back into the local dialect.

"Dunno," Mr. Hilton replied. "Tried to get him up but couldn't, an' didn't have time to keep on tryin'. These here folks was in a bad way, figgered I better get them in outta th' cold soon as I could. Might jist be mired down, it's a pretty deep ditch, long about thar. Figgered these folks couldn't see whar they was a goin', way th' wind was a blowin' th' snow around."

Clemmy brought filled plates to both the man and his wife. They began to eat voraciously. The man's hands trembled visibly, but he was able to manage. So far I had not heard him speak a word.

Davy buttoned his coat up to the neck and put his cap on. As he pulled on his gloves, his eyes met mine, and I stifled the protest that rose to my lips. He didn't like me worrying about him, especially in the presence of others. I rephrased the question I was about to ask.

"Are you going out to look for their mule?"

"Got to. He'll die for sure if he's left mired down in that ditch." He looked at the man. "What you wantin' me to do if his leg is broke?"

The man cleared his throat and spoke in a raspy voice. "Guess you'll jist have to shoot him," he answered.

Davy nodded and reached for a rifle on the far wall. He inserted a couple of shells and put the gun over his shoulder. He also took up a big flashlight. His eyes lifted briefly to mine, then he smiled and touched my arm and went out the door. I swallowed and turned to pour fresh coffee for the visitors.

CHAPTER TWO

Hill Stories

*I*t seemed that Davy was gone forever, but the door opened at last and he came in. He was snow-covered and chilled through, but he was all right. He propped the rifle in the corner and came quickly to the warmth of the stove. I poured a cup of hot coffee and handed it to him. He took a grateful sip or two.

"Mule's all right," he told the man, who had straightened in his chair and was looking expectantly at him. "A little lame, but I put him in th' barn an' rubbed him down good an' fed an' watered him. I think he'll be all right by mornin'."

The man nodded. It was obvious that he was grateful, though he spoke no words of thanks. The cold air Davy brought in with him seemed to revive everyone. The woman sat up straight and pushed her chair back from the stove a little. She attempted to straighten her hair, which hung in grey wisps around her face. I judged her to be about sixty. I wondered who they were. No introductions had been made; I didn't even know if my in-laws knew them.

"You'll spend th' night," Clemmy was saying. It was a statement, not a question. The woman looked at her with gratitude and spoke a brief "Thankee."

Clemmy served the chocolate cake and Jell-O. When Mr. Hilton was finished, he rose from the table and pulled his chair up to the stove and sat back down. He pulled his pipe from his breast pocket and a pouch of tobacco from his hip pocket, then proceeded to fill his pipe and tamp it down. He struck a match on the side of the stove and held it to the pipe, making a soft puffing sound as he drew on it. When it was lit to his satisfaction, he tossed the match in the stove, leaned his chair back and took a few contented puffs. He eventually removed the pipe and spoke.

"Good thing you folks went into th' ditch there by that ol' shack," he drawled. "I take cover there many a time when th' weather is bad. That's where I was headed when I come on you. Reckon some day hit'll fall down an' won't be of use to no one no more. Been some right interestin' things happen in that ol' shack."

He puffed a few times on the pipe while we all waited expectantly. Mr. Hilton was renowned for the stories he could tell, but I had been privileged to hear very few of them. I drew my own chair up to the stove and sat down. Davy had removed his coat and hat and was standing near the heat, still chilled. Clemmy bustled about, clearing the table. She wouldn't allow me to help her this time.

"My brother's boy, now," Mr. Hilton continued, "he come from Kentucky to visit us one time. Had to walk all th' way from town an' got caught in th' dark 'fore he could get here. Well, he was a walkin' along th' road when all of a sudden he hears a wolf howl nearby, an' then another one. First thing he knowed, he was surrounded by a whole pack of wolves, a snappin' an' a snarlin' an' a circlin' him. Well sir, he don't have no gun ner nothin' with him, so he picks up th' only thing he can find, a clod of dirt, an' throws it at them wolves. He hollers an' flaps his arms, a tryin' to scare them off, but they ain't a scarin' too good. He throws another clod and hits one, an' it yelps an' runs off a ways. He sees a openin', so he takes off a runnin' an' a yellin' with that pack of wolves right on his heels. Jist as they was about to get him, he sees that ol' shack an' runs inside an' slams th' door in their faces. Course it was in better shape in them days. Anyhow, he had to spend th' night there with his back again' th' door, with them wolves right outside, a circlin' an' a snappin' an' a snarlin' an' throwin' theirselves again' th' door from time to time. Said when he looked through a knothole, he could see their big teeth an' their eyes a shinin' in th' moonlight; his hair fair stood on end. That boy was tough—he didn't scare easy—but he was shore scared that night. Made sure he didn't get caught out in th' dark around here without his gun after that."

"Were there really wolves when you first came here?" I asked.

"Shore was. Woods was full of them."

"When we first come here," Clemmy said, her hands busy in the dishwater, "there wasn't no glass in that winder in th' back door there. Folks said th' man who lived here before us got drunk one night an' kicked it out. Anyways, there was jist a piece of rotten canvas tacked over it, an' one side was loose. One night I was here, jist me an' my three babies. Dad was off a huntin', an' he had th' hounds with him. I had me a little dog named Pupsy. He slept in a box there on th' back porch. Well, that night he started a whinin' an' a scratchin' at th' back door, so I lifted th' corner of that canvas an' looked out. I saw what I thought was one of them big German shepherds. He was jist a standin' there a starin' at th' house. I opened th' door to let Pupsy in an' I yelled 'you get!' to that big dog. He jist turned around an' loped off; but my little dog was jist a tremblin' an' a whinin' like all get-out. He run straight for th' bed an' got under it. Next day I told one of th' neighbor men about it an' he said 'Why didn't you shoot it?' He said that wasn't no dog, that was a wolf, an' they kill little dogs. He said won't no dog challenge 'nother dog in its own territory. After that, when Dad was off huntin', I made sure I let Pupsy in th' house at night. I never went outside myself or let any of th' little ones go out, either. It wasn't safe."

Mr. Hilton put his pipe away and took out a plug of chewing tobacco. He took a bite and passed it to the other man, who also took a big bite. I suppressed a small shudder of revulsion. It was bad enough when Mr. Hilton chewed, but now there were going to be two of them doing it.

Instead of giving the plug of tobacco back to Mr. Hilton, the man passed it on to his wife. She took a bite, then offered it to Clemmy. Clemmy gave it back to Mr. Hilton, then reached under the stove and brought out a red coffee can, putting it on the floor between the three of them. I gave Davy a horrified look and saw his eyes twinkling back at me in amusement. I looked at the woman again. She was chewing away, her eyes on Mr. Hilton, who had launched into another story.

"If they all three start spitting into that can, I'm going to be sick," I thought. I stood up. I would have liked to stay and listen to more of their stories, but my stomach rolled at the thought of those three mouths spewing forth that awful brown tobacco juice.

"Excuse me," I said. "I think it's time I went home. It's been very nice meeting both of you. I hope your horse—mule—is all right and you'll be able to get home safely."

I reached for my boots and sat down to put them on. Davy helped me, then brought my coat and held it while I put it on. The woman bent and picked up the can, bringing it up to her mouth to spit. She had a little more finesse than Mr. Hilton, but it still turned my stomach queasy.

"Thank you so much for supper, Clemmy," I said. "It was delicious. Good-night."

I tied my scarf under my chin and pulled on my gloves. Davy put his coat on and took up the lantern, and we went out into the cold night air. The wind had died down, but the temperature had dropped with it. Davy took my arm.

"What's th' matter, little prude?" he asked, laughing. "Never see a woman take a chew of plug tobacco before?"

"No, I haven't, and I hope I never do again. It's a disgusting, nasty habit for a man, but for a woman! How could she?"

"Be surprised how many women do it."

"No women of my acquaintance have ever done it," I retorted. "I'm glad you don't, Davy. I couldn't take it."

"Tried it once. Come to th' same conclusion: it's nasty."

The moon peeked out from behind a cloud. In the distance a coyote howled. I drew closer to Davy.

"Are the wolves really all gone from here?" I asked.

"Yep. All killed off years ago. That was a coyote."

"Yes, I know."

"Want to hear a really disgustin' chewin' tobacco story?" he inquired with a touch of humor.

"No thank you."

"I had this here friend, a backwoods hillbilly like me, ya understand. Well, he decided a few years back it was time he got hisself a wife. So he looked th' girls over an' saw one he liked th' looks of, an' he ast her to go to the drive-in movies with him. She said yes, so he went out to her place in his pick-up truck an' took her to th' drive-in. They was a gettin' along real good, but he noticed she kept sort of twitchin' her head over to th' right an' kinda pullin' at th' top of her blouse. He figgered maybe she was jist a little nervous, goin' out with him for th' first time like that. Then he thinks maybe she's gettin' a little cold, 'cause it had turned off a mite chilly an' she was wearin' a blouse without sleeves. Well, he slides over in th' seat real careful like an' puts his arm around her. She don't object, so he gets a little bolder an' slides his hand up her arm. She's still doin' th' neck twitchin' thing, but he's got used to it by now an' don't hardly notice it no more. She cuddles right up to him, so pretty soon he slides his hand up her shoulder an' sorta slips his fingers up under th' edge of her sleeve. He feels somethin' wet an' sorta slimy on his hand, and he wonders what in tarnation. Thinks maybe she's bleedin' or somethin', so he straightens right up an' turns on th' inside light an' looks at his hand. There ain't no blood there, jist some sort of brown stuff. Then he looks at her, an' there's a wet brown stain down th' front of her blouse. What she's been a doin' all that time was spittin' tobacco juice down th' front of her blouse. Guess she didn't want him to know she chewed or somethin'. Well, he's a tobacco chewin' man hisself but that near gags him. He starts up that pick-up without a word an' drives her home jist as hard an' fast as he can go, then dumps her out an' goes on home. He ain't never asked no other girl out for a date since then, far as I know. He's still a bachelor to this day, an' that's been near ten years ago."

"You made that up."

"Gospel truth, I swear it. He told me so hisself."

"That's disgusting. I don't blame him for deciding to stay a bachelor."

There was a sudden high scream that sounded like a woman in mortal fear or pain. I gasped and stood stock still, clutching at Davy, knowing exactly what it meant to feel as if the hair was standing straight up on the back of the neck.

"Don't be scared," Davy said, "It's only a panther."

"What are we going to do?" I whispered in panic.

"Ain't goin' to do nothin', except keep on walkin'. He won't hurt us. There's enough food in these hills that panthers don't have to go around huntin' people. Only time they'll attack is if they're cornered or lame an' can't hunt regular game."

"How do you know this one isn't lame?"

"Wouldn't be up in them trees if he was."

"W-which trees?"

"Them right over there behind th' house. He's jist out prowlin' around, seein' what he can see. Th' dogs heard him, hear them howlin'?"

"Davy, I'm scared. Let's go back."

"Ain't nothin' to be scared about. He won't come near th' light, but don't be surprised if he screams again. Panthers seem to enjoy doin' that, now an' again."

He did scream again just before we reached the house.

He sounded so close. I would have run the last few yards, but Davy literally held me back.

"You might slip an' fall an' hurt yourself or th' baby. Don't never run from a wild animal, Anne. He might decide to chase you, jist out of curiosity. Best thing to do is to jist stay calm an' act like nothin's botherin' you."

When we were inside, I locked the door and stood for a few minutes with my back to it, my heart pounding wildly in my breast. Davy lit the lamps, then stood with his hands on his hips, grinning at me.

"So," he said. "You've heard your first panther scream. How did you like it?"

"I'd have liked it a lot better if I'd been inside, behind closed doors," I retorted.

"Jist think, a few years from now, you'll be sittin' 'round th' stove yourself, tellin' your own kids stories about what these hills was like way back in th' good ol' days. Won't have no stories to tell if you don't have a few excitin' experiences like that."

He turned to the wood box and built up the fire. I removed my outdoor clothes and moved closer to the fire.

"I'm surprised Dad ain't out with his gun," Davy observed, adjusting the damper. "Maybe he's enjoyin' storytellin' too much, or maybe he's had enough of th' cold for one night. To him, a panther's scream is usually like wavin' a red flag in front of a bull."

"Why does he hunt them? Does he sell their pelts?"

"No. They ain't worth nothin' anymore. He jist kills them to be killin' them, I guess. Considers them pests."

"You don't?"

"No. They're a real pretty animal, prettiest animal there is in these parts, I think, except for horses maybe. An' like I said, they ain't hurtin' no one. Goin' to be all gone like th' wolves before long."

"That's too bad. I'd like to see one someday."

"Someday maybe you will."

"Behind closed doors, of course."

"Well, I don't know about that, but I'll take care of you. Like I said, they ain't dangerous to humans 'less you corner them."

"By all means then, let's make sure he doesn't feel he's cornered."

CHAPTER THREE

A Fire in the North

I woke toward morning and heard Davy fumbling around in the dark. Then I heard the swish of his jeans as he pulled them on. I was accustomed to hearing him get up to replenish the fire at least once during the night, but he didn't get dressed to do that. I sat up.

"Is something wrong?" I asked.

"There's a big fire somewhere to the north of here," he answered, sitting on the edge of the bed to pull on his socks and shoes.

"A fire?"

"Yes. I let Brownie out an' he started barkin' to beat th' band, so I looked out an' saw it. Th' whole sky is lit up."

"What do you think it is?"

"This time of night I'm afraid it can only be someone's house or barn."

"Whose house or barn?"

"Don't know. Might be Granny Eldridge's, but I don't think so. It looks farther away than that."

"Whose then?"

"Maybe th' Anderson's, but I can't say for sure."

"Oh no!" I exclaimed, throwing the covers aside. "All those children! Wait, Davy, and I'll come with you."

"You stay here an' get some hot coffee or hot soup or somethin' ready. They'll need it if they're out in th' cold. Got any old blankets I can take along?"

"But Davy."

"I don't want you goin'. You might get hurt an' more than likely there won't be anything you can do. I may have

17

to bring them back here, so you can start gettin' ready for that. Bring me that big bucket from th' back porch, will you?"

I did as he asked. He put his coat on and took the blankets and the bucket and went out. I heard the truck start up, then I went to the window and looked to the north. It was as Davy had said: the whole sky was lit up. I watched the truck disappear over the hill, then looked at my in-laws house. It was in darkness. Evidently they hadn't heard Brownie, who was still barking.

I was wide awake by then, so I got dressed and made a pot of coffee. I heated a pan of milk for hot cocoa, then went back to the window. The glow in the north gradually faded, replaced by a column of black smoke. There was no sign of Davy returning in the truck.

As soon as I saw a light flickering in Clemmy's kitchen window, I put on my coat and boots and walked to her house. It was still very cold, but the day was going to be bright and sunny.

"Why child, what is it?" Clemmy asked in surprise when she answered my knock.

"There's a fire. See the smoke? Davy went to see about it over an hour ago and he hasn't come back. He thought it might be the Anderson's house."

"Mercy me," she exclaimed. "Come on in then. You'll catch your death standin' out there."

"I don't know what to do. Davy wouldn't let me go with him, and I'm getting a little worried."

"Best stay here until he gets back. Likely he's doin' all that can be done. Your turn'll come later. I do hope if it's th' Andersons, they got all them young'uns out in time."

"I just hope Davy didn't try to go in after any of them."

"Likely it'd be too late for anything like that, time he got there. Them old houses go up in flames mighty fast, once they get started. I'll get Dad up. He can hitch up the mules an' go see about it. Sit down. Coffee will be ready in a minute. Don't you worry about Davy none. He'll be all right."

I went to the window to look out. Black columns of smoke still ascended, but the road to the north remained empty. Mr. Hilton came into the room, pulling one overall strap over his shoulder. His hair was in wild disorder, his chin bristling with several days growth of beard. He yawned widely and accepted the cup of coffee Clemmy handed him.

"What's this about a far?" he asked.

"Davy got up about an hour and a half ago and saw a bright glow in the north. He thought it might be the Anderson's house burning, so he took the truck and went to see about it. He hasn't come back yet."

He made no comment but sat down to pull his rubber boots on over heavy woolen socks. Clemmy set an iron skillet down on the stove and began putting thick slices of bacon in it. The biscuits were already made and sitting in a pan ready to go into the oven. I felt worried and impatient. Evidently Clemmy was going to fix his breakfast before he went to see about the fire and Davy.

I heard the sound of a vehicle and ran to the window. It was Davy in the truck, and he was alone. Perhaps it hadn't been a house after all. I felt tremendously relieved. He stopped the truck and got out. When he came in, his hands were black with soot. His face had a black streak down one side, and his expression was solemn.

"Davy, are you all right?" I asked. "Was it the Anderson's house?"

"Yes," he answered soberly to both questions. "Pour me some water, will you?"

"The children? Mattie and the boys and the little ones? Are they all right?"

"They're all okay, 'cept for ol' man—Mr. Anderson."

"Do you mean ... Is he? ..."

"'Fraid so," he said, beginning to wash his face and hands.

He said no more until he finished washing and sat down at the table. Clemmy was scrambling eggs and making gravy. I poured Davy a cup of coffee and sat down beside him. Mr. Hilton drew out his chair and sat down also. As we waited for Davy to speak again, I remembered what the old woman had said the night before about the hoot owl and someone close-by dying within a few days. A shiver went through me.

"By th' time I got there, th' whole house was up in flames," Davy said tiredly. "Mrs. Anderson an' th' kids was standin' out in th' yard barefoot in their night clothes, jist a watchin'. I asked where Mr. Anderson was, an' she pointed at th' house. Wasn't no way I could get in there to get him out. Wasn't no use even tryin'. No one coulda still been alive in that."

"But the children all got out?"

"Yes, she was able to get them all out."

His mother put the bowl of scrambled eggs in front of him. He put some on his plate and passed it on to his father. He took several pieces of bacon, split two biscuits in half, covered them with gravy and began to eat.

"I had them all get up in th' back of th' truck an' wrap th' blankets around theirselves. By that time, Ol' Man Horton had come, Tom an' Ellen, too. They had more blankets. None of them was hurt, they was jist cold, scared an' tired."

"We asked Mrs. Anderson what happened. She said she got up in th' night to put some wood in th' stove an' went back to bed. Her ol' man was still layin' on th' sofa in th' livin' room where he'd been th' evenin' before, dead drunk. She was jist about asleep again when she heard a loud thump. She said she jist figgered he'd tried to get up an' fell; she didn't go in to check an' see. She went on back to sleep, an' th' next thing she knew, she woke up to see th' whole room lit up, flames leaping through th' door to th' livin' room. She jumps out of bed, grabs up th' baby an' starts screamin' at th' kids, pullin' them out of bed an' tellin' them to get on outside. When she gets them all out, she gives th' baby to Mattie an' runs back to th' house, yellin' at her husband. She couldn't see past the flames to where th' sofa was, but she sees a piece of th' stovepipe on th' floor. She figgers that must of been what she heard fall an' what caused th' fire. The whole room was on fire. She couldn't go in, so she run around to th' back, but when she tried to go in th' flames shot out at her an' caught th' front of her hair on fire. By the time she put that out with snow, th' whole house was up in flames; th' heat was so bad she had to get back from it. An' that's about th' time I got there."

"She didn't actually see Mr. Anderson still lying on the sofa?" I asked.

"No, th' room was full of flames, but she saw him there when she built up the fire, so there ain't much doubt that he was still there. He sure wasn't nowhere outside. Anyhow, th' house burned clean to th' ground. Only thing they got left is th' clothes on their backs. We asked her if she had any relatives she could go to, an' she said no. Then we asked her where she wanted to go, an' she said she didn't have nowhere to go. Tom an' Ellen an' Ol' Man Horton an' me, we jist looked at each other, then we stepped away from th' truck an' looked at each other some more. Bill Horton said he couldn't take them in 'cause of his wife's bad heart. Ellen said they didn't really have room for nine extra people, an' Tom said outright he wouldn't have them in his house. Said he'd never seen so many ragged, snot-nosed, dirty kids in his life; they probably had head lice to boot. Then they all looked at me. I said I couldn't have them either, cause you wasn't feelin' too good, bein' pregnant an' all."

"Davy," I chided, though I couldn't help feeling relieved.

"Well," Clemmy began a little doubtfully, "I suppose we could ..."

21

"No, Mom," Davy interrupted. "I told them you couldn't take them in either 'cause you got them other folks here that was stranded in th' storm last night. So I took them over to th' schoolhouse."

"To the schoolhouse?"

"Yes. Couldn't think of nowhere else, an' schools are s'posed to be used in times of disaster, ain't they? Anyhow, I built up th' fire an' got it goin' good an' brought them in some water an' left. They're cold an' dirty an' prob'ly gettin' pretty hungry by now. Ellen asked if I could bring a tub, some soap an' towels an' somethin' for them to eat. She'll try to round up some towels for them too."

"Well, at least I can help with that. I'll get some things together and go right over."

"Hold on there," Davy said, rising. "I'll help you—we'll take them over in th' truck."

"I can get some things together an' come with you," Clemmy said.

"You better stay here, Mom, since your company will be gettin' up soon an' wantin' breakfast. If you want to make a batch of corn bread or somethin', we can take that over to them."

"I'll send over some canned peaches an' some of that wild plum jelly to put on th' corn bread. You come back over here an' get it 'fore you go. I might have some clothes around here she can use, too."

"Thanks, Mom. That'll be a big help."

Davy and I went home to gather up towels and shampoo and soap. I included a few clothes that I thought they might be able to use; there were two boys about Davy's nephew Calvin's size. I included a dress that I thought Mrs. Anderson might be able to wear, plus a couple of sweaters and several pairs of socks. Davy loaded it all in the truck, along with the washtub Ellen had requested, and we drove back over to Clemmy's.

She had scrambled a big pan of eggs to send along with some bacon and the corn bread and peaches. With the coffee and hot cocoa I brought, I thought the Andersons would probably eat better this morning than they had in a long time. Clemmy also sent a big stack of flour sacks that she said could serve as diapers for the baby, and a few odds and ends of clothing.

When we arrived at the schoolhouse, the Andersons were alone. They were gathered around the stove, a couple of the little ones quietly crying, their noses running unheeded. Mrs. Anderson cradled the baby against her and looked at us through dark-circled, anxious eyes. The front of her hair and her eyebrows were badly singed, but she bore no other burn marks that I could see. All of them had clean faces and hands—I supposed Ellen had seen to that—but their clothes were filthy and soot-blackened. The room reeked with the smell of unwashed bodies and smoke from the fire.

"I'm so sorry about your loss, Mrs. Anderson," I said, depositing the pans I carried on my desk at the front of the room. I didn't know if I should mention her husband or not, so I left it at that. She made no reply. "We've brought you some breakfast. You're probably getting pretty hungry, after being up half the night. If you'll have each of the children sit at a desk, I'll give them a plate of food. Davy's mother, Clemmy, fixed it. I think it will be all right for you to lay the baby on the ping-pong table for now. I'll put a blanket on the far edge by the wall, and we'll keep an eye on him in case he wakes. How old is he now, about two months?"

She nodded as she laid the baby on the blanket. I handed a plate to her. She seated herself at a desk and took the next youngest child, a girl of about two, onto her lap and started to feed her.

When they each had a full plate in front of them, I poured the cocoa into the clean tin soup cans Clemmy had provided. Clemmy always kept a supply of these at the back of her cabinet for just such an emergency. They were unbreakable and easy to transport. She told me once they were all she had in the way of drinking glasses when her children were small.

There was a thud on the outside door, and I went to let Davy in. He carried a bucket of water in one hand and an armload of wood in the other. He dumped the wood in the wood box and put the bucket of water on top of the stove. Then he opened the stove door and built up the fire. The baby woke and began to cry.

"He's hungry," his mother said, lifting him up in her arms.

"Is he bottle fed?"

"Yes. I didn't get a chance to go back for no bottle."

"No, of course not. Clemmy always keeps a spare bottle or two in her cupboard. Davy, will you go back for them? I'm sorry I didn't think of it earlier. What kind of milk do you give him?"

"Canned milk with half water," she answered.

"Have your mother fill the bottles before you bring them, if she doesn't mind. It will be easier. Half canned milk and half boiled water. If she doesn't have any canned milk, we do, at the back of the cabinet. Bring whatever is left over for later. Also, you might bring along some kind of line or rope, about four sheets, some large pins and a hammer and nails. We'll partition off this corner of the room for the baths. I think, too, we'd better start passing around the word that school will be closed tomorrow, until we can find a place for the Andersons to go."

Davy nodded. "Anything else?"

"That's all I can think of right now, unless you want to bring back a couple more pans to heat water in."

"I'll bring th' tub in an' fill it when I get back."

I cleared the desks and wet one of the flour sacks to wipe

them clean. The children were quiet—their hunger appeased—but by the time Davy returned, the baby was red-faced and screaming with rage; no amount of jiggling or walking him did a bit of good. He was hungry, and he wanted to eat now. Davy thrust one of the bottles at Mrs. Anderson, which she put in the baby's mouth. The screaming was replaced by loud sucking and gulping. The baby waved his tiny fists as he noisily ate.

Clemmy had come back with Davy. She carried a chamber pot in one hand and a stack of towels in the other. *"Trust Clemmy to know exactly what was needed,"* I thought affectionately.

Davy brought the tub in and began filling it. He drove two large nails in the walls on each side of the stove and tied a light rope from one to the other. I pinned the sheets up while he brought in more water. Soon that corner of the room was curtained off from curious eyes, and the tub was almost full enough of warm water to start the baths.

"Tom brought these," Davy said, coming in with a pile of clothing in his arms. "When they got back home this mornin', th' baby was sick an' runnin' a fever, so Ellen couldn't come back herself."

"That's all right. We'll manage. Did you tell your brother to pass the word around about no school tomorrow?"

"Yes. He said he'd go around to let some of th' folks know an' tell them to pass it on. I'll go chop some more wood. If you need any more water, jist holler."

"We probably will. With all that black soot, it won't take long for the water to get filthy. Would you like to go first or last, Mrs. Anderson?"

"Last. I'll have to help with some of them. Likely they'll fight it. It's been so cold an' drafty in that ol' house, ain't been able to do any more that wash their faces an' hands for a long time."

I didn't say anything, but I knew from having them in my school that she didn't bother to bathe them as much as once a week, even in the summertime. I had sorted out the clothing and thought there would be enough to outfit all of them in clean, dry clothes. My sister-in-law, Ellen, had been very generous.

Mrs. Anderson put the now-sleeping baby back on the ping-pong table and joined Clemmy on the other side of the half-filled tub. They stripped the two-year-old and put her in the bath. Several minutes later, I wrapped her naked body in a large, warm towel and sat down to dry and dress her. She was a pretty child with all the grime removed. Her hair was short and fine, light brown in color now that it was clean. Her eyes were getting heavy, and her thumb was in her mouth before I finished. I laid her on a quilt on the floor and covered her warmly. She was asleep almost immediately. I went back to receive the next child, another girl of about four. They called her Clarie, so I supposed her name was Clara.

Tears were pouring down her cheeks, and when I tried to comb out her long, tangled hair, she began to cry in earnest. I laid the comb aside and wrapped the towel around her tighter and held her against me.

"Mrs. Anderson," I said, raising my voice above the racket that was coming from behind the curtain. "Do you mind if I cut Clara's hair? It's so tangled I don't think I'm going to be able to comb it out without really hurting her."

"You can if you want to," she replied breathlessly. Jackie, the next youngest child, was evidently putting up quite a fight against his bath.

"Mattie, will you bring me the scissors out of my desk drawer, please?" I asked the oldest. "Now then, Clara, this won't hurt a bit. It will be much easier to comb your hair after it's cut. Hold real still, there's a good girl."

I cut it off about halfway down her neck, not worrying too much about whether it was perfectly even. When it was cut and I had managed to get it combed, I dressed her and put her down beside her sleeping sister.

I heard a sharp slap, and Jackie's howls turned into shrieks. A moment later he shot through the curtain, stark naked. As he ran for the door, tears of rage poured down his cheeks. I caught him as he passed me, holding him firmly while he kicked and fought.

"That's enough now, Jackie," I said in my no-nonsense schoolteacher's voice. "Stop it this instant. There's nothing to cry about now. It's all over. Let me dry you and get you into some nice, warm clothes, then you can play with some toys I have here. Would you like that?"

He didn't stop crying immediately, but gradually the fight went out of him and he submitted to being dressed. I gave his hair a quick lick or two with the brush, holding him by one arm while he ducked and dodged. Still holding him, I went to the cloakroom and took down a box of small toys I kept there, setting them before him on a blanket on the floor. He was soon occupied with a couple of small cars.

After the next boy, Frankie, had his bath, we had to change the water. Mattie then had her bath with her mother's help, followed by the two older boys. Since the older children didn't want Clemmy with them while they bathed, she poured out a pan of fresh warm water, picked up the baby, and began to bathe him, cooing over him and talking softly while she worked.

When Mrs. Anderson was finished with her own bath, I pulled the sheets aside and bent to gather up the pile of soiled clothing, Davy emptied the water again and put the tub back in the truck.

"Mrs. Anderson, I'm afraid these clothes will have to be burned," I said, handling them gingerly. "If you don't mind, I'll have Davy take them outside and burn them now."

When she nodded, I helped Davy carry them out. Using the kerosene that we started the morning fires with, Davy doused the clothes and threw a match on the heap. We stood and watched them burn.

"They're not a bad-lookin' bunch, once they're cleaned up," Davy observed.

"Mrs. Anderson must have been quite pretty when she was a girl. Davy, what on earth are we going to do with them? They can't stay here."

"Don't know, but you better go back inside. You'll freeze without your coat."

"I'm not cold. In fact, the fresh air feels pretty good after that overheated room."

"Has she said anything 'bout her ol' man?"

"Not a word."

"S'pose it ought to be reported. I mean, you don't jist see a man die an' not say a word about it to th' authorities."

"Do you suppose there'll have to be an investigation?"

"Don't know, but I s'pose tomorrow I better go to town and find out what has to be done. I can pick Calvin up an' bring him home at th' same time. He's probably thinking we've abandoned him by now."

"I wonder—Davy, do you remember when I was there once last fall, Granny asked me if I knew of anyone who might like to rent her house? She said she didn't want to sell it because she wanted Calvin to have it when he grows up, but she would like to rent it until then. Do you suppose she'd let the Andersons live there, since they don't seem to have any other place to go?"

Davy scratched his head. "You know Granny," he said. "She ain't a gonna let anyone live there unless they're able to pay, an' I don't s'pose Mrs. Anderson has any money. Well, I know she don't now—don't have nothin'. It all went up in smoke."

"But they get federal aid, don't they? I remember you saying so once. Shouldn't she get more now that her husband is dead and she has eight children to provide for?"

"You'd think so."

"Will you ask Granny, Davy? Go in as early as possible

tomorrow and ask her if she'd consider it. She might, since the house has been sitting there empty for close to a year. There's still quite a bit of furniture left there."

"Might work. I'll ask, but I know Granny. She'll be wantin' that first month's rent right off."

"We could pay that, or the neighbors could all chip in. I'm sure some of them would be glad to. At least ask her, Davy, because they can't stay here beyond tomorrow evening."

"You think I should ask before we mention it to Mrs. Anderson?"

"Yes. We don't want to raise false hopes. Besides, she doesn't seem to be able to come up with any kind of solution. She's waiting for someone to do it for her, and I guess that's us."

"Okay. I'll do it first thing tomorrow."

CHAPTER FOUR

Gossip

*T*he entire Anderson family was asleep: Mrs. Anderson and the seven older children wrapped in blankets on the floor, the baby in a cardboard box on the ping-pong table. Clemmy and I cleaned and straightened the room, while Davy chopped wood and refilled the wood box.

Neighbors began to arrive with food and clothing. They all wanted to stay awhile and talk about the fire. They whispered about the death of Mr. Anderson, glancing covertly at the sleeping form of his wife.

"You don't s'pose she done it on purpose, do you?" one woman whispered to me.

I looked at her in surprise. "Did what on purpose?" I asked.

"You know. Her ol' man. He wasn't no good, wouldn't work an' was always gettin' drunk. Some folks say he beat her an' th' young'uns, too. Couldn't no one much blame her for wantin' to get shed of him."

A cold chill went through me. I was ashamed to admit it, but the same thought had occurred to me. I knew what Mr. Anderson was and that his wife had no use for him. I straightened and spoke a little tersely.

"It was an accident," I said. "The chimney fell down and that's what started the fire. Mrs. Anderson was able to get all the children out with the help of the older ones, but she couldn't get her husband out because he was passed out drunk in the room where the fire started. You know how fast an old wood-frame house can burn, once a fire gets started."

"That's what she said, but wasn't nobody else saw it, was there?"

"Of course not, it was very early in the morning. I do know that when I was there a couple of months ago, I saw that stovepipe, and it was sagging then. You said yourself Mr. Anderson wouldn't work; he never repaired anything. It was an accident, nothing more. Please don't repeat to anyone else what you've just said to me. It could do irreparable harm to Mrs. Anderson. She's going to have a hard enough time as it is, caring for those eight children alone."

She shrugged defensively, a little offended. "I'm only sayin' what ever'body else is thinkin'. Ever'body knowed she'd come to fair hate him, th' way he treated her an' them young'uns, an' her havin' another baby ever' year or two."

"That may be true, but she didn't set the fire. It was an accident. If you hear anyone suggesting otherwise, be sure you set them straight. Tell them the teacher said so. Davy was the first one there, and he saw how it was." I added with only a slight twinge of conscience, "I've come to know Mrs. Anderson well enough to believe that she wouldn't do anything like that."

"I was of th' opinion that no one knowed her very well. She's always been sorta stuck-uppish 'bout visitin' with th' neighbors, an' wasn't no one wantin' to go visitin' her, with th' mess that house was in an' him always drunk."

"I've become acquainted with her through the children, and what I've said is fact, not gossip. Now if you'll excuse me, I'll go help Clemmy sort out the rest of these clothes. Thank you so much for what you brought. Mrs. Anderson will be grateful."

She turned away, her back stiff. I knew I had offended her, but I also knew how gossip like that could spread in these hills and the damage it could do. In spite of what I had said, her words revived that little nagging doubt in my own mind. I remembered that I'd even told Davy after my visit there at the beginning of school that the place should be burned to the ground. Had Mrs. Anderson, in her despair, come to the same conclusion? Had she seen it as a convenient way—the only way—to get rid of a drunken, abusive husband? I gave myself a mental shake and went to greet my sister and her husband, who had just entered with a full grocery sack.

"Liz, how nice," I said, going to her and giving her a hug. "It seems a long time since I've seen you. How are you?"

"I'm fine, and how are you?"

"Good."

"We just got groceries yesterday, so we thought maybe the Andersons could use some of them."

"Thank you. Yes, they can use whatever they get. They lost everything, you know."

"I heard Mr. Anderson ..."

"Yes, I'm afraid so."

"How is she taking it?"

"I think she's still pretty well dazed. They're all very tired from being up since early morning. I don't suppose the reality of it has really hit her yet."

"You don't s'pose she done it on purpose?" my brother-in-law, Jim, asked me low-voiced, glancing at the sleeping figure of Mrs. Anderson lying on the floor.

"Jim!" I whispered reproachfully. "Don't say that! Don't even suggest it. Of course she didn't."

"Wouldn't nobody blame her if she did."

"Jim, No! Do you think she'd risk her own life and the lives of her children like that?"

"Never can tell what a body might do if they get desperate enough."

"No, Jim. It really was an accident."

"Okay, teacher, if you say so."

We didn't get to talk much more because people were arriving bringing clothing and food. I thought it ironic that people were so willing to think the worst of Mrs. Anderson, yet they were so generous in offering help. Perhaps it was the lack of outside stimulus, the monotony in their lives that made them so eager to gossip, so quick to see the sensational in something that was quite easily explained.

The baby awoke and cried. Mrs. Anderson got up immediately and picked him up. I wondered if she had been lying there awake, listening to what people were saying. I profoundly hoped not, but I was afraid to ask. Clemmy handed her a bottle and she sat down at one of the desks, her head bent over her baby. Her face was pale and drawn, the front of her hair frizzy from the singeing it had received in the fire. The dress and sweater she wore hung loose on her, making her look slight and somewhat frail and helpless. My heart went out to her. She was going to have some hard times ahead, but perhaps not as hard as those in the past. I was determined that Davy and I would help her as much as we could.

People came and went through the middle of the afternoon. Nearly all of them stayed to visit for awhile, but few of them made an attempt to talk to Mrs. Anderson. Perhaps it was because they didn't know what to say, or perhaps it was her own aloofness that kept them from approaching her. She sat cradling her baby with her head down toward the back of the room, seemingly oblivious to all that was going on. I thought she was probably suffering from other's reactions, perhaps wishing everyone would go home and leave the family in peace. I heard no more gossip about the fire being deliberately set, but I saw a few people off in the corner with their heads together, and I could imagine what they were talking about. On behalf of Mrs. Anderson I thanked everyone for what they had brought, making sure everyone knew that school would be closed the next day and would resume again on Tuesday. When no one came after four o'clock, I was relieved. I was beginning to feel very tired myself.

The ping-pong table was piled high with clothing and blankets, and my desk top was covered with foodstuffs. The five-gallon pail that Davy had used to carry water in for the baths had flour-sack diapers soaking in it. Clemmy had washed some of them, rigging up a temporary clothesline where the curtains for the baths had hung. My well-ordered schoolroom had been turned into a temporary shelter for the homeless, without the knowledge or consent of the school authorities. But with no telephone service, there had been no time to notify anyone. I was sure the superintendent, Mr. Cooper, would be very understanding when he found out.

When Clemmy, Davy and I were preparing to leave the family for the night, I noticed tears coursing silently down Mrs. Anderson's cheeks. I went to her and put my hand on her shoulder.

"You know, I don't even know your first name," I said. "I feel ridiculous calling you Mrs. Anderson, when we're so close to the same age. I surely must have heard your name, but I don't remember it."

"It's Jeanette," she said, wiping the tears away with the backs of her hands.

"That's pretty. I've always liked Jeanette. May I call you that?"

She nodded.

"And you can call me Anne, if you'd like. I'm sure you're worried about where you're going to live, but try not to, okay? Davy and I have an idea. He's going to check into it early in the morning, and we'll let you know what he finds out as soon as possible. There's plenty of food here for tonight and the morning. I've put the things that might spoil in the cloakroom, where it's cooler. Will you be comfortable enough sleeping on the floor? There are more blankets on the table if you need them; just don't let any of the children sleep too close to the stove. Is there anything else you need before we go?"

She silently shook her head. I would have liked to hear a word or two of thanks from her, at least to Clemmy and Davy for all they had done, but she said nothing. I knew it wasn't lack of gratitude, simply lack of training, so I tried not to feel resentful.

"Davy's brought in a bucket of fresh water, and there's plenty of wood to keep the fire built up. The chamber pot is in the cloakroom, so there's no need for any of you to go outside. I'll be back sometime in the morning. I hope you rest well. Good-night."

I followed Clemmy and Davy out the door. We all got into the truck and started home. We were silent for awhile.

"Did your company leave?" I asked Clemmy.

"They got up right after you an' Davy left an' went on home," she answered.

"I never did hear their names. Do they live around here?"

"Ain't right sure where they live, don't recall them sayin' anything about it."

"Oh."

"They live further back in th' hills," Davy said. "Seen them a few times, think their name's Smith. There's a whole settlement of them back there. They don't mix much with other folks, stick to theirselves, mostly."

"I see." I was thoughtful for a minute, trying to understand that kind of mentality. "Would they have helped you if you had an accident like that in their territory?" I asked.

"Shore, but then they might not a had anythin' to do with you again, even if they was to see you on the road or in town or somethin'."

I shook my head. There was still a lot to learn about the area and the people where I had chosen to make my home. I puzzled over it a few minutes, then my thoughts went back to the Anderson family. If Granny Eldridge decided not to let them rent her house, I wondered where in the world they would live. Mrs. Anderson didn't seem to have any initiative of her own. It would probably be up to Davy and me to find a place for them.

CHAPTER FIVE

"He's From the Police"

*I*t was late morning when Davy came back from town the next day. Clemmy and I were at the schoolhouse with the Anderson family when he drove up. I happened to be standing by the window and saw that he had two people with him. One was Granny Eldridge. The other was a man, a stranger. Calvin, Davy's nephew who lived with us, was not with them.

The men got out on either side of the truck, and it took both of them to help Granny out. She seemed to have grown even heavier since I had seen her. They came toward the schoolhouse, Davy holding Granny by one arm and the stranger holding her by the other. Because of her weight and her rheumatism, Granny found it difficult to get around, and the ground was still slippery underfoot because of the recent snow. I went to the door and held it open for them. Granny was panting with the effort of coming up the steps. She had to stand on the porch for a minute and catch her breath before she could come on inside.

"Hello, Granny." I greeted her with a smile and an effort at cheerfulness. She was not one of my favorite people. "How are you?"

"Fair to middlin'," she managed to say when she was inside the door. "Or at least I was, 'til your man come an' drug me out here. Got so wallered around in that truck of his, ain't sure but what my insides ain't turned upside down."

I looked at Davy, who gave me a rueful grin.

"Where is Calvin?" I asked.

"Stayed in town. There wasn't room for him in th' truck. I'll bring him home when I take Granny an' Mr. Griffin back. Mr. Griffin, this is my wife, Anne."

The man removed his hat and took my hand. He was a small man, rather nondescript, perhaps in his forties. He seemed pleasant enough.

"Hello, Mr. Griffin," I said. "Granny, would you like to sit here in my chair? I think you'll find it comfortable."

When I had her seated, I looked back at Davy and Mr. Griffin. "Mr. Griffin is here to ..." Davy began, then paused and looked over at Mrs. Anderson, who was watching us. "To look into ... to check out the details of the fire."

"He's from th' police," Granny interjected with obvious relish. I saw the alarm that crept into Mrs. Anderson's face and had to grit my teeth. Granny was not known for her tact.

"Then I suppose you'll want to talk to Mrs. Anderson," I said, as matter-of-factly as I could. "Jeanette, this is Mr. Griffin. Mr. Griffin, Jeanette Anderson."

He held out his hand to her, and she took it almost fearfully. I pulled out one of the two metal chairs we had and offered it to Mr. Griffin. He thanked me and sat down, taking a notebook out of his briefcase. I reached for the baby, but Mrs. Anderson made an inarticulate protest and held him tighter, so I didn't insist. I put my hand on her shoulder and gave it a reassuring squeeze; there was little else I could do. The other children, who had been occupied with various toys and books, sat looking up at their mother and the stranger.

"Now then, Mrs. Anderson," Mr. Griffin said in a brisk-but-kind voice, "Mr. Hilton told us what happened, but his was a second-hand account. We'd like to hear it directly from you. Tell me exactly what happened on the night of the fire."

She moistened her lips, glanced over at me then back at him, and began to talk hesitantly. She told basically the same story Davy told, her words audible to all in the room. Granny was listening avidly. I wished there was some way I could get her away, but that was impossible. The children were quiet, sitting wide-eyed, watching this stranger question their mother. Clemmy was rinsing out diapers over in the corner, seemingly oblivious to what was being said. Davy sat on the long bench in front of my desk, watching Mr. Griffin and Mrs. Anderson. I busied myself at the ping-pong table, sorting and folding a pile of clothes and putting them in paper sacks.

"Your husband was in the room where the fire started?" Mr. Griffin asked when Mrs. Anderson's story ended.

"Yes."

"Did you try to wake him?"

"I hollered at him."

"And he didn't answer you?"

"No."

"Why was that, Mrs. Anderson? You would think the heat and the light and the noise would have disturbed him. Was he an unusually sound sleeper?"

"He was drunk."

"How drunk was he?"

"Dead drunk," she snapped, then gasped and put her hand over her mouth.

"He had passed out, would you say?"

"Yes."

"And when was this?"

"'Fore we went to bed."

"Would you say your husband often drank excessively?"

"He'd been drunk most ever' night since way before this last baby was born."

"So he was in the room where the fire started—passed out on the sofa—when you went to bed?"

"Yes."

"You're quite certain he was still there when the fire

started?"

"Yes."

"There's no chance that he might have woke and gone outside, or somewhere else, before the fire started?"

"He was still a layin' there when I got up to build up th' fire."

"And that was how long before the fire started?"

"Maybe a hour, I ain't sure."

"All right, Mrs. Anderson," he said, closing the notebook and putting his pen in his pocket. "That's all for now. Mr. Hilton is going to take me to the scene of the fire so I can look around a bit, then I'll be back. I may need to talk to you again. You'll be here?"

She nodded, her eyes fastened on him in fear.

"Would you care for a cup of coffee before you go, Mr. Griffin?" I asked.

"Thank you, that sounds good," he said, sounding relieved at the change of subject.

"Black, or cream and sugar?"

"Black."

He took the cup from me and lifted it to his lips. The room was eerily silent.

"Granny, there's just about one more cup left in the thermos. Would you like it?" I asked.

"I give up coffee when I moved in with my daughter. Th' doctor says it ain't good for my heart," she answered.

"Davy?" I asked.

"Okay."

I poured out the rest of the coffee. Davy rose and came to take it from me. I put my hand on his arm and let it rest there for a moment, wondering what kind of ordeal he was about to face. Would there be anything left of Mr. Anderson's body? Would something have to be done with it? Whose unpleasant task would that be? Surely not Davy's.

When Davy and Mr. Griffin were gone, Mrs. Anderson

gave a strangled whimper and put her hand up to her face. "What is he gonna do?" she asked. "Do they think I done it?"

"No, of course not," I replied. "It's just routine. They have to investigate when someone dies. They have to be sure of all the facts, so it will be legal and all."

"Them women yesterday, they was over in th' corner an' they thought I was sleepin'. I heard them talkin' about it an' a wonderin' if I done it on purpose, but I didn't! I didn't!"

"Of course you didn't. If anyone said anything like that it was just idle gossip that doesn't mean a thing. You know how some people are, they're not happy unless they're talking about someone, usually making mountains out of molehills. Now you just relax and stop worrying. Everything is going to be all right."

"They was sayin' maybe I ain't a fittin' mama an' maybe they'll come an' take my kids away from me an' put them in a orphan's home an' ..."

"Hush," I said, putting my arm around her shoulders. "The children will hear you. Of course they won't take them away from you. We'll all pitch in and help. It will all work out, you'll see. You can't let what people say bother you like that, they don't mean half of it. How could they possibly know what happened; they weren't there. Now you just stop worrying."

"But what am I gonna do? Where am I gonna go?"

"I think maybe Granny can shed some light on that for us," I said, straightening and looking over at her. "Can you, Granny? I assume that's why you came back with Davy."

She sniffed. "I come back with him 'cause he ast me to," she snapped.

"But he did explain why he asked you, didn't he?"

"He said as how Miz Anderson here might be rentin' my house. I ain't sayin' I will now. I ain't aimin' to have it tore up or messed up by a bunch of rambunctious young'uns who don't have no respect for other folks belongin's. I aim for Calvin to have that house when he's growed up enough to be out on his own, an' I don't aim for it to be tore up or burned down 'fore that time comes."

I winced for Mrs. Anderson, but her expression didn't change as she stared dully at Granny. There was a moment of silence, then Granny's expression seemed to change and soften.

"I 'member when you first come here," she continued, her eyes on the younger woman. "You was jist a kid, no more'n fifteen years old an' pretty as a pitcher. You was so proud of yerself for catchin' a man at sich a young age. You uster come over to visit with me most ever' day there at first, remember? You was so full of plans. You scrubbed that ol' house an' fixed it up best you could. Put pitchers up on th' walls an' made curtains outta flour sacks; you pieced together a tablecloth an' put it on that ol' table. You even ast me to teach you how to crochet so's you could make yourself some scarves an' doilies to cover up them holes in th' arms of that ol' sofa you had."

I sat and listened in amazement. Clemmy was hanging the flour-sack diapers she had washed on the make-shift clothesline, her face impassive. Evidently this was not news to her. Mrs. Anderson sat silently with tears running unchecked down her cheeks, her eyes on her baby.

"Then th' babies started comin', one right after 'nother," Granny continued. "After 'bout th' third one, you changed. Didn't keep your house up no more, didn't drop in for a visit, didn't smile no more. Couldn't help my heart achin' over you but wasn't nothin' I could do. Ain't your fault your man turned out to be lazy an' no good. Ain't surprisin' you fell for him in th' first place, either. He had a way about him 'fore th' whiskey got sich a hold on him."

Granny paused and seemed to give herself a shake. Her voice lost its softness.

"I got to have me fifty dollars a month if you want to live in my house," she said. "An' I got to have your promise that all these young'uns won't tear things up. You usta be a right good housekeeper, you can be again. This here oldest girl of yours is big enough to help an' so is them two bigger boys. There's some stuff I left there that you can use, but I don't want no bed wetters sleepin' on that feather bed an' ruinin' it. Th' teacher here an' her man can help you get things squared away, bein' as how it was their idea to rent it to you. They'll be checkin' up on you from time to time to make sure you're takin' proper care of things. If you ain't, you'll have to move out."

I opened my mouth to protest, then closed it again. What could I say? The Andersons had to have someplace to stay, and I had suggested it.

"I ain't got no money," Mrs. Anderson stated flatly.

"You get them checks from ADC, don't you? You'll be gettin' more now that your man's dead, won't she, Teacher?"

"But I don't know nothin' about that. Jack always picked up th' money same time he picked up them commodities."

"Teacher here'll help you figger all that out. You got to pay reg'lar ever' month, now, or you won't be able to stay there no more."

Mrs. Anderson looked hollow-eyed and haunted. I put my hand on her shoulder to reassure her.

"Davy and I will help all we can," I said.

"When will you be wantin' to be movin' in?" Granny asked.

"This afternoon," I replied before she could answer. "Before dark. We have to resume school tomorrow, you know."

"I don't know as how I can allow them to move in without payin' first."

"The neighbors have been quite generous," I said curtly,

thinking she could be more magnanimous herself. "Not only have they brought food and clothing, some of them brought money. Fifty dollars, did you say?"

I reached for my purse. A few of the neighbors had given money, but in no way would it be close to fifty dollars. However, I thought I might have enough in my purse to make up the difference. I counted it out and had a few dollars left over. I handed the fifty to Granny.

"There you are. The first month's rent is paid. Just to make it official, I'll make up a receipt for you to sign."

I drew a half sheet of paper toward me and wrote swiftly. Then I read what I had written aloud, not knowing if Granny or Mrs. Anderson was literate.

"Now if you'll just sign your name here, Granny, it will all be legal and official," I said, unsure whether that was true. If Granny was going to make me at least partially responsible for Jeanette Anderson, I was going to see that she was dealt with fairly.

She waved the paper away. "That ain't necessary," she said.

"Oh yes it is; that way no mistakes will be made. Shall I sign it for you?"

"I don't keer," she said begrudgingly.

I bent again to the paper. "Signed Granny. No, that won't do. What is your first name, Granny? I don't think I've ever heard it."

"It's Mildred Martha."

"Signed Mildred Martha Eldridge, by Anne Hilton. Now if you'll make an x there, Granny, to show you agreed to my signing for you, it will be finished. I've put in the date, the period the rent covers and when the next payment is due. I'll just keep it here in my desk, so we'll be sure it doesn't get lost in the move. And thank you very much, Granny. I'm sure we're all relieved that the Andersons will have a decent place to live."

CHAPTER SIX

A Pile of Rubble

When Davy and Mr. Griffin returned, all eyes turned toward them. Their expressions were sober. It was Davy who spoke.

"Nothin'," he said. "Jist a pile of rubble, still smoulderin'. Impossible to do any lookin'."

"I think it's safe to say that no one left in that could have survived," Mr. Griffin added. "Needless to say, Mrs. Anderson, I'm very sorry about your husband."

She nodded but didn't speak.

"There were no other witnesses to the fire? No one else who saw what happened?"

"No."

"It was three or four o'clock in the morning, Mr. Griffin," I felt compelled to add.

"So your husband informed me. I understand, Mrs. Hilton, that you were probably more in touch with the family in recent months than anyone else. I realize, of course, that you didn't witness the fire, but if you don't mind, I'd like to get a deposition from you, just for the records."

"Of course," I replied calmly, but my heart began to beat more rapidly in my breast, wondering what kind of questions he was going to ask me. "What do you want to know, Mr. Griffin?"

He glanced around at all the faces turned toward us. "Er, is there someplace we could go to talk privately?"

"Davy, perhaps you could go ahead and take the Andersons to Granny's house? It's settled that Granny is going to rent it to them. And Granny, perhaps you'd like to go along to show Mrs. Anderson where things are and how you want them kept?"

"I knowed th' Andersons here a sight longer than th' teacher," Granny informed Mr. Griffin resentfully. "Reckon I could tell you a sight more about th' family than she can."

"Thank you," he replied, "but it's only the recent months we're interested in, and I understand you haven't lived here since last summer. I think a statement from Mrs. Hilton will be all that's necessary."

She gave a disgruntled snort and struggled to rise. Davy went over and helped her.

"Can you take these boxes and sacks of clothing, too, Davy?" I asked, relieved to see her going. "I can bring the food over later in my car."

"Okay, but wrap th' kids up good in them blankets. They'll have to ride in the back of th' truck, an' it's cold out there."

"Excuse me, Mr. Griffin. This won't take long."

I helped bundle the children up, and we all made several trips out to the truck, carrying the little ones and the things the neighbors had brought. Mr. Griffin helped Davy get Granny out to the truck. Clemmy got in after her, carrying the baby. When they were all loaded, Davy said he'd be back in an hour or so to take Mr. Griffin back to town.

"What do you want to ask me, Mr. Griffin?" I asked when we were back inside and seated.

"I understand you visited the Anderson home recently?"

"I was there at the end of August, about a school matter, then again briefly in January when she had the baby."

"And how would you describe the family?"

I hesitated. He was making notes in his notebook, and I wanted to make sure I didn't say anything that would hurt Mrs. Anderson, while at the same time being truthful. How was I to describe the family honestly without casting suspicion on Mrs. Anderson—perhaps unwittingly providing a motive for murder?

"They were very poor," I said. "He was disabled. They lived on ADC."

"His wife said he drank heavily. Did you see any evidence to substantiate that?"

"Yes. When I was there in August, he was lying on the sofa in the living room. I thought he was asleep and was afraid of waking him, but Mrs. Anderson said he was drunk, and nothing would wake him. I soon saw that was true. There was an empty whiskey bottle on the floor beside the sofa where he was lying. One of the little boys picked the bottle up and lifted it to his mouth. I went over and took it away from him because I saw that there was a small amount of whiskey left in it. He started to cry—scream would describe it better—I guess I scared him. Anyhow, he was standing right beside his father, but his father didn't wake up, he didn't even stir. In fact, he never moved the whole time I was there, and the children were making quite a lot of noise."

"You felt certain he was drunk, rather than just a sound sleeper?"

"I know he was. He reeked of whiskey and there was the empty whiskey bottle on the floor right beside him."

"I see. And did you ever see him drunk on any other occasion?"

"No, but three of the children are in my school here, and Mattie, the oldest, has told me on several occasions that her father was drunk."

"Did you see Mr. Anderson on the occasion of your second visit?"

"No. He wasn't there."

"Can you tell me the condition of the home? Mrs. Anderson stated that the stovepipe had fallen to the floor. Do you think that likely?"

"Much more than likely. I didn't notice it the first time I

was there because it was summer, but when I was there the second time, I did. The stovepipe sagged and the stove itself was overheated. I thought at the time that it was dangerous, but I didn't say anything because ... well, because one hates to interfere. I wish now I had."

"Would you say Mrs. Anderson was irresponsible?"

"No, I wouldn't. She's a young woman who's wholly responsible for eight children between the ages of two months and ten years. Her husband was a drunken, shiftless, no-good person who did nothing to help her. The house was old and drafty and the doors didn't fit tight. Some of the windows were broken out and she'd covered them with cardboard. The stovepipe sagged, and the chimney probably hadn't been cleaned for years. She had a new baby so she built up the fire as hot as possible in an attempt to keep her children warm, that's all. If you'll remember, it was a bitterly cold night."

"So you would say the possibility of an accident such as Mrs. Anderson described was very high?"

"Yes, I would."

"Very well, Mrs. Hilton, I think that's all we'll be needing from you. If you'll just read over what I've written to make sure it's accurate, then sign and date it, I'll be on my way."

I read, signed and dated it and gave it back to him, relieved that it was over.

"Do you think there will have to be any further investigation?" I asked, as he closed the notebook and returned it to his briefcase.

"I don't think that will be necessary. The evidence seems clear enough. However, if there is, I presume you'll be here if we need to talk to you again?"

"Yes, of course. I teach school here and I live just over the hill."

"A pretty place. Your husband pointed it out to me."

"Thank you. Can I fix you a sandwich or something to eat? It's past lunchtime, and I'm not sure when my husband will return."

"No thanks, I'm fine. Had a late breakfast, but you go ahead. I'll just sit here by the fire until he does return, if you don't mind."

While I went around straightening up and packing the food into boxes, Mr. Griffin sat gazing about the room. Presently he rose and asked if he could look around. He stuck his head in the cloakroom, opened the bookcases and thumbed through the books, then walked down one of the aisles, his hand brushing the tops of the desks.

"Brings back old memories," he said. "I went to a school like this many years ago, didn't know they still existed."

"There aren't too many of them left."

"I thought these little country schools were consolidated years ago."

"Most of them were, but this area is so isolated that it wasn't included."

"How much longer do you think it will be before it is included?"

"I don't know. There's been some talk of it. It all depends on when they get the new county road through."

"As a teacher, are you for or against it?"

"I'm not sure. A few years ago I would have been all for it, but that was before I came here to teach. People in general seem to think the children who go to these one-room schools are underprivileged, deprived of a good, basic education. I used to think that myself, but I'm not sure I do anymore. There's something about these schools, a cohesion, a ... oh, I don't know exactly how to explain it, but here families are not divided up and sent off in all different directions. Older brothers and sisters look after the little ones, making them feel safe and secure. They walk to and from school with them, keep an eye on them during recess, help them with their homework. It helps keep families together, not separated and divided, and I'm beginning to think that's important. Besides, the teacher gets to know the children, so she is able to meet their needs in ways not possible in larger schools. There are disadvantages, of course, but if I have any say in the matter, I think now I'd be in favor of retaining the one-room country schools."

"You're not a native of these parts, I gather?"

"No. I was born and raised in St. Louis."

"It must have been quite a change for you. Did you come here especially to teach in a one-room school?"

"Yes."

"How many years have you been here?"

"This is my second year. I stayed because I met and married my husband here."

"And you love it?"

"And I love it."

Davy drove up then, Granny beside him. I went out with Mr. Griffin, feeling as if I were saying good-bye to an old friend. Before he drove away, Davy told me they had the Andersons settled in as much as possible, and he'd be sure to bring Calvin back with him. I said good-bye to Granny— still a little huffy—and to Mr. Griffin, then went back inside to carry the rest of the things for the Andersons out to my car. It was after one o'clock. The children were sure to be hungry.

CHAPTER SEVEN

A Foggy Night

*I*t was after four o'clock when I started for home. It was already growing dusky. Heavy fog had gathered at the tops of the hills and was beginning to drift down into the valleys. Visibility would be very poor in an hour or so. I hoped I would find Davy and Calvin already there when I arrived home.

They were not there. The house was dark and cold when I entered. The electricity was still off, so I lit a lamp then bent to build up the fire. Only a few live coals were left below the ashes. I managed to get a flame going by adding a few crumpled newspapers and some kindling, then lay down on the sofa, pulling the quilt up around my shoulders. I was exhausted; I would lie there until the house warmed up some, then I'd get up and start supper.

When I woke it was six o'clock. The lamp was sputtering and the fire had died down, but there was no sign of Davy and Calvin. I got up and opened the door to look out. I was greeted with heavy, sinuous fog that seemed to enter the door and curl around me. I could see nothing beyond the end of my nose. I shut the door again, fretting about Davy and Calvin. Perhaps they'd decided to stay overnight in town because of the fog. I hoped they hadn't had an accident.

I tried not to dwell on that thought. Davy didn't appreciate it when I worried about him. I knew he was sensible and would use good judgment. If he thought it too dangerous to drive, he wouldn't be on the road, but there was no way for him to get word to me. I would just have to stay calm and wait.

I put on a heavy sweater and built up the fire. Realizing I

was hungry, I went into the kitchen to make myself a sandwich. There was no point in making supper now because I was sure Davy and Calvin would not be coming home until morning.

The house was eerily silent. I wasn't used to being alone in the evenings. If Davy was late with chores, Calvin was almost always there, or if not actually there, ready to burst through the door at any moment. The silence was so absolute that I almost felt as if I was alone in the world. I couldn't even see the lights from Davy's parent's house, as I usually could when I looked out the north window.

I took my sandwich back into the living room and curled up in one corner of the sofa with the quilt draped around me. As I began to eat, I picked up a magazine from the coffee table and soon became engrossed in an article I found interesting.

An hour crept by. I laid the magazine aside and prepared some schoolwork, finding it difficult to concentrate. The only sounds in the room were the loud ticking of the clock and the occasional crackle of the fire. I got up and looked out the door again. The fog was as thick and impenetrable as it had been earlier.

I went to the bookcase and drew out a volume called *The Complete Stories and Poems of Edgar Allan Poe*. I loved his writings and thought I might find some of them appropriate to read to my students. I was trying to inculcate a love for reading in them by reading aloud at the end of each school day.

I went back to my corner of the sofa and curled up with the book, perusing some of the shorter stories. I read "The Telltale Heart" and "The Pit and the Pendulum" and decided neither would be appropriate for some of the younger ones. Perhaps some of the poetry would be better. I reread several of the poems and finally decided "The Raven" would be my best choice. I laid the book aside and rose, taking up the lamp and carrying it into the kitchen. My footsteps on the bare floor sounded loud in the silence. A slight chill went up my spine. Was there an echoing footstep behind me? I looked around but there was nothing. I had to laugh at myself. Perhaps it hadn't been such a good idea to read Edgar Allan Poe when I was completely alone.

I set the lamp on the counter and turned on the water above the sink, intending to do the few dishes there. There was no water; I had forgotten that the electricity was off. I could do the dishes in the morning, but suddenly I was thirsty for a drink of water. There was the pump outside, but I decided I wasn't that thirsty and settled for a glass of orange juice. I usually made the coffee in the evenings so all I had to do in the morning was plug it in, but I couldn't do that, either. I would go to bed and perhaps do a little more reading, but not Edgar Allan Poe.

Outside the circle of light cast by the lamp, the room was in darkness. I reached for the lamp, almost dropping it when there was a sudden scratching at the window. I gave a muffled cry and froze, my heart in my throat.

The sound came again, and I recognized it as a tree branch brushing against the glass. I let my breath out with a long, relieved sigh. "It is the wind and nothing more," I quoted, giggling nervously. I was being ridiculous. Here I was, a grown woman, afraid to be alone at night. What would my husband say? I told myself I wouldn't have been so jumpy if only the electricity would come back on. It was just the awful silence and the night's blackness that was getting on my nerves.

We never locked our doors at night, but now—still feeling a little foolish—I locked both the front door and the back. I put another stick of wood on the fire, adjusting the damper as Davy had instructed me. Then, carrying the lamp with me, I went into our bedroom and got ready for bed.

This time I choose a less daunting novel and snuggled down under the covers. I soon grew warm and sleepy. Laying the book aside, I blew out the lamp and was soon asleep.

It must have been several hours later when I suddenly woke, lying there with my heart pounding in my throat and my mind filled with dread. It was still night because the room was totally dark. I longed for a light, but I just lay there—too scared to move—clutching the covers tightly under my chin. I lay still and listened, then I heard a low moaning sound, so eerie that the hair on the back of my neck seemed to stand on end, cold chills chasing up and down my spine. I couldn't move. I waited for the sound to come again, which it soon did, louder this time: a low moaning that ended in a rising wail.

I lay there, stiff and scared, trying to think rationally, trying to figure out what on earth it could be. It wasn't coyotes; I'd heard their howling before. It was an eerie enough sound, though it wasn't anything like this. Was it the panther Davy and I had heard the other night—on the prowl—perhaps joined by another? Was it wolves, perhaps not as extinct as Davy and his parents thought? Whatever it was, it was coming closer, because the sound came again, louder and more bone-chilling than before. It was accompanied by a slight, stealthy creaking. Was someone in the house?

I lay there trying to conquer my panic, telling myself that no amount of wolves or panthers could hurt me inside the house. But if it was a person in the house, I might be in grave danger; just laying there frozen to the bed wasn't going to help matters at all. The sound came again, louder, ending with a dash of rain against the window.

I threw the covers aside and rose, shivering, fumbling for the matches. When I had the lamp lit and my warm bathrobe wrapped around me the sound began again. I forced myself to go to the window. Immediately I felt the draft. The window had been left open just a crack, and cold wind was whistling under it. I pushed the window down and the sound stopped. Limp with relief, I felt the impulse to either laugh or cry, I didn't know which.

I had panicked over nothing, but I knew I wouldn't be able to sleep another wink until I had checked the whole house to make sure there was no one there.

I picked up the lamp and went through the house. Checking first to make sure the doors were still locked, I inspected all the windows and even looked under Calvin's bed. I resisted the impulse to put a chair under the doorknobs; what would Davy think if he came home unexpectedly? I put another stick of wood on the fire, then went back into my own bedroom and looked under the bed. There was nothing. I felt extremely foolish, but when I went back to bed, I still left the lamp burning. I lay awake for hours, finally falling asleep toward morning.

I woke to bright light: the electricity had finally come back on. I sat bolt upright, so startled that it took me a few minutes to get my bearings. I had slept heavily, but not restfully, for a few hours. My body felt weighed down with fatigue; my eyes felt gritty. The lamp was still burning, the globe blackened from being on for so long.

Shivering in the cold, I got wearily out of bed and pulled on my warm bathrobe. I wasn't used to getting up to a cold house; Davy always built up the fire before he went out to do the chores. I slipped my feet into warm slippers, blew out the lamp and went into the living room to build up the fire. I unlocked the doors and peeked out. The sun was coming up and the fog was gone. It looked as if it was going to be a beautiful day.

I made the coffee and got myself dressed. I was just starting breakfast when Davy and Calvin drove up in the truck. I went to the door to greet them.

"Well, Calvin, how are you?" I asked when I had given him a hug. "You were gone a lot longer than we planned. Did you have a nice visit?"

"It was okay."

"If you'll hurry and get yourself ready for school, I'll have breakfast ready in a few minutes."

"We already et."

"Ate, Calvin, not et," I corrected.

"Granny fixed us bacon an' eggs an' biscuits an' gravy," Davy added as Calvin went off to his room, dragging his suitcase behind him. "You all right?"

"I'm fine."

"Sorry I couldn't get ahold of you to let you know where we was," he said, taking hold of my upper arms and drawing me to him. "Was you worried?"

"I was a little concerned, but I thought you probably stayed at Granny's or went to your brother's house because of the fog."

"We stayed at Granny's. I was goin' to try to make it home, but she wouldn't let me take Calvin, so I had to stay."

"I figured it was something like that."

"How'd you get along without us?"

"Fine."

"No problems?"

"Why should there be a problem?" I asked, as if surprised. "I did some reading, then went to bed, that's about it."

"Sleep good?"

"Why ever not?"

"Jist crossed my mind you might be a little scared, bein' out here all by yourself like that."

"I'm not a child, Davy. I'm perfectly capable of taking care of myself too, you know."

"Didn't even notice I was gone, huh?"

"I didn't say that. Of course I missed you, but I was all right."

"I'll go ahead an' drive you an' Calvin in to school this mornin'. It's a loblolly of mud out there, with th' snow meltin' all at once like that, but it looks like it's goin' to be a real pretty day. Maybe spring is finally on th' way. While I'm at th' school, I'll go ahead an' build up th' fire for you, even if you are a self-sufficient woman who can take care of herself."

"Thank you, Davy. I'd appreciate that."

I went off to the bedroom to finish dressing, smiling to myself, remembering the night I'd had. In the light of day it seemed pretty foolish. Perhaps someday I'd tell Davy about it.

CHAPTER EIGHT

Lewis Disappears

I was very tired at the end of the school day, so I was glad to see Davy drive up in his truck with the high school students, Evelyn and Todd. Now I could get a ride home without appearing to be a helpless female who always had to have a man looking out for her.

When we arrived home there was a car parked in front of our house. I recognized it as the older model that the Proctor family had bought a short time before. Sue Proctor got out of the car, lifting her baby up in her arms, while the two girls got out of the back seat. They stood waiting for us, and when I saw the expression on Sue's face, I knew something was wrong. I felt a little stab of dismay; I had so looked forward to a quiet evening at home with my family.

"Hello, Sue," I said as I approached her. "How are you?"

"Not so good," she replied.

"Is something wrong?"

"Let's wait a minute," she said softly, indicating the girls.

"Well, come on in. I missed the girls today."

"I'd like for Davy to come in, too. I need to talk to you both."

"All right. Davy, can you come inside for a few minutes, please?" I asked. He looked up and nodded. I led Sue and her family into the house.

"Take your coats off," I invited. "I'll get some toys and puzzles for the children, then we'll go into the kitchen where we can talk. Calvin, why don't you go get the cookie jar. You and the girls can have a cookie in here and you can play host to them while we visit with Sue."

The expression on his face suggested he wasn't overly pleased, but he made no audible objection. He was not yet at an age to appreciate having to entertain girls. I gave him a smile and led Sue into the kitchen.

"Sit down," I invited, pulling a chair out from the table. "I'll make some coffee, shall I? Davy should be here in just a minute."

I busied myself with the coffee then sat down at the table across from Sue. Her baby lay half-asleep in her arms; she seemed to be concentrating on his head. Davy came in and pulled a chair out to sit down with us, looking first at her then inquiringly at me.

"Sue wants to talk to us," I explained. "What is it, Sue?"

She swallowed, her lower lip trembling as she made an effort to speak.

"Didn't see anything of Lewis today," Davy commented casually. "Is he sick or jist catchin' up on some of his own work?"

"I don't know where he is," she replied in a thick, shaken voice. Tears welled in her eyes and rolled down her cheeks. She wiped them away with the back of her hand. Davy and I exchanged puzzled glances.

"You don't know where he is?" I repeated.

"No."

"But what's wrong, Sue? How long has he been gone?"

"Since Sunday."

"Since Sunday? But that's three days. He may have had an accident or something."

"No."

"No?"

"It was because of the fire."

"Because of the fire? But what did the fire have to do with your husband?"

"Nothing, but he was afraid they might think it had."

"Who might think it had?"

"Anybody. Everybody. The police."

"The police? But why in the world? ..."

Davy put his hand on my arm. "Jist let her tell us what happened," he said, interrupting me. "Why would the police be interested in Lewis as far as th' fire was concerned, Sue?"

"He was there the evening before the fire."

"At the Anderson's?" Davy asked.

She nodded. "He'd been into town. Coming home he saw her, Mrs. Anderson, out in the yard trying to chop some wood. He felt sorry for her; it was so cold and windy and starting to snow. He drove on by but it bothered him, so he went back to help her. He said he took the ax from her and told her to go back to the house; he'd take care of the wood. He was there about an hour, chopping up all the wood she had then carrying some of it inside. He said all the kids were huddled around the stove, trying to keep warm in that drafty old house. He hated to ask them to carry in the rest of the wood, so he just did it himself. When he had carried in the last armload and was putting it in the woodbox, Mr. Anderson came in. He had been drinking, and he started yelling at his wife, something about her having other men in while he was away. He even said ..."

Sue stopped and swallowed. I rose and briefly put my hand on her shoulder, then went to pour three cups of coffee.

She continued after taking a sip of coffee. "He said he had always suspected that the last baby wasn't his. He guessed now he knew whose door to lay it at. Mrs. Anderson just stood there and didn't say a word. Lewis tried to explain why he was there, but Mr. Anderson ordered him out of the house and said if he ever came back again he'd shoot him. Then we heard about the fire and Mr. Anderson's death and the rumors that maybe Mrs. Anderson had deliberately set the fire."

"That's not true," I spoke up quickly.

"Lewis was afraid he might be accused of being an

accomplice?" Davy asked.

"It's because of his prison record, you know," Sue explained, her eyes lifted toward Davy. He reached out and sympathetically put his hand briefly over hers. I felt a little pang of jealousy. She hadn't come to me for help; she had come to Davy. I mentally shook myself. Being pregnant was making me feel unattractive and insecure: vulnerable. It was true that Sue was my friend and often came to me with her problems, but Lewis and Davy were good friends too, so there was no reason in the world why she shouldn't look to Davy now for help.

"Lewis was afraid that if it became known that he was there the night before and that Mr. Anderson had made those accusations ..."

"Don't seem too likely anyone would mention that. Nobody heard it but th' family, did they?"

"No, but he was afraid one of the children might say something, and you know how people out here like to gossip. Neither of us really knows Mrs. Anderson and what she might say or do if she's accused of ... of causing her husband's death. She might implicate Lewis, just to avert suspicion from herself."

"That wouldn't help her any, that'd jist make her the accomplice. I don't see that Lewis has got that much to be worried about."

"But you don't understand, Davy, you don't know. Lewis wasn't guilty the last time either, but that didn't prevent him from going to prison. It was all circumstantial evidence and being in the wrong place at the wrong time. It could happen again, and Lewis says he can't—he won't—risk going to prison again. He doesn't think he could survive it."

Davy rubbed his chin thoughtfully. "Guess I can understand that," he said. "When you've been in jail for somethin' you didn't do, it'd have a tendency to make you want to steer clear of th' so-called justice system. Is that why he took off?"

"Yes, and he said if they came looking for him, I was to tell them he was gone and I had no idea where he was, which I don't," she ended, with a fresh rush of tears. "It's been three days. I haven't heard a word, and the weather has been so bad. I don't know if he's had anything to eat, if he's had an accident or if he's lying somewhere frozen to death ..."

"Easy," Davy said, patting her hand again. "Don't let your imagination run away with you. I'll go look for him. I got an idea where he may be."

"If you're thinking he may be at the old house, he isn't. I've already been there."

"Doubt he'd go there. That'd prob'ly be th' first place anyone would look, but there's a cave back in th' side of one of them hills at th' very back of th' farm. Me an' him talked about what a good hideout it would make if a person needed one. Dad uses it sometimes when he's out huntin'. I got a inklin' he may be there." Pushing his chair back, he reassured her, "Don't you be worryin' none. I'll find him an' bring him back."

"But what if you don't? What if? ..."

"Then I'll keep lookin' 'til I do." Davy turned to me. "Fix up a Thermos of hot soup or coffee or somethin'," he said. "Likely he'll be in need of somethin' hot an' nourishin'. I'll go get th' lantern. If I ain't back before dark, don't go to worryin'. It might take awhile."

He left the room. I rose and opened a can of chicken noodle soup and put it on the stove to heat. I took out two Thermoses, and while I busied myself at the stove, Sue sat quietly at the table sipping her coffee, her baby asleep in her lap.

"The police did come, didn't they?" she asked presently.

"Yes. It's routine, you know, when someone dies accidentally like that," I replied, pouring hot coffee into one Thermos.

"Did they ... do you know what they said?"

"Yes. I was there. A man named Griffin came to the

schoolhouse, because that's where Mrs. Anderson and the children stayed for a couple of days after the fire."

"What did he say?"

"Just routine questions," I answered, pouring the hot soup into the other Thermos. I took out a loaf of bread and quickly made a couple of thick sandwiches and wrapped them in waxed paper. "He asked what caused the fire, why Mr. Anderson didn't get out with the rest of the family, that sort of thing."

"Did Mrs. Anderson say anything about Lewis?"

"No, not a word. She just said she'd gotten up to build up the fire in the night, and gone back to bed. The next time she woke, the living room was on fire. She'd heard a thump earlier and saw that the stovepipe had fallen to the floor. She got all the children out but couldn't rouse her husband, because he was drunk and passed-out on the living room sofa. She couldn't get to him because of the fire's intensity."

"Did he believe her?"

"I'm sure he did. There was no reason not to. He more or less asked me to confirm some of her story, since I'd had some recent dealings with the family."

"What kind of questions did he ask you?"

"Did I know for a fact that Mr. Anderson was frequently drunk, the condition of the home, was it likely that the stovepipe had fallen, that sort of thing."

"And no one mentioned Lewis having been there?"

"No one. I wasn't aware of it myself, and Mrs. Anderson didn't say a word about it. He didn't question the children."

"Were you there the whole time he was questioning her?"

"Yes. He did take Davy with him when he went to look at the house. I don't know what was said then, but you can ask Davy if you'd like."

"Ask me what?" Davy asked, coming back into the room with his coat on and a lantern in his hand. I had packed the things I prepared into a bag with a shoulder strap. Now I draped it over his shoulder so his hands would be free. I knew he would likely take his rifle, too.

"I packed an extra sandwich for you," I said. "Sue was wondering if anything more was said about the circumstances of the fire when you were alone with Mr. Griffin."

"Not much. Nothin' that was important, jist what I'd seen when I got there."

"Lewis wasn't mentioned?"

"Nope. Far as I know, Mr. Griffin ain't even aware of his existence."

Sue sighed with relief. "Thank you," she said. "I feel a little better."

"It might not look so good though, him disappearing like that right after the fire," I said, feeling troubled.

"No, I know," Sue agreed mournfully, while Davy gave me a warning look from beneath his lowered brow.

"But since no one else knows about it, it's all right," I added reassuringly. "Nobody else does know, do they?"

"No, I haven't told anyone but you two."

"Then that's all right."

"I'll be back as soon as I find him," Davy said, bending to give me a quick kiss on the cheek. "Keep your chin up," he added to Sue as he went out the door. A minute later we heard the truck start up. I turned back to the table and gathered up our coffee cups.

"I don't want to go home and be alone," Sue said a bit forlornly.

"Then don't go home," I replied with only a moment's hesitation. "Stay and have supper with Calvin and me. I'll get a blanket so you can put the baby down on the living room floor, then you can come help me."

"Thank you so much, Anne. You and Davy are the very best friends in the whole world. I've turned to you so many times for help. I hope you know how much I appreciate it."

"You're quite welcome," I replied, feeling my slight resentment and jealousy evaporating. I was just overly tired, that was all. I'd feel better when I'd had something to eat and could relax.

It was after eight o'clock when Davy finally returned. Sue, the children and I had eaten and cleared away the dishes. For the past hour, Sue had restlessly paced to and from the window. I tried to reassure her, but I was beginning to worry myself.

When the truck drove up and Davy came in alone, I saw Sue's face crumple. A lone tear rolled down her cheek. I spoke the words she was unable to utter.

"Didn't you find him?"

"Yep, I found him. He's all right."

Sue slumped in relief and wiped the tear away. Davy grinned at her. "He wanted me to take him home before I come after you," he said. "Guess he didn't want you girls to see him in all his dirt and whiskers. I'll take you on home now, if you're ready."

"Yes, I'm ready," Sue said, beginning to gather up her belongings.

"I'll fix a plate for him," I said. "He's probably hungry."

"He ate that food you sent like a man half-starved. Otherwise, ain't nothin' wrong with him that a bath an' a shave won't fix up. Got anything left for me? I'm near starvin' myself."

"I'll have it warmed up for you when you get home."

He took the covered plate I handed him and went out to the truck, followed by the two girls. Sue held the baby in one arm and hung the diaper bag over the other. She lingered long enough to give me a hug and thank me again.

"Will you and Davy and Calvin come have supper with us next Friday evening?" she asked. "I know how busy you are, but we'd just love to have you. It's been so long since you've been over."

"Yes, I know, too long. I'll check with Davy, but unless I let you know otherwise, we'll be there. What time?"

"About six?"

"That will be fine. Bye, Sue. If there's anything more we can do, let us know."

"I will. Thanks again."

I closed the door and went back into the kitchen to fix a plate for Davy, reflecting on the events of the past few days. So many things had happened: the bad weather, the fire, then Lewis's disappearance. Surely things would quiet down for awhile now and get back to normal. I profoundly hoped so; I felt utterly worn out.

CHAPTER NINE

A Visit With Jane

Although the weather was warmer, the rest of the week brought intermittent rain and drizzle. Several students were absent from school because of colds, but on Friday, when Jimmie and Johnny Decker were absent for the third day in a row, I became worried.

They lived some distance from school. Their mother was expecting another child very soon, and they had no means of transportation. That and the bad weather would be explanation enough for their absence under ordinary circumstances, but the Decker's circumstances were not ordinary. Jane Decker's good-for-nothing husband, Jesse, had walked out on his wife and four children months ago, and no one had seen or heard from him since. My concern turned to dread as the day wore on. At the end of the day—when I saw Davy drive up in the truck—I suddenly decided there was nothing to do but go out and check on them. When he took my arm to help me up into the truck, I broached the subject immediately.

"Trouble?" he asked.

"I don't know. The boys have been absent for three days in a row. Neither of them showed any signs of illness that I noticed on Tuesday. I just need to go out and check on them to make sure they're all right."

"Okay."

"Thank you, Davy."

"You worry too much about people though, you know."

"I don't think so. Besides, I didn't say I was worried, just concerned. They're so alone out there."

"Okay."

He closed the door and went around to get in on his side.

Calvin sat between us, silent as usual.

The road was muddy and deeply rutted from all the rain. Davy drove slowly, the truck barely creeping along. I knew he was being careful because of me but I could barely contain my impatience. The conviction that there was something terribly wrong kept nagging at me.

We finally rounded the last bend in the road, and the Decker house came into sight. It sat silent and isolated, looking bare and abandoned except for the thin stream of smoke that rose from the chimney. Not even their old dog came out barking to meet us as he usually did. I leaned forward, my pulse quickening in apprehension, but I could tell nothing from the external appearance of the house.

"Take it easy," Davy said as he drew up into the yard and brought the truck to a stop. "Don't go jumpin' out an' hurtin' yourself. If somethin's wrong, another minute or two ain't goin' to make no difference. You wait an' let me help you down."

I opened the door but waited while he came around the front of the truck to help me. As he almost bodily lifted me down, I saw the front door of the house open and Jane's familiar figure, far advanced in pregnancy, standing there.

"You folks sure picked a nasty day to come a callin'," she greeted cheerfully as the three of us made our way toward the house. Davy had me by the arm, carefully steering me around the puddles of water that stood in the path, but Calvin plowed right through the biggest one, sending mud and water splashing up on the front of my coat.

"Calvin," I exclaimed in exasperation, stopping to look at the damage.

"Sorry," he mumbled, giving me a sidelong glance as he continued on.

"Guess boys is th' same the world over," Jane commented

with a touch of humor. I was so relieved to see that every-thing seemed all right with her that I forgot about the mess on my coat. "You folks come right on in outta that drizzle," she continued. "Don't know but what a day like this ain't a lot more bone chillin' than a outright cold day, if th' sun's a shinin'."

"We really can't stay, Jane," I said. "I just wanted to make sure you and the boys were all right."

"Come on in," she insisted, standing aside and holding the door wide. "You cain't come all this way out here an' not come in an' sit for a spell."

"Well, just for a little while then. Calvin, stand on the newspapers. Your boots are all muddy."

"Can't hurt these floors none," Jane said, closing the door behind us. "Take your coats off an' come on over by the fire. Boys, go drag up a couple of them chairs from outta th' kitchen for th' teacher here an' her family."

All four of her boys were there—standing around watching us—and everything seemed normal. I was relieved, but felt a little foolish for bringing Davy and Calvin all that way for nothing. But perhaps it wasn't for nothing, I thought, as I took in Jane's beaming face. She was pathetically glad to see us.

Calvin sat on the floor and removed his boots. He shed his coat and left it lying on the floor, then went to join the Decker boys.

"Calvin," I started, then stopped and bent to retrieve the coat myself. Jane and I exchanged rueful smiles.

"I'm glad to see I ain't th' only one has trouble gettin' th' boys to pick up after theirselves," she said. "I'll jist hang these coats behind th' stove here so they'll be nice an' warm for you folks when you're ready to leave. Sit down, Mr. Hilton. Mighty nice of you to bring your family out here jist to see if we're all right on a nasty evenin' like this."

"That's okay," Davy said. I could sense the uneasiness in

him that Jane always seemed to arouse. I turned my attention to the boys.

"How are you?" I asked. "We've missed you the last few days."

"They both had colds," Jane answered for them. She opened the stove door and added a piece of wood. The room was as bare as usual; the only furniture consisting of the stove and the few chairs grouped around it. But it was clean and reasonably neat. There were a few toys scattered around the room, but the coats were neatly hung on nails along the wall behind the stove. Jane took a chair. Her body was swollen and awkward, but her manner was relaxed and pleasant. "I figgered it was better to keep them home for a few days than to send them out in th' rain an' maybe all of them end up sick, jist about th' time th' baby's due to put in an appearance," she added.

"Yes, I thought that was probably what it was," I said, "but I just wanted to make sure. I brought some homework out for them if that's all right."

"Sure. It'll give them somethin' to do. They was a wantin' to go back today, but I figgered it wouldn't hurt to keep them home one more day. You folks want somethin' to drink? All I got's some canned orange juice or water, but you're welcome."

"No thanks, Jane, we're fine."

"Usually have some goat's milk, but Dinah seems to have run off again. Didn't catch sight of her by chance on your way here, did you?"

"Your goat has run off?"

"She's done it two or three times this week. Guess she's lonely; goats are social animals, you know, an' we ain't been able to pay much attention to her lately, with th' boys bein' under th' weather an' me bein' so clumsy in th' mud an' all. She's always come back before, but she's been gone most all day an' I'm some worried. She's a good milker, an' I don't want to lose her. These young'uns of mine gotta have milk."

"I'll go look for her," Davy volunteered, rising and reaching for his coat.

"Now I wasn't aimin' for you to have to do that," Jane said. "Likely she'll turn up 'bout milkin' time."

"I don't mind. Any idea where she might be?"

"She's been goin' over to where them cows of Mr. Miller's are, th' other side of them woods," she answered, pointing. "Goats is herders, they like to be with other animals. I knowed I shoulda kept her last kid, but I had to sell her to get money to pay some bills. Sure didn't mean for you to come over here jist to send you out in th' wet again, though."

"I don't mind a bit. Got some feed or somethin' I can take along to lure her back?"

"Only thing I got is some table scraps. Johnny, go get Dinah's bucket. She'll recognize it th' minute she sees it, even if she don't recognize you," she added as Johnny, the oldest boy, handed Davy a small galvanized bucket.

Davy took the bucket and went out. Jane came back to the stove and sat down.

"Hate to have him do that," she said, "but I am some worried. It's awful hard goin' for me in all that mud."

"You shouldn't be out in the mud at all, Jane, in your condition. What if you should slip and fall?"

"Wouldn't be th' first time. Guess I'm 'bout as tough as whet leather. Don't nothin' ever seem to interfere with th' babies comin' regular an' right on time."

"Haven't you been to a doctor yet?"

"Can't afford no doctor. 'Sides, ain't likely he can tell me anything I don't already know."

I opened my mouth to protest, but closed it again. I had been trying to get her to go to the doctor at least for a check-up all through this pregnancy, but she was proud. She wouldn't go without the money to pay and she wouldn't accept any kind of financial help from Davy and me.

"What about yourself?" she asked, brightening. "You feelin' all right?"

"I'm fine, just tired all the time. I'll be glad when the school year is over and I can have a couple of months to relax and get ready for the baby. So far I haven't had much time to even think about it, I've been so busy with other things."

"Wisht I could be as glad about my own young'un as I am about yours. Yours'll have a good home, a good mama an' a daddy at least."

"Jane, you're a good mother. You've had some very difficult circumstances to deal with, that's all. I wonder how well the rest of us would do under the same circumstances. I have nothing but admiration for you and how well you've managed without Jesse."

"Don't know how you can say that, after all th' things you know I done," she said in a gruff voice.

"But that's in the past, isn't it? You're doing much better now, aren't you?"

"Reckon I am, but it's funny. I'm doin' better cause I ain't tryin' so hard. Seems like it don't matter so much any more if th' house gets messed up or if th' meals ain't right on time. If th' boys get loud an' rowdy, I jist kinda tune them out less it gets really bad. I don't even interfere much any more when they get to squabblin'. Figger sooner or later they'll work it out for theirselves, or else get tired of it an' quit their wranglin'."

"Maybe you've learned the secret to being a good mother. Relax and don't try to do everything perfectly. Kids are only young once; they should be allowed to be kids, that is, most of the time. Your boys are good, Jane, and they're good students. I think you're doing just fine."

"You goin' on teachin', even after th' baby comes?"

"Not for at least a year, possibly even two. We'll just

have to wait and see how it goes."

"You goin' to like that, I mean stayin' home an' bein' a wife an' mama?"

"I'm looking forward to it. I love teaching, but I think I'm ready for a change. There just doesn't seem to be enough time to get everything done anymore."

Jane and I sat and talked while the five boys played with some toy trucks on the floor. I felt more relaxed than I had for several weeks. I liked Jane, and we had always been able to talk comfortably together, which was a source of amazement to Davy. He was always uncomfortable in her presence.

She had a pot of beans on the stove, which she got up to stir a couple of time. Each time she got up, she went to look out the south window to see if she could see any sign of Davy and the goat.

"He's got her," she said, the last time she looked, "but looks like she's givin' him quite a tussle. She sure can be ornery when she wants to be."

I got up and joined her at the window. Several yards away I saw Davy, bent over with his back to us, literally dragging the goat forward by the horns.

"She don't know him," Jane said. "I wonder if I might ought to go out an' help him."

"He'll manage," I said. "Davy's pretty determined. See? He's got her almost to the gate."

While we watched, Davy retained his hold on one of the goat's horns while he reached to unlatch the gate with his other hand. While his back was temporarily turned to the goat, she lowered her head and lunged forward, butting him in the seat of the pants. The gate flew open and Davy plunged through it, landing sprawled-out on the ground. He retained his hold on the goat's horn, and she landed on top of him. Jane and I both gasped, but before we could do anything, Davy was up, his front covered with mud, his expression grim. He slammed the gate shut and locked it, then dragged the goat toward the shed. Jane and I exchanged glances, then we both began to laugh.

Fortunately, the boys were occupied with their own interests and oblivious to us. When we saw Davy come out of the shed and start toward the house, brushing the front of his coat, we both quickly stepped back out of sight.

"Poor man," Jane said, her voice unsteady. "Don't never let him know we was watchin'."

"No, of course not," I agreed.

We were back in our chairs by the stove when Davy stuck his head in the door.

"You found her?" Jane innocently asked.

"I found her. She's needin' to be milked. If you'll hand me the milk bucket, I'll take care of it."

"That ain't necessary. You done enough an' I'm thankin' you for it but ..."

"I'll do it," Davy interrupted. "I'm already wet, no point in you havin' to get out in th' rain too."

"Better get it for him," I said low-voiced. She rose to go into the kitchen. She came back with the milk bucket and handed it to him. He closed the door, and Jane and I exchanged glances and giggled a little more.

A short time later, Davy came back with the milk bucket and set it inside the door, closing it again. A moment later we heard the sound of him chopping wood.

"Lord love th' man, what's he doin' now?" Jane asked.

"Getting rid of his frustrations," I said. "Better leave him to it."

"Why don't you folks stay to supper?" she asked. "There's jist beans, but there's a plenty an' you're sure welcome."

For some reason, I felt a small prick of conscience when she said those words. It puzzled me. Was there something I was forgetting? I thought about it for a minute and came up with nothing, so I dismissed it from my mind. It must not have been important.

"Thank you, Jane, but I'm not sure we can. It will be up to Davy."

"I'll go ahead an' get th' corn bread in. After all that work, he'll likely be starvin', an' it'll be awhile before you can get home an' get your own supper made. It ain't nothin' fancy, but a big hearty bowl of navy beans can be real satisfyin' after a hard day's work."

She went into the kitchen and I followed her. We could hear Davy carrying armloads of wood to the back porch and stacking it along the inside wall. Presently, he rapped on the back door then stuck his head in.

"You ready to go?" he asked me.

"Jane has asked us to stay to supper," I said.

"It's jist beans," Jane repeated apologetically. "but I'd sure be beholdin' to you if you'd stay. Don't get too much company out here, so when I do, I kinder hate to let 'em go."

Davy glanced at me. "It's up to you," he said.

I looked at Jane. I knew we'd hurt her feelings if we didn't stay. Besides, I was suddenly hungry myself, and the beans simmering on the stove smelled very appetizing.

"All right, Jane," I said, "we'll stay, but I'm afraid we'll have to leave soon after that. Davy still has his own chores to do at home."

"You can leave jist as soon as you've et. It's all ready. You can hang your wet coat there behind th' cookstove. I'll pour some warm water in th' dishpan for you. Sure am beholdin' to you for goin' after th' goat an' choppin' an' carryin' all that wood for us."

"That's all right."

In a short time, we sat down to steaming beans served in cracked bowls of various sizes, and canned orange juice served in clean soup tins. The corn bread sat in the middle of the table, along with a bowl of chopped onions and grated cheese. Davy crumbled a piece of corn bread into his bowl, added a spoonful of the grated cheese and the chopped onions and began to eat voraciously. I saw that Jane and her boys were eating their beans the same way and decided to try it myself. I found it very good and even had a second bowl along with everyone else.

"That was delicious, Jane," I said when I was finished. "Thank you for inviting us. I'll be glad not to have to cook supper tonight. I'm always tired at the end of the week."

"I'm proud you could stay," she said gratefully. "Like I said, I don't get company out here very often."

"I'll have one more scoop of them beans, if you got any left," Davy said. His request conveyed more gratitude than any words of thanks he might have spoken. Beaming, Jane rose immediately to refill his bowl.

We sat and talked while Davy finished his last bowl of beans, then we rose to leave. Jane wouldn't hear of me helping with the dishes. As we were leaving, she thanked us again for coming. *"It takes so little to make some people happy,"* I thought as we drove away. I knew Jane was lonely, and I was determined to spend more time with her when the school year was over.

On the way home, my thoughts drifted back to our unexpectedly pleasant evening. Suddenly I sat bolt upright and put my hand over my mouth.

"Oh no!" I cried.

"What is it?" Davy asked, slowing the truck.

"I forgot! Oh my goodness! Sue invited us to her house for supper tonight and I completely forgot about it."

"Is that all? Warn me before you screech like that again, will you? You almost gave me a heart attack."

"Is that all?" I wailed. "Sue will never forgive me. She invited us when she was at the house earlier this week, and I said we'd come unless I let her know otherwise. I completely forgot about it. I hope she didn't go to too much trouble."

"You know Sue."

"Yes, I know Sue," I moaned. "Candlelight, flowers, her

best dishes and a meal served in courses. She probably spent all day on it. Oh, how could I have forgotten?"

"First I heard about it."

"I tell you I totally forgot about it until this minute. She asked me just before you took them home. You were gone awhile, and I was tired so I went to bed early. It never entered my mind again until now. She'll be so hurt. Do you suppose we could swing by there now?"

"It's late an' I got chores to do, remember? You can run over there tomorrow."

I groaned. "I'm afraid she'll never forgive me."

"Never's a long time. She'll forgive you, but it may take her awhile, she seems to be one of them sensitive women. I'm glad I'm not in your shoes."

"Thanks a lot," I said grumpily, as I settled back to try to think how best to frame my apology.

CHAPTER TEN

Another Goldie Sutton?

On my way to the Proctor's house the next morning, I was still trying to think of an explanation to give Sue that wouldn't hurt her feelings too much or actually be lying.

"You see, Sue," I said, practicing the words aloud, "I was really worried about the Decker family. She's expecting her baby any day now, and she's all alone out there with those four little boys and no transportation. The two older boys had been absent from school for three days. I was afraid something might have happened, so I had to go out and check on them. When we got there, Jane's goat had run away and Davy had to go find her because they're dependent on that goat for the only milk those boys get. Then she needed some wood chopped because—you know yourself—being nine months pregnant and trying to chop wood just isn't a good idea. By the time Davy had the wood chopped, it was too late to come to your house, and besides, Davy needed to get home to do his own chores and check on that cow that he's expecting to calve any day now."

It didn't sound too bad, and it was mostly the truth. It might just work, and if it saved Sue's feelings, wasn't it worth a little white lie?

I pulled up in front of her house and got out. I had to knock twice before she came to the door, though I was sure I had seen her peek out the window when I drove up.

"Sue, I'm so terribly sorry," I said as soon as I was inside. "What happened? Is something wrong?"

"Well, you see, I had to ..." I stopped and drew in a deep

breath, then blurted out the truth. "I'm sorry, Sue, I forgot."

"You forgot?"

"Yes. I'm sorry. I know that sounds terrible; it sounds as though your invitation wasn't important to me, but it wasn't that at all. It's just that there's been so much going on this week with the fire and all. I've been so tired, and I was worried about Jane and her boys ..." I recounted the rest of the story, emphasizing how isolated Jane was and how hard it must be for her raising her four boys alone. After all, Sue was a mother, too, so I hoped she would empathize with Jane, and in the process forgive me. I finished my explanation in the same way I had begun it: apologizing.

"That's all right. I know you like Jane and worry about her," Sue said dejectedly.

"But I like you too, Sue. You're one of my best friends, and we always enjoy coming over here for a meal, but I ... The truth of the matter is, Sue, I totally forgot your invitation. I had so many other things on my mind, I guess it didn't really register. I even forgot to mention it to Davy. We did go over to Jane's, as I said, Davy did have to go hunt down her goat and chop wood for her, but that had nothing to do with our not coming. I simply forgot."

Sue just stood and looked at me. I knew I had hurt her feelings immensely. Might as well finish my confession and get it over with, then see what kind of amends I could make. She'd hear soon enough that we'd had supper with Jane.

"Jane invited us to stay for supper. It was just beans and corn bread, but she really wanted us to stay, so we did. It wasn't until we were on our way home that I remembered your invitation."

"You had supper with Jane, when I had already invited you over here first?"

"Yes. I'm sorry. As I said, I totally forgot your invitation. I must be getting senile."

"Well, I guess I know now how I rate."

"Please don't say that, Sue. It was nothing like that."

She didn't answer immediately. She just stood and looked at me, a hurt expression on her face. I felt awful.

"I'm sorry," I repeated. "I feel awful about it. Will you please forgive me?"

"Well, I guess so. What else can I do? Next time I'll send you a written invitation," she added tersely.

"At least write me a note, and I'll stick it up on the refrigerator. I find I have to do that any more if I'm going to remember anything."

"People do seem to run to you every time they have a problem, including me. I guess I can understand how you could forget."

"Thank you, Sue," I said with relief. I went to hug her, and she returned the hug warmly. "I hope you didn't go to too much trouble," I added.

"As a matter of fact I did, but that's all right. I had fun doing it, and it wasn't a total loss. It was a pretty special dinner if I do say so myself. When you didn't come, we made a family party of it. The girls were thrilled because they got to stay up late and ... well, it was kind of nice. We all enjoyed it. I would have enjoyed it more, of course, if I hadn't been so worried about you. I even sent Lewis over to check on you, but you weren't home."

I shook my head. "I can only say again how sorry I am. I hope you'll invite us again sometime, and next time I promise I won't forget."

"Can you stay now for a cup of coffee? There's some cherry pie left over, too, if you'd care for a piece."

"That sounds lovely."

I followed her into the kitchen and sank into the chair she pulled out for me.

"Where are the children?" I asked.

"Still asleep. We were up past midnight last night. I don't know that we've ever done that before. I haven't been up long myself. You look tired," she added, setting the pie and coffee in front of me.

"I am tired. The days just don't seem long enough anymore. I've been trying to spend some time with the Andersons; Granny made it a requirement when she agreed to rent her house to them. I've been over there twice this week. I'll have to confess I didn't sleep too well last night, worrying about how angry you were going to be with me."

"I'm not angry. Maybe I could help with the Andersons."

"Could you? That would be wonderful. She's doing quite well so far, but she needs someone to just drop in once in awhile to check on her and see if there's anything she needs. Davy has sent Lewis over there a couple of times with wood, so that's a big help to her."

"Yes, I know about that."

There was an odd clipped note in her voice. I put my cup down and looked at her in surprise.

"Is something wrong?" I asked.

"No," she said slowly, "not wrong really, it's just that ..."

"It's just that what?"

"Well, do you remember when Lewis stopped to chop wood for Mrs. Anderson the day before the fire?"

"Yes."

"I found out later that wasn't the only time he'd done it. He'd stopped to help her a couple of times before that."

"So?"

"So why didn't he tell me? Why did he keep it a secret?"

"Probably because he just didn't think it was important."

"Maybe."

"Sue! What are you thinking?"

She shrugged. "Nothing really, I just think it's odd that he didn't mention it to me."

"If he didn't tell you, how did you find out?"

"Mrs. Adams told me."

"And how did Mrs. Adams know?"

81

"She said Mrs. Wilson told her, and that she'd said everybody in the community knew about it. Only I didn't know about it and I'm his wife."

I groaned and put my head in my hands. "Sue, haven't you learned by now this community thrives on gossip? Most of these folks are good people, but some of them just aren't happy unless they're stirring up trouble. I don't know why that is. Maybe it's just a lack of excitement in their lives, but you can't afford to listen to half the things they tell you. Have you asked Lewis about this?"

"Yes. He said he did stop once before, a few weeks ago. One of their dogs was lying by the road hurt; he thought someone had probably run over its hind legs. He went up to the house and told her about it, then she asked him if he'd chop up a little wood for her because her man had been gone for several days and they were almost out. He stayed and chopped the wood, then he left. At least that's what he said."

"Don't you believe him?"

"She said—Mrs. Adams said—he'd been seen going into the house with her."

"Probably carrying in some wood for her."

"I asked him about it and he said he didn't go inside at all that time. He said he'd never been inside the house except that last time, the day before the fire."

"Don't you believe him?"

"Well yes, but why would Mrs. Adams say that, if there wasn't some truth to it?"

"Mrs. Adams didn't see it herself, she's admitted that. Mrs. Wilson told her and someone else probably told her. The whole thing has been blown way up out of proportion. Someone said something and someone else enlarged on it— perhaps embellished it would be a better word. It had to be made to sound exciting, you know, otherwise the story wouldn't be worth repeating. Forget it, Sue. There isn't a word of truth in it, except what Lewis told you."

She was silent a moment, her coffee cup forgotten in her hand, her head lowered. I frowned.

"Sue, you know Lewis loves you. He wouldn't look twice at another woman. What's gotten into you?"

She sighed. "I don't know," she admitted. "Maybe I've been alone too much and my imagination is running away with me, but I can tell you one thing. I don't like that woman, and I don't trust her."

"Which woman?"

"Jeanette Anderson."

"Jeanette Anderson has been a victim of gossip just as much as you have, Sue. As soon as her house burned down and her husband was killed people started speculating on whether she had done it deliberately to get rid of him. There wasn't a word of truth in it, it was purely accidental; but no one was willing to give her the benefit of the doubt. As I said, they seem to have to make something sensational out of the most ordinary things. Not that all of this was ordinary, but Lewis stopping to chop wood for her certainly was."

"I still don't like her. There's a certain 'oh poor helpless me' attitude about her when there's a man around. Haven't you noticed it? A man can be a real pushover for that."

"No, I haven't noticed it. I think your imagination is running away with you," I said, feeling a little exasperated, as well as amused. "The woman's just lost her home and her husband. She has sole responsibility for eight young children. That's enough to overwhelm anybody, you know. I think I'd be feeling a little like 'oh poor helpless me' in the same circumstances, wouldn't you?"

"Maybe, but I don't think she acts like a woman who's mourning the loss of her husband too deeply."

"No, perhaps not. You can't really expect her to mourn the loss of a drunken bum who refused to provide for her and the children and who regularly beat her in the bargain."

"Have you ever thought there might be a reason why he drank and beat her?"

"Sue!"

"Well, have you?"

"There can be no adequate reason for a man to be a drunk, or a wife-beater either, in my opinion."

"Oh, of course I agree, but you know what I mean."

"No, I don't know what you mean. Mrs. Anderson seems a basically decent person to me."

"I'm still not going to let Lewis go over there alone any more. I've told him that if Davy asks him to take over a load of wood or do something else for her, he has to stop by here first and take me along."

"Sue, you don't really think ..."

"No. I trust Lewis but I don't trust her. While we're there, I'll go in and visit with her a little and see if there's anything she needs help with while Lewis takes care of things outside. I'm not risking having her lure him into her den."

I did laugh then, almost choking on my coffee. I couldn't believe Sue was genuinely jealous of Jeanette Anderson. She was so attractive herself, and Lewis was obviously devoted to her.

"Laugh if you want," Sue said defensively, "but I intend to make sure what's mine remains mine. Men can be such pushovers for helpless, clinging woman. It's a dog-eat-dog world, and there seems to be a slight shortage of men out there. Look at what Goldie Sutton tried to do to you and Davy."

"I wasn't worried," I said, suppressing the remembrance that there had been a few times when I did worry. "Besides," I added, "Jeanette Anderson is not another Goldie Sutton."

"That's where you're wrong. Jeanette Anderson is just exactly another Goldie Sutton. Just watch her next time you and Davy go over there. See if she doesn't pay a lot more attention to him than she does to you, even after all you've done for her. Watch her eyes and the way she looks at him."

"Sue, I don't believe this."

"You'd better. Davy's not immune, either. No man is."

"I don't agree with you."

"You don't have to. Just do as I say; watch her next time."

"All right, I will. Then I'll come back and tell you you've got rocks in that silly blond head of yours. Sue, she can't begin to compare with you in looks or anything."

"That isn't always what counts. More coffee?"

"Thanks."

"More pie?"

"No thanks, but it was wonderful. I know we missed out on a delicious meal, but Jane's beans and corn bread were good, too. She was so pathetically glad to have us come to visit and then stay to supper. Please stop by and see her sometime when you're out that way."

"I will."

"Thanks. I have to go now. I've got the laundry to do yet today, but why don't you and the family come over next Saturday evening and have supper with us? Maybe we can invite my sister and Jim, too. We've seen so little of them since their marriage."

"I see them fairly often, since we live so close. Sometimes they stay in town over the weekend, like this one. They're still on their honeymoon."

"They seem to be doing all right?"

"They seem very happy. They're really fixing that old house of Jim's up nice. You'll have to stop by soon and see all the changes they've made. Of course, the outside still looks pretty bad, but Jim says they're saving that part of it for summertime. The parts they've done inside are just darling."

"I'll have to do that. I feel guilty, neglecting them as I have, but I haven't wanted to intrude. I figured if they wanted to visit they'd stop by the house, since they drive by every day on their way home from work, but they've only stopped once. I guess, as you said, they're still on their honeymoon and don't need anyone else. Well, Sue, thanks for the coffee and the pie. Most of all, thanks for being so understanding. Do you think you can come next Saturday? It won't be anything special, but it will be a chance for all of us to sit down and catch up on some visiting."

"We'll come. What time?"

"About five or so. We'll look forward to having you."

I drove home slowly, pondering what Sue had said about Mrs. Anderson. I didn't believe a word of it. If people only realized the harm that gossip could do, perhaps they'd be more careful about what they repeated. It was definitely a problem out here in the hills.

"Was she mad?" Davy asked a little later, coming into the kitchen where I was washing up the breakfast dishes.

"A little at first, but she forgave me. I've invited them over here for supper next Saturday. Is that all right?"

"All right by me. What're we havin' for lunch? I'm starvin'."

"You're always starvin'," I mocked. "What do you want?"

"I'll have me an old-time hamburger, if you got th' makin's."

"I don't have any buns. Will sliced bread do?"

"I guess so."

"Where's Calvin?"

"Left him over to th' Anderson's."

"You've been over to the Anderson's, have you?" I asked, pausing to glance over at him.

"Yep. Had to take her over a load of wood. Asked Lewis to do it yesterday but guess he forgot. Calvin was helpin' stack it on th' back porch. He'll be home soon."

"Did you see Mrs. Anderson, Jeanette, I should say?"

"That her name? Never did hear her called nothin' but Miz Anderson. Yes, I seen her. She come out an' talked awhile."

"You didn't seen her, you saw her, and she didn't come

out, she came out," I corrected, turning the hamburger in the skillet.

"Yes ma'am," he replied meekly, pulling a chair out from the table and seating himself.

"You really didn't know her first name was Jeanette?"

"Nope, can't say as I did."

"But you've been neighbors more or less for years."

"Never was interested in huntin' or farmin' or doin' much of nothin', far as I could see. She used to do some visitin' with Mom, but that's been years back."

"How does she seem to be doing?"

"Okay, far as I can tell. She's needin' a ride into town to pick up them commodities and her ADC check. Ast if I was goin' in soon. Told her I wasn't, but you might."

"I can't go in today. I still have the laundry to do."

"Don't want to have to make a special trip into town, but I may have to. She says she's gettin' real low on supplies. I told Mom, an' she's takin' a few things over to hold her 'til Monday."

"Mustard or catsup?" I asked, preoccupied, as I put the hamburger patty between two slices of bread.

"Both, plus some pickle, onion an' a slice of cheese."

When I set his sandwich on the table in front of him, I drew out another chair and sat down across from him.

"Ain't you havin' any?" he asked.

"I'm not hungry. I had coffee and pie at Sue's. Davy, do you see any resemblance between Jeanette Anderson and Goldie Sutton?"

"Huh?"

"I said, do you see ..."

"You feelin' all right? Them two don't look nothin' alike."

"I wasn't talking about looks. I was talking about, well, personality, behavior."

"Miz Anderson an' Goldie?"

"Yes. Do you see any resemblance?"

"They're about as different as night an' day, far as I can see. Why?"

"Because Sue seems to think Jeanette Anderson is like Goldie, in that she's man-hungry, and not too particular about whose man she goes after."

"What?"

"Sue thinks she's after Lewis," I said, watching him with amusement. "Or perhaps you," I added.

Davy choked. He put his sandwich down and reached for his glass of milk.

"You gotta be kiddin'," he said in disbelief.

"No."

"Well, great day in th' mornin'! What'll you women think up next?"

"I didn't think it up, Sue did. There's been talk."

He groaned. "When hasn't there been talk?" he asked. "What're they sayin' now?"

"That Lewis has been seen over there several times. The local women seem to think there's some reason for Sue to be concerned."

"She don't believe that."

"Not really, but she's going to take precautions from now on. She isn't going to let Lewis go over there alone any more. That's probably why he didn't take the load of wood over yesterday. She thinks I'd better keep an eye on you, too."

Davy just sat and looked at me, his expression stunned. I had to smile.

"Maybe it's Jeanette you need to be wary of instead of poor old Jane," I teased.

"That ain't particularly funny."

I put my hand on his arm. "No, I'm sorry. However, Sue is convinced she's not to be trusted around our menfolk."

"Women," Davy snorted, picking up his sandwich again.

"Can't live with us, can't live without us, huh?" I asked,

rising and giving his arm a pat. "Just thought I'd mention it, but don't tell Sue, will you? I don't know that I'd mention it to Lewis, either; it might upset him."

"Don't worry, I won't," Davy said curtly. "Talk about a lot of nonsense."

CHAPTER ELEVEN

Dirty Laundry

*B*efore my sister Liz was even through the door, she blurted out, "I have a surprise for you."

It was Saturday evening. I had been working all afternoon getting the house ready and a meal prepared for the company we were expecting. Lewis, Sue and their family had not yet arrived. Liz and Jim were almost an hour early.

"What is it?" I asked, smiling at my sister. She was looking very pretty and happy. Her husband, Davy's best friend, stood beside her, looking fatuous.

Liz threw her jacket open and struck a pose, saying "Ta da."

I looked blankly at her. What was this? Had my sister become an exhibitionist? Then I noticed that she wore a loose top, almost like a maternity top. I looked closer. It was a maternity top.

"Liz!" I exclaimed. "Are you? Is that a maternity outfit you're wearing?"

"Sure is," she said proudly. "You're not the only one who can have a baby."

"Liz! This is wonderful," I said, hugging her. "I had no idea. How far along are you?"

"Three months. We've kept it a secret. You're the first one to know."

"I'm so happy for you. And you, Jim, how are you going to like being a father?"

"I'm proud as a peacock. We're plannin' on havin' about ten, ya know."

"Ten?"

"Yep. This bein' a only child is for th' birds. Kids need

lots of brothers an' sisters to grow up right, I'm thinkin'."

Davy came over and hugged Liz, then gripped Jim's hand and slapped him on the back. We were still standing there exclaiming over the news when the Proctor family arrived and had to be filled in.

"I've suspected it," Sue said, "but I didn't say anything. I thought you'd want Anne to be the first to know."

"Why did you suspect it?" Liz asked her. She and Sue were good friends and next-door neighbors. "We haven't told a soul."

"No, but when I was over that day last week, one of those rooms you were papering was starting to look suspiciously like a nursery. Little animals on the wallpaper, you know."

"Oh. Well yes, it is a nursery. It's all so much fun—being a housewife, and now, getting ready to be a mother. I'm having a ball."

I felt a little stab of envy. I hadn't had the time to do very much as far as getting ready for my own baby, and I was three months further along than my sister. Davy and I hadn't even talked about a nursery yet, or much of anything else as far as the baby was concerned. We had talked a little about names, but that was about it.

We sat down to supper, and the talk was still about babies. I was glad to see my sister and Jim so obviously happy. I wished my parents could see them now. My mother had been concerned about their marriage, and my father had been adamantly against it. But it looked as if everything was working out very well.

After supper was over and the dishes done, Liz, Sue and I went back into the living room where the men and children were. Calvin and the girls were playing a board game. Sue's baby, little David, was fast asleep on a blanket on the floor. The men sat back, talking in a relaxed way. It was a pleasant scene—peaceful and quiet—with a contented atmosphere.

There was a knock on the door. Davy and I exchanged

surprised looks. We weren't expecting anyone else, and if it was one of Davy's family, they usually just walked in without knocking. Davy rose and went to the door.

"I understand this is where Liz Davis's sister lives," a male voice said.

Liz gasped audibly, and her hand went up to her mouth. Her face paled and her eyes grew large.

"Her name is Liz Baker now," Davy answered. His voice didn't sound overly friendly.

"I wasn't sure of her married name. Can you tell me where she lives? I'm an old friend."

Davy looked over at us. The visitor wasn't visible to us, but I knew from Liz's expression that she recognized his voice and that she was quite upset.

"If I could just talk to her sister," the stranger persisted when Davy didn't answer.

Jim's eyes were on Liz's face. His expression was sober, but not shocked or surprised. He reached over and took her hand. Sue and Lewis were looking at her, too.

"She's here," Davy said then.

"Can I speak to her, please?"

Davy stepped back and held the door wider. The man who came in was young and very good looking. His face was rather square, his hair blond and curly; he had the build of an athlete. He stepped tentatively inside, looking extremely nervous as he faced the battery of eyes that were turned on him.

"Hello, Liz," he said quietly. "I've evidently come at a bad time. I'm sorry."

Liz attempted to speak, but no words came out. There was a long moment of uncomfortable silence.

"Could I speak to you, please? Privately?" he persisted.

Liz found her voice. It came out clipped and harsh. "No," she said bluntly. "I have nothing to say to you."

"But I have something to say to you. I wanted to explain. ..."

"I don't think you have anything to say that I want to hear," she said, her voice strengthening. "You're not welcome here. Get out."

"Liz," Jim said quietly. "Maybe you should talk to him."

"Why?" she flashed, turning on her husband. "This is the jerk who let me think he was free and single, while all the time he had a wife and even a baby back home in Chicago. Why should I listen to him?"

"It wasn't quite like that," the young man said, sounding desperate. "If you'll only let me explain ..."

"There is no explanation—exactly how is one not quite married and the father of a child?"

"You don't understand."

"I understand perfectly. You were married but you forgot to tell me that. You let me think you were free and available. Fool that I was, I even thought you wanted to marry me."

She ended on a small, almost hysterical laugh, her face hard and angry.

"If we could just go somewhere private and talk, Liz, I'd like to explain, like to try to make you understand. But I can't talk to you in front of all these people," he said.

"All these people are my husband, my sister and brother-in-law and my good friends. I didn't ask you to talk in front of them. I didn't ask you or want you to come here at all. Get out!"

"Liz, my wife and I were separated, had been for a long time. We were going to ..."

"You couldn't have been separated all that long and had a baby just a few months old. I have no desire to listen to any more of your lies. I've asked you to leave; now please do."

"Liz, I really did love you. I didn't tell you because I didn't think you'd understand."

Liz laughed bitterly. "You're right there, I wouldn't have understood. Davy, or Jim or Lewis, will you please escort this ... this thing out to his car?"

"Liz, please listen to me. I know what I did was wrong, but I was going to tell you."

"I have nothing further to say to you," Liz said, her expression haughty. "You've embarrassed and humiliated me enough in front of my friends. That seems to be what you specialize in. If you don't leave immediately, then I will. Davy ..."

Davy opened the door and stood beside it. The stranger looked from him to Liz, then back to him. He shrugged and took a step toward the door.

"I'm sorry I hurt you," he said remorsefully. "I didn't mean to. It could have worked. I really loved you. I still do."

"Tough," Liz said, her voice hard. "I'm married, you know, and quite happily, but I forgot; marriage means nothing to you, does it? I'll also let you in on a little secret. I'm going to have a baby. But," she slapped her forehead, "I forgot again. Babies aren't important to you either, are they?"

"We could have worked it out," he said doggedly.

"Davy, do I have to listen to any more of this? Is he more welcome in your house than I am?"

Davy nodded toward the door, his hard eyes on the stranger. The man seemed to hesitate, then he shrugged again and went out the door. Davy closed it firmly behind him.

There was a long moment of silence. Even the children were quiet, looking up at the adults.

"Sorry to air my dirty laundry in front of all of you like that," Liz said apologetically. Then she uttered a strangled sob and rose, rushing for the bathroom. We all heard the lock turn, then the sobs that came from behind the closed door.

"That isn't good for her or the baby," I said finally.

"No," Jim agreed, rising. "I want all of you to know, I knew all about this. We talked about it th' very first time we met, that time you all had th' housewarmin' an' I took her for a ride an' showed her my houses. I told her about my first marriage an' she told me about him. She didn't do nothin' wrong except fall in love with a scoundrel. She really didn't know he was married."

He went forward and turned the knob of the bathroom door, knocking softly.

"Liz, honey, can I come in?" he asked quietly.

"No," came the muffled cry.

"Please unlock th' door. It ain't good for you or th' baby for you to be upset like that."

We held our breath; I was prepared to supply Jim with the key to the bathroom door if she didn't open it soon, but we heard the lock turn, and Jim went in. We all heaved a sigh of relief. We could hear Jim's soft, soothing voice. The sobs seemed to have stopped.

"I'm so sorry," I said helplessly to Sue and Lewis.

"It's all right," Sue said. "you couldn't have known he was going to come."

"No," I agreed bleakly. "Please don't think poorly of Liz. It was just one of those things."

"We don't think poorly of her," Lewis spoke up. "How many of us don't have something in our past that we're not exactly proud of? That young man doesn't seem to have much of a sense of what's appropriate behavior and what isn't. I can't imagine talking like he did in front of a bunch of strangers. She's better off to have found him out when she did."

"I hope she's all right," Sue said, sounding worried.

"She'll be all right," I said, with more confidence than I felt. "I don't have to ask you not to repeat any of this and to caution the children. You know how people out here like to gossip. Liz and Jim don't need that."

"We won't say a word," Lewis said. "It's none of our business. I think it's time we went on home; it's about bedtime for the girls. Thanks so much for the evening, Anne. We've enjoyed it."

I went for their coats. While they were putting them on, Liz and Jim came out of the bathroom. My sister's pretty face was red and puffy from crying. She gave us a rather wobbly smile.

"I'm so sorry I spoiled your evening," she said.

Sue went over and hugged her. "You haven't," she said. "It wasn't your fault. Are you all right?"

"I'm all right."

"We've got to go but we'll see you soon. If you need anything, just run over to the house anytime."

"Thanks, but there's nothing I need. I'm fine, actually. It's just that for a few minutes he brought back all the memories of what a fool I made of myself."

"We all make fools of ourselves at one time or another. You take care now."

Lewis shook hands all around and we said good-bye. When they were gone, I went to my sister and put my arms around her.

"All right?" I asked.

"I'm all right, but I'd like to go home now. Will you get my coat?"

"Of course."

I brought their coats, and after Liz had apologized again for ruining the evening, they were gone. Davy and I stood for a few minutes looking at each other. I sighed and felt my shoulders slump.

"Bedtime, Calvin," I said.

He needed no urging. When we were alone, Davy and I sat down together on the sofa.

"Well, at least now the mystery is solved," I said.

"What mystery?" he asked.

"Mom said Liz was in love with someone and talking marriage, then all of a sudden something happened and it was over; she didn't know why. Well, now we know why. She found out he was already married. Poor Liz."

"She'll be all right."

"You think so?"

"Yes, I do. You heard Jim say she told him all about it th' first time they met. If she hadn't told him, that mighta been a horse of a different color. As it is, he's got no call to be upset with her."

"But she cried so hard."

"Be good for her to get it out of her system, maybe once an' for all. Might be jist what she needed. Now she can put it all behind her an' forget it."

"I hope you're right. Jim was sweet about it, wasn't he?"

"He's crazy about her. They'll work it out. They was honest with each other from th' beginnin'. That's th' most important thing."

I sighed. "What terrible timing, though. I was so looking forward to a nice, quiet evening together."

"We can do it another time. I'm jist glad it was Lewis an' Sue that was here an' not someone else who'd spread it all over th' countryside."

"So am I," I said. "Profoundly glad."

CHAPTER TWELVE

A Breach Birth

I had just gotten up and gone into the kitchen to make coffee on the following Wednesday morning when I saw my sister and brother-in-law drive up in their small red truck. Liz got out with a large bag over one arm and a blanket-wrapped baby in the other. Jim got out on his side, and several children piled out of the back of the truck. They all started toward the house.

"What on earth?" I exclaimed aloud, going to open the door.

"Mornin', Sis," Jim greeted me cheerfully. "Glad to see you're up an' around, 'cause you got company."

"So I see," I replied, seeing that the children were Jane Decker's four boys and Sue Proctor's two girls. "What's going on?"

"Jane is in labor," Liz informed me. I looked closely at her. I hadn't seen her since the night I'd had them over to dinner. She looked fine, bright and smiling, as if she hadn't a care in the world. I was relieved. "Sue went over to stay with her while Lewis went for the midwife. Here."

She handed me the bag and put the baby in my arms. Little David was sound asleep. I looked from him to my sister, who was dressed for work.

"You asked Sue and me to help keep tabs on Jane and we have," she said. "But I have to go to work today, and Sue had to stay with Jane. We didn't think it would be a good idea to have all the kids there, and we didn't know what else to do but bring them to you. Lewis or Sue will come for them as soon as they can."

"Well, all right. How is Jane?"

"I don't really know; I didn't see her. She sent Jimmie over to the Proctor's and Sue sent him over to get me. We just stopped in a minute to pick up the boys. Sue thinks maybe Clemmy should come, just in case they can't locate the midwife. We'll stop to tell her, but someone else will have to take her there, we're running late already. Bye. Have fun."

"Bye."

I closed the door and looked at the children's upraised faces. In an hour I had to start for school, and what was I going to do with seven extra children—including a baby—if Sue or Lewis didn't come for them before then?

"Have you had breakfast?" I asked.

Six heads moved from side to side. I heard the alarm go off in Calvin's room and knew he'd soon be joining us.

"Take your coats off and wash your hands there in the bathroom, then come into the kitchen. I'll start breakfast."

I laid the sleeping baby on a blanket on the floor and covered him warmly. Calvin emerged from his room, his hair tousled, and stopped short in surprise.

"Good morning, Calvin," I said.

"Good mornin'."

"The Decker boys and the Proctor girls will be here for breakfast. Jane is going to have her baby today. As soon as you're dressed and ready, come to the table. You may have to help me a bit with the littler ones. We're going to have to hurry."

I went back into the kitchen and poured eight glasses of orange juice and set them around the table. Then I filled eight bowls with cornflakes. I topped them with canned peaches, added sugar and milk and set them around, too. The children began to file in. I put the smaller ones in chairs and let the older ones stand. While they were eating their cereal, I put on bacon and scrambled some eggs, knowing that these children were accustomed to a large country breakfast. I glanced up at the clock, beginning to feel a little harried. So this was how mothers with large families felt in the mornings. I hadn't even had the added chore of getting them up and seeing that they were properly dressed. I was still in my bathrobe and hadn't had time to do more than wash my hands and splash cold water on my face. How was I ever going to get ready on time?

Davy came in and put a bucket of foaming milk on the counter. He looked from the children to me with raised brows.

"Jane's in labor," I explained, "and Sue is with her. Lewis went for the midwife, so Jim and Liz dropped the children off here. Hurry and wash, Davy, so you can have your breakfast before your mother gets here. Sue wanted her to come in case they couldn't locate the midwife, so you'll have to take her out there. I don't have time."

"What are you goin' to do with th' kids?"

"If you go right away, maybe you can get back before I have to leave for school. If not, come after them, will you? It'll just be the two younger Decker boys and little David."

"Don't know if I know how to take care of a baby."

"Well, it's time to learn. Besides, it probably won't be for long. Hurry now, Davy, your mother will be here soon, if I know her."

He went off to the bathroom. Clemmy came just as he finished a quick breakfast. I was left with a table full of dirty dishes, a roomful of small children with sticky hands and faces, a crying baby, and still I'd had no time to get myself dressed. I grabbed a handful of washcloths out of a drawer and thrust them at Calvin.

"Wet them and give one to each of the children and tell them to wash their hands and faces, will you? And if you have time, you might clear the table for me. Just put the dishes in the sink."

I rushed into the living room to pick up the baby, who

was crying in earnest now. He quieted only for a moment. After studying my face, he opened his mouth in another frustrated and bewildered wail. His older sister Lori appeared in the doorway.

"He's hungry," she said.

"Very likely. I hope your mother sent some bottles."

"They're in the bag there."

"Thank goodness. Go warm one, will you, while I change his diaper."

When Lori came back with the warmed bottle, I handed the baby to her. She sat down with him in a corner of the sofa and put the bottle in his mouth, and the wails ceased. I rushed to the bathroom for a quick wash, then to the bedroom to dress. With only a light application of make-up and a quick brush through my hair, I was ready. I looked out the window. Davy had not returned. I would have to take the children to school with me.

The baby had to be changed again. While I did that, I set Calvin, Johnny and Lori to brushing the hair of the younger ones. The children hadn't brought toothbrushes so I gave them each a piece of gum to chew until we got to school. By the time we were all out the door, I was exhausted.

Lori volunteered to carry the baby, and her sister Becky took the diaper bag on her shoulder. It bumped against her knees as she walked, but she didn't complain. Josh, the youngest Decker boy, lagged behind. I picked him up once but soon put him down again. He was a chunky little boy.

We were ten minutes late getting to school. All the children were milling around the schoolyard, wondering what had happened to Calvin and me. I unlocked the door and let them in. I quickly assigned Johnny and Jimmie each a younger brother to look after, left Lori in charge of the baby and called the children to order. Once the familiar routine was under way, I felt my tension begin to subside. Surely someone would be coming after the little ones soon.

First recess was over and still no one had come. I began to worry whether something might have gone wrong with Jane. However, there was nothing I could do but wait.

Little David was getting fussy, so I took him from Lori. While the children studied for a spelling test, I put him over my shoulder and walked with him, humming softly in his ear. He had been very good so far, but I knew that since he was normally breast-fed, he missed his mother. He threw himself around a little, then finally fell asleep on my shoulder. I laid him on a blanket on the floor, then went back to my desk. A few minutes later I saw my car drive up, but it was Sue who came in instead of Davy.

"Sue!" I exclaimed. Remembering that the Decker boys were present, I lowered my voice. "Is something wrong?"

"It's a breach birth," she said. "The midwife wasn't home, so Lewis went to look for her. Clemmy sent Davy in to get the doctor. They just got back, so I thought I'd better come after the children. I didn't want to leave Clemmy alone with Jane while they were gone, in case there was something I could do."

"Is Jane all right?"

"It was just awful. She's been in such pain, but the doctor gave her a shot, and it had eased her some when I left. I guess—I hope—she'll be all right and that it will be over soon."

"Oh, poor Jane."

"She's tough, I'll give her credit for that, but she should have gone to the doctor so she would have known about this."

"I tried to get her to go."

"We all tried, but she said she couldn't afford it and she didn't anticipate any problems since she hadn't had any trouble with the other four."

"Yes, I know. Jane is proud, poor thing."

"Well, I'll take the extra kids off your hands now. Sorry about sending them off to you like that, but I didn't know what else to do, and I thought I'd be able to come after them sooner. I hope they haven't been too much trouble."

"They've been very good. Sue, you'll let me know? About Jane, I mean."

"Yes. Davy will have to have the car to take the doctor back to town, but we'll keep you informed as best we can. It's old Doctor Connors who came out, the one who came after David was born, remember?"

"Yes, I remember. What a day that was. Sue, just think, if this had happened to you."

Sue shuddered. "I don't think I could have borne it. Poor Jane has really suffered, but hopefully the worst is over. I'll keep you posted. Thanks again."

She left with her baby and Jerry and Josh Decker. I reassured Johnny and Jimmie Decker, explaining that the baby hadn't come yet, but it would soon. I gave the spelling test then, but I was worried about Jane, feeling that I should be there for support and reassurance. Not that she would expect it of me, she asked so little for herself. I liked and respected her so much; I would have liked to be able to stand by her now, as I knew she would want to stand by me in similar circumstances.

Soon it was lunchtime. It was a mild, springlike day, so most of the children had gone outside to play after they had eaten. Lewis and Davy drove up in my car. Davy got out, waving to Lewis as he drove away. He came toward the schoolhouse.

"Is Jane all right?" I asked, rushing out to meet him.

"She's all right now. Sleepin'. Mom's with her."

"Thank goodness. And the baby? Is it all right?"

"He's fine, sleepin' too. Both of them was pretty well wore out."

"Another boy?"

"Yep."

"Oh dear, and after all she went through. She was hoping this one would be a girl."

"After th' mornin' she put in, she wasn't worryin' none about whether it'd be a boy or a girl, just so it was all right. Seemed to think th' Lord might be punishin' her for not wantin' th' baby in th' first place. Went to howlin' right along with th' baby. When Doc swatted it on th' rear an' she knew it was okay, she didn't care none then that it was another boy."

"It must have been pretty scary."

"Guess it was. I didn't go in, but when I took th' Doc to th' door an' heard her groanin', that was enough for me. I went to th' woodpile an' chopped her a bunch of kindlin'."

"But she's all right now?"

"She's fine. She's gonna have to stay in bed for a week or two, but Doc says there shouldn't be any complications. Lewis is takin' him back to town. Guess he's had to give up drivin', his eyesight ain't so good any more. I went ahead and paid him for comin' so you can tell Jane when you see her that there ain't gonna be no bill, Doc said. She don't need to know why."

"Thank you, Davy, that's good of you."

"Don't go tellin' her. I don't want her feelin' she's beholden to me."

"All right, I won't tell her."

"I'll tell you one thing," he continued. "You're not stayin' out here to have our baby. You're goin' in to the hospital, even if we have to stay at a hotel for a week or two beforehand. I ain't riskin' puttin' you through anything like that. I couldn't stand it."

"I probably couldn't either. Thank you, Davy, for coming to tell me about Jane. I've been worried. Is your mother going to stay with her for awhile?"

"She'll stay, long as she's needed." He leaned over and gave me a quick kiss. "Well, see you later. I'm goin' on home an' get started on them cabinets I'm s'posed to be makin'. I told Lewis to bring th' car back here an' leave it for you.

Figgered you'd be wantin' to go out an' see Jane after you get off school."

"I would like to do that. I won't stay too long."

"Okay. See you later."

"Bye."

I took up the hand bell from my desk and went out to stand on the porch and ring it. That was the signal for a last-minute rush to the toilet or to the pump for a drink before the children came inside. I had seen Davy pause in the schoolyard beside Jimmie Decker, who had run up to him. Davy put his hand on Jimmie's shoulder and spoke to him. I knew he was telling him that he had a new brother and that his mother was all right. Johnny ran up to join them. Davy spoke to him, too, then strode on out of the yard and down the hill toward home.

"Congratulations," I told the boys when they came inside. "Did Davy tell you about your new brother? If you want to wait and ride with me, I'll be going out to see your mother for a few minutes after school."

They nodded, taking their seats as I called the first grade up to the front for a reading lesson.

CHAPTER THIRTEEN

Jesse Decker Returns

We were relaxing in the living room in an unusual moment of leisure. I looked up at Davy, who had lowered his newspaper and was looking at me with a certain amount of amusement in his eyes.

"Betcha can't guess what th' latest gossip is," Davy said.

"I don't want to hear it," I said firmly. "People around here do entirely too much gossiping. If I didn't know better, I'd think the hills themselves talk, the way news, good or bad, gets around so quickly."

"Sure you don't want to hear it?" he persisted, his voice teasing. "It's about your friend Jane."

We'd enjoyed several weeks without anything too eventful happening. Liz and Jim seemed to be fine, perhaps even more settled and happy than before our unexpected visitor. The Anderson family was coping. Jeanette, with the help of the older children and a little coaching and support from a few of the neighbor women, was keeping her home and her children relatively clean and properly fed. Calvin seemed to be doing well. He was at an age when he was striving for his own independence. Sometimes that was harder for me to accept than his dependence, but Davy had taken him in hand and he seemed to be thriving on the rules he had laid down. Jane was well and her baby was thriving; she was up and around and able to take care of her own responsibilities again. Therefore, when Davy said what he did, I felt a vague foreboding. Perhaps things had been going along too smoothly.

"Well, what is it?" I said impatiently. "What about Jane?"

"Thought you didn't want to know."

"You shouldn't have mentioned it in the first place, unless you know for a fact that it's true, or unless you saw it yourself or heard it first-hand from someone who did. Things get so distorted after they're repeated several times."

"Heard it from a pretty reliable source."

"Well, what is it?"

"They're sayin' that Jane's ol' man has come back."

I sat up straight and dropped the magazine I had been holding. "Jesse Decker is back? No, he couldn't be. Jane wouldn't take him back, after all he's done."

"Accordin' to th' grapevine, though, she has."

"I don't believe it."

"Lewis hisself told me. Said Jim told him he was drivin' by an' saw him there. Jesse waved to Jim, big as you please, jist like he belonged an' was makin' hisself right at home."

"I don't believe it," I said again. "Jane has more sense than that. How could she take him back after what he did, selling the pig I gave her and taking all the money they had, leaving her alone there with those four little boys to take care of, and with another baby on the way? She'd have too much pride to take him back after all that."

"Some women jist gotta have a man, I guess, don't seem to matter much what kind of man he is. You said that yourself, remember?"

"I said that?"

"Yep. You was talkin' about Goldie Sutton an' Miz Anderson, if I remember right."

"Oh. But I don't think I said any kind of man, I said it didn't seem to matter whose man ... Oh, nevermind, it's not important. I can't believe this about Jane. Are you sure Jim would recognize Jesse? After all, he's never been around very long at a time. Maybe it was Jane's brother. He does visit them sometimes, you know."

"Lewis said Jim said it was Jesse."

"Well," I said, picking up the magazine and putting it on the coffee table before getting clumsily to my feet. "I still don't believe it. I'm going out there to see for myself."

"Best not interfere. She won't thank you for it."

"Jane's not like that. She and I are friends."

"Maybe so, but he's her husband. They're still married, ain't they?"

"Well, yes, I guess so, but ..."

"Go pay her a visit if you got to, but I'd stay out of their personal business, if I was you. It might cause trouble."

"Trouble! Trouble is that man's middle name."

"Maybe I better go along."

"Why?"

"To keep you outta trouble."

"I don't need you to keep me out of trouble. I know my place."

"Uh-huh."

"What do you mean, uh-huh? Am I in the habit of interfering in other's personal lives?"

He looked at me with his tongue in his cheek and a twinkle in his eyes. I picked up the magazine and threw it at him.

"I try to help when help is needed, that's all," I said loftily. "I don't interfere. I can talk to Jane. We're friends."

"If you say so."

"I do say so. And I also say I know Jane better than to think she'd go back to a scoundrel like that."

I took up my car keys and went out the door. The weather was beautiful: spring had finally arrived. The sun was shining brightly, a soft breeze was blowing, and birds were singing. The only thing that marred the beauty of the day was the nagging possibility that Jesse Decker had returned. I simply would not believe it unless I saw it with my own eyes.

When I arrived at the Decker home, the four older boys were outside playing. They stopped and looked at me; I smiled and spoke and went on up to the house. The door was closed. A thin spiral of smoke ascended from the chimney, but the house was silent. I knocked, then stood stunned for a moment when Jesse Decker opened the door.

"It's the teacher, isn't it?" he said, in the smooth, insinuating way I remembered. "It's a pleasure to have you come to visit us. Jane has told me how helpful you've been. Come in, come in."

He held the door wide and stood aside. I entered, mute, unable to think of a word to say. The living room was empty.

"Jane is napping with the baby right now," he volunteered. "We had a rather late night last night, family talk you know, catching up on things. This last job of mine took me away from home much longer than I had intended."

"Sure," I thought with contempt. *"It took you away for the better part of a year, with not a word to your family, as far as I know. And where has all the money from this so-called job gone, I'd like to know. None of it to the support of your wife and sons."*

"I just stopped by to see if she needed anything."

"That was kind of you, but I'm here now. No need to worry yourself about her any longer."

"I'm not worrying myself," I snapped. "Jane and I are friends. I like to stop in now and then, just to visit."

"I'll tell her you were here. I'd wake her, but the little one was colicky during the night and she lost some sleep. Perhaps you can come by another time."

"I'll certainly do that. Tell her I was here, will you?"

"I ought to say 'welcome back' or something like that," I thought, but the words stuck in my throat. I turned toward the door.

"Jesse, is that Miz Hilton?" called Jane's voice from the nearby bedroom.

"Yes, my dear, it's the teacher. She just stopped in to say hello," he answered.

"Tell her to come in, will you? It's been a spell since I seen her."

I didn't wait for his invitation, but stepped into the bedroom. Jane was in bed, propped up on two pillows, the sleeping baby cradled in one arm.

"How are you, Jane?" I asked.

"Fair to middlin'," she answered. "S'cuse me for not gettin' up. Th' baby was colicky last night an' is jist now sleepin' good. Musta been them beans I et for supper. Pull up a chair an' sit down."

"I really can't stay. I just ran by for a minute."

"I know what you're a thinkin'," she said, low-voiced. "An' I don't blame you a bit. I been thinkin' 'bout th' same thing myself."

"I don't understand," I said helplessly.

"No, I don't s'pect you do. Ain't too sure I understand it myself. If you'd a told me a few weeks ago that he'd come back an' I'd take him, I'd a said you was crazy, but a body does get lonesome, jist bein' around kids all day ever' day."

"But Jane, after what he did?"

"I ain't forgettin' that. I ain't never goin' to be as trustin' of him as I usta be, but ain't no man ever paid no heed to me 'ceptin' Jesse, an' ain't no man ever likely to. I ain't pretty like you, I ain't got nothin' to offer a man. I don't talk right, I got no education. I can't even read an' write. I been too ashamed to tell you that before, but it's true."

"But Jane, you could learn, and besides, those things are not important here. You have honesty and integrity and industriousness. ..."

"Don't reckon I rightly know what them last two things are, but it don't matter anyhow. I know no man but Jesse will ever look twice at me, and a body does get lonesome."

I looked at her, troubled, unable to think of what to say.

"You're not to be a worryin' about me now. You an' your man done a awful lot for me an' I'm beholden to you, but likely things'll be better for us now. Jesse's got him a good job, so there'll be money to pay th' bills an' maybe a little somethin' extry. I been worryin' some about th' cost of that doctor a comin' out here to help with th' baby. I know you said it was took care of but ..."

"It was taken care of. There is no doctor bill from that, Jane. Dr. Connors is retired, he doctors part time just to keep himself occupied, so you can forget about that."

"It was good of him. Folks has been awful good, but I hate to be beholden to anyone. Maybe now I can repay some of th' kindness that's been done for me, now that Jesse's back."

I didn't know what to say, but I felt infinitely sad for Jane. I felt certain she was doomed to disillusionment. What kind of empty promises had he made to her, and how could she possibly believe them? There was nothing I could do, though. I rose and put the chair I had been sitting in back in the corner.

"Kindnesses are not done to be repaid, Jane," I said gently. "You are well liked around here; people wanted to help. I'd better run along now. I just stopped by for a minute."

"I'm thankin' you an' I'm hopin' you'll come again sometime."

"Of course I will," I said, touching her shoulder. "You and I are friends, Jane, and if you ever need anything, you let me know, all right?"

"An' you do th' same. I'm hopin' I can be of some help to you when your own little one comes. That's one thing I do know somethin' about."

"I'll probably need your help. Good-bye, Jane. Take care."

When I re-entered the living room, Jesse rose from his chair and more or less escorted me to the door. I wondered if he'd overheard any of our conversation, although I didn't care if he had. It was all I could do to hide my contempt for him and be civil until I was out of the house.

"Well?" Davy asked when I arrived home.

"I don't want to talk about it," I answered gloomily.

"So he has come back?"

"Yes. He met me at the door, as oily and slick-tongued as ever, talking about regretting that his last job had taken him away from home for so long. He's filled Jane's head with promises of good times to come, a good job and all that. Poor Jane, how she could believe him I'll never understand. I wonder how long it will be before she has to start picking up the pieces again. He'll probably just stick around long enough to start another baby, then he'll do his disappearing act again. I'd like to shoot him. I had an impulse to ask him how much money he got from Rosy when he sold her, but I didn't."

"Good girl," Davy said. I made a face at him.

"She said no other man has ever looked twice at her, and she gets lonesome. Can you believe it?"

"Yep. Told you so, remember?"

"Don't you 'I told you so' me," I retorted. "No man is worth it, certainly not Jesse Decker."

"Are you gonna wash your hands of her?"

"No. I like Jane and I respect her. I just don't understand this."

"Need for a man, any man?" he mocked.

"Oh, be quiet," I said. "I'm not in a good mood and I don't want to talk about it."

"Yes ma'am," he said meekly, disappearing behind his newspaper with a grin.

CHAPTER FOURTEEN

A Mountain Out of a Molehill

*D*avy was taking a load of wood to the Anderson's, so I went along. Although the weather had become warmer, most of the people out in the hills still cooked with wood. My sister-in-law, Ellen, had been spending some time with Mrs. Anderson, helping her with the smaller children and the housework. But according to Granny's terms, I was required to check in on her from time to time.

It was a Saturday afternoon in late April, a fine spring day. We had both the windows down in the truck; the fresh wind blew my hair about my face and the sun shone warmly on my right side. It was pleasantly relaxing to be with Davy like this, my other responsibilities temporarily put aside.

When we drew up before the house, all looked peaceful and quiet. Several of the older children stood silently in the yard, watching us. Calvin jumped down from the back of the truck and went to join the two older boys. He had become better acquainted with them since the fire and sometimes stayed awhile and played with them after he and Davy had been there.

Davy came around the truck to help me down. I was now seven months into my pregnancy, and my body felt heavy and clumsy. I was finding it increasingly difficult to keep up with all my responsibilities. For the first time, I would be glad when school was out. I loved teaching, but I was tired, and anxious to begin getting things ready for the arrival of our baby.

Jeanette Anderson met us at the door, and I had to take a second look to make sure it was her.

She wore a clean cotton dress, obviously cheap, but bright and pretty. Her hair was cut and curled, and she wore a light application of powder and lipstick. She was smiling rather shyly.

"Why Jeanette," I heard myself saying with a note of surprise. "How very nice you look."

"Thanks," she said, her voice low and uncertain. Her eyes left mine and shifted toward Davy's. Her smile seemed to deepen, and a curious light came into her eyes. I glanced quickly at my husband and saw him return the smile. His eyes were warm and kind. I felt excluded: there seemed to be a special bond between them. A little pang of jealousy smote me. The two of them were evidently a little better acquainted than I had realized. Just how often had Davy been coming over here?

I remembered dismissing what Sue had said about this woman as having no foundation. Had I been too busy with my own life and responsibilities? Was Sue perhaps more tuned-in to what was going on than I had been?

I mentally shook myself and tried not to feel fat and awkward and ugly. I knew that Davy loved me and I trusted him, but was this woman not to be trusted, as Sue had intimated? Or was I, as I had accused her of doing, letting my imagination run away with me?

"Come on in," she said, standing aside for us to enter.

"I'll go ahead an' unload th' wood," Davy said. "Is there anythin' else you're needin' done while I'm here?"

"I can't think of anythin' today," she said softly. "you been so good, fixin' everythin' up like you done."

"If you think of anythin', let me know. I'll chop you up some kindlin'."

Davy turned and strode away; her eyes followed him. Then, almost reluctantly it seemed, her eyes turned back to me.

"Come on in," she said again, but her voice had lost its

animation. I went inside, attempting to suppress my galloping imagination.

She offered me a chair, and I sat down and glanced around. The house seemed to be in reasonably good order.

"How are things going for you?" I asked, striving to make my voice pleasant. "You seem to be doing very well."

"Ever'body's been real good," she answered briefly.

"And the children, the little ones? How are they?"

"Th' baby's been a little sickly but I reckon it's jist th' croup. Kept me up some durin' th' night, but he's sleepin' now. Mattie's got th' others down by th' crick."

"I see. Who did your hair? It looks very nice."

"Ellen done it, Miz Hilton. She's been comin' over some an' helpin' out."

"That's good. Ellen's a very special person."

In view of my own feelings about this woman, I wondered what Ellen's were. Her husband had a well-known weakness for women; did Ellen worry that her own contact with Jeanette Anderson might result in her husband becoming involved with her? Goodness knew she had more to be concerned about in that area than I did, but it hadn't stopped her from coming over and doing her duty. Perhaps I should take a lesson from her.

I tried to make further conversation, but it was difficult. She had nothing to volunteer, so I had to keep asking questions, which she answered only briefly. The two of us didn't seem to have much in common, although I hadn't been aware of any particular restraint between us before.

Her whole demeanor changed when Davy came in. Her face quite literally lit up; an attractive, shy smile curved her lips. A slow anger began to burn in me. I had to suppress an urge to get up and throttle her.

"You wantin' a drink of water or a cup of coffee, or somethin'?" she asked him. She hadn't bothered to offer me anything.

"No thanks," Davy replied easily. "I had a drink out at the pump. You ready?" he asked, glancing over at me. "Unless," he added, turning back to her, "there's somethin' you've thought of that you're needin' done."

"No, not today."

"If I hadn't been along, I'll bet she would have thought of something," I thought grimly, struggling to rise. Davy reached out to help me, but I ignored his hand and took hold of the arms of the chair, pushing myself to my feet. I looked at Mrs. Anderson and forced a smile to my lips.

"It's so nice to see you doing so well," I said. "If you need anything, be sure and let us know."

When we were outside, Davy again reached for my arm as we walked toward the truck, but I pulled away. "I'm not an invalid," I almost snapped. "Calvin, come on," I called, raising my voice. "Let's go home."

"I told him he could stay for awhile."

"Suppose I don't want him to stay?" I snapped back.

"Didn't think you'd mind. He's done it before, then walked home. It ain't that far."

"It's not the distance I'm concerned about. Calvin, come on."

Calvin came running up, looking from one to the other of us. "You said I could stay," he said to Davy.

"Sorry. Anne wants you to come on home."

"But we was goin' down to th' crick to do some fishin'. Matthew says he knows where there's some big 'uns an'..."

"They'll have to wait," Davy said. "No arguin' now. You can do it another time."

Calvin gave me a hateful look, and my heart smote me. I'd never seen him look at me like that before. I wanted to relent, but something wouldn't let me. Calvin climbed into the back of the truck and threw himself down against the cab, his arms crossed over his chest, his face belligerent and frowning.

I had to accept Davy's help up into the truck. He closed the door, then went around to get in on his own side and start the truck. We maintained an uneasy silence for several minutes.

"What happened in there?" Davy asked finally.

"Nothing."

"Musta been somethin'. You was in a good mood before we got there."

"I just don't think Calvin should associate with the Anderson boys."

"First I ever heard of it."

"I didn't know he was playing with them that much. How often have you—has he—been going over there?"

"Jist whenever I go over to take her some wood, or fix somethin' that needs fixin'. Granny let th' place get pretty run down, you know. I take Cal along, cause I think it looks better than me goin' over there alone, an' sometimes I've let him stay an' play awhile."

I felt relieved and somewhat foolish, but I didn't know what to say. I couldn't tell Davy how jealous I had been.

"Th' boys ain't that bad," Davy continued. "I can't see that it's hurtin' Cal any to spend some time with them."

"They've had almost no training or discipline. They've been let run and do as they please for most of their lives."

"But ain't that 'bout what Cal was let do, 'til we got him? Ain't that much mischief to get into out here. Fishin' an' playin' around in th' woods ain't gonna hurt any of them that much, far as I can see."

"I just want him to limit his association with them, that's all. I know them perhaps a little better than you do. I've been their teacher for nearly two years now."

"Okay. If you feel that strong about it, I'll make sure he comes home when I do from now on."

"I don't think you should be spending so much time over there, either," I snapped, before I could stop myself.

He looked at me in surprise, and I knew it was genuine. Again, I felt that little prick of shame. I had no reason to doubt my husband, but I understood now what Sue had meant about Jeanette Anderson.

"What're you sayin'?" he asked. "I thought you wanted me to help her."

"You've helped her enough. Let someone else take a turn."

"I was sendin' Lewis, but he refuses to go anymore. Who else is there to send?"

"I don't know, but find someone."

He was silent, but I felt him look at me several times. I kept my own eyes focused straight ahead.

"You can't be jealous," he said finally. His tone was incredulous, with a hint of amusement.

"Of course not. It's just that I, well, I don't think it's wise for you to go over there so much. It might cause talk."

"I don't go over there that much an' there's always talk."

"Not about you and her. At least, there'd better not be."

He shrugged, but there was a little smile playing about his mouth. It irritated me.

"Don't act so pleased with yourself," I said shortly. "Sue was right. That woman is not to be trusted."

"Miz Anderson? You gotta be kiddin'."

"No, I'm not. You stay away from her."

"If you say so, but you oughta know you ain't got no reason to be jealous. I never looked at any woman but you."

I snorted, and he looked a little hurt.

"When have I ever looked at another woman?" he asked. "Since I met you, I mean."

"I'm not accusing you of looking at another woman, but she is certainly looking at you."

"You're lettin' your imagination run away with you. I sure ain't seen her lookin' at me. She's been friendly an', well, grateful for th' help I've give her, but that's all."

"That's what you think. Men are so naive."

"I don't know what you're talkin' about. Give me a fer instance."

"For instance, she was all smiles every time you were around. She didn't bother to smile for me, and I've done as much or more for her than you have. She offered you a drink, but she didn't offer me anything."

"That's because you was jist settin' there an' I was out workin' in th' hot sun," he replied with amusement.

"It wasn't just that."

"Well, what?"

"The way she looked at you. The way her eyes followed you."

"You got rocks in your head," he said. "What's got into you anyhow? You been listenin' to Sue again?"

"No, but perhaps I should have listened to her in the first place. I heard things about Mrs. Anderson when I first moved here, but I didn't pay any attention. I wish now I had."

"You're gonna hear talk, no matter what you do or don't do," he said impatiently. "Haven't you learned that by now? Thought you were th' one who told me not to listen to gossip."

"Nevertheless, I want you to stay away from her."

"Yes ma'am," he said, sounding amused again.

"I mean it. I don't want there to be trouble."

"There won't be any trouble, far as I'm concerned. I think you're makin' a mountain out of a molehill, but Mom told me that women in your condition get funny notions an' I got to humor you, so consider it done."

"Oh you." I left the sentence unfinished, but hit him lightly on the arm. I sighed. Perhaps there was something in what his mother had said.

"Maybe I am making a mountain out of a molehill," I said presently. "But she did look at you as if you were, well, her salvation or something. I suppose it's perfectly natural for her to feel grateful. After all, you are a very attractive man, and you're kind; I'm not surprised that she likes you."

"But you think maybe she likes me too much?" he asked.

"Don't joke about it. It's not funny, at least not to me."

"Is to me."

"Why?"

"'Cause. Great snakes, woman. Here's th' whole country-side knowin' I'm downright crazy about my wife, who's pretty well got me wrapped around her little finger, an' you're worryin' about Jeanette Anderson?"

"I'm not worrying exactly, just warning you that you need to be careful. Besides, I do not have you wrapped around my little finger. You're your own man; you do as you please, at least for the most part."

He laughed. "I ain't complainin'," he said, giving my hand a squeeze. "So I'm to stay away from Miz Anderson, am I?"

"Yes."

"Okay, but you'll have to find someone else to help her then, an' it'll have to be someone who won't succumb to her charms, like me an' Lewis supposedly did."

"I didn't say you succumbed to her charms, I just said ... Well, you'll have to admit that she has started to be more concerned about her appearance. She's had her hair cut and curled and she had on lipstick and powder today. That's a first, as far as I've seen. Did she by any chance know you were coming today?"

For a moment he looked discomfited. "Guess maybe she did," he admitted. "Told her last week I'd bring her some more wood today."

"You see?"

"Don't see nothin'. Ain't it natural for a woman to want to look as good as possible?"

"Yes, but she obviously hasn't cared about her appear-ance for a long time. Now, all of a sudden, she cares again."

"That don't mean nothin'. Things are lookin' up for her now: she's gettin' some of th' help she's been needin' for ages, an' she has a little time to think of herself. Besides, it was Ellen who offered to fix her hair an' encouraged her to take some time for herself. She didn't do it jist for me or for Lewis or any man, like you're implyin'. She done it for herself."

I was silent, feeling more ashamed by the moment. I couldn't argue with what he was saying. It was perfectly understandable that Jeanette would feel better about herself and want to look accordingly.

"She looked very nice," I acknowledged begrudgingly.

Davy glanced again at me, as if surprised. "She looked all right," he said. "Can't no woman compare to you, though."

"It's nice of you to say so, at least."

"What do you mean by that? I wouldn't say it if I didn't mean it."

"Oh Davy, I feel so fat and awkward and ugly," I said.

"You, fat an' awkward an' ugly?" he asked incredulously. "Why, you're prettier than you've ever been. Don't you know that?"

"No."

"Ain't I been tellin' you that all along?"

"Yes, but I know you've just been trying to be kind."

He laughed again. "You goose," he chided, covering my hand with his. "I don't ever say things jist to be kind. If I can't say somethin' nice an' mean it, I jist don't say anything. I thought you knew me better than that."

Tears came to my eyes. I bit my lip to keep it from trembling and turned my hand so that I was holding his. I sniffed forlornly.

"What is this?" he exclaimed, puzzled. "Don't you know I think you're th' most beautiful woman in th' world an' I'm crazy about you?"

"I know you used to think so."

"Nothin's changed, except I love you more now than I ever have. After all, you're gonna have my baby, an' that's th' most wonderful thing in th' world."

"Is it, Davy?"

"You know it is. Haven't I told you enough times?"

"Not lately you haven't."

"I have too. Maybe you jist haven't been listenin'."

I sighed. "Maybe I haven't. There's been so much going on, too much. I'm tired, and I guess your mother is right. I have been getting funny notions. I'm sorry."

"It's all right. I'm glad you care enough about me to be a little jealous now an' again, jist don't overdo it, you hear? You got no reason in th' world to be jealous of Miz Anderson."

"All right, Davy, but I still want you to stay away from her. I don't trust her a bit."

"But you trust me, don't you?"

"Yes, of course, but you can't be too careful."

He sighed. "I'll be glad when this baby comes, in more ways than one," he said.

"So will I," I admitted. "I'm sorry, Davy. I'll try to be less temperamental."

"Okay, an' I'll stay away from Jeanette Anderson, jist to please you, not that there's anything there to worry about."

"Thank you, Davy. It will make me feel better."

"Then that's all there is to it. Well, we're home, an' if I ain't much mistaken, you got some explainin' to do to Cal. From th' looks of things, he ain't too well pleased with you."

"No, I know."

"Want me to handle it?"

"No, I'll do it. I've been wanting to have a talk with him about the Anderson boys; this is as good an opportunity as I'll get. I'll keep in mind what you said about them, perhaps they aren't such bad friends for him as I've been thinking."

Davy shook his head. "Does a man ever get to th' place where he understands how a woman thinks?"

"Probably about the time a woman gets to the place where she understands a man," I replied.

"Men ain't that hard to understand. They're straightforward an' reasonable an' not devious."

"And women are? Perhaps you're right, but women are wiser. Men can be so naive when it comes to other women."

He sighed again and shook his head. He got out of the truck and came around to help me. When he lifted me down, he hugged me for a moment, then bent and kissed me on the cheek before he turned away, leaving me to confront an angry and resentful adolescent boy. The next half hour or so was going to be anything but pleasant, but I felt up to it now. Davy had reassured me so successfully that I felt foolish about the whole episode. Nevertheless, I was still determined that my family's association with the Andersons was going to be strictly limited from now on.

CHAPTER FIFTEEN

That Anderson Woman

*I*t was the noon hour. Most of the children had finished their lunch and were outside playing. Mrs. Miller had stopped by on her way home from visiting with one of the neighbors. There was an air of suppressed excitement about her.

"Hear tell you're thinkin' about takin' these young'uns to town to see one of them picture shows."

"Yes, Mrs. Miller, I am. I thought it would be a nice end-of-the-school-year treat for them."

"There's some folks think them picture shows are from th' devil."

That gave me pause. Davy warned me that I might face opposition from Mr. Sutton, the father of two of the boys in my school, but I hadn't expected it from Mrs. Miller.

"I know some people feel that way, Mrs. Miller," I said, "and of course, there are some movies that wouldn't be appropriate for children, but the movie I want to take them to is about a dog named Lassie. It has been approved by the school board as appropriate for children. I've seen it myself and I didn't find anything objectionable about it. I've read the book about Lassie to the children here at school, and they loved it. And after all, it's only a story put into pictures. Of course, if any of the parents don't want their children to go, that's perfectly all right."

"Oh, if it's jist about a dog an' you've seen it, guess there ain't no reason why my girls can't go. But how you gonna get all them kids into town?"

"Davy will take the older ones in the truck. He'll put the

sideboards on and strap benches inside them for the children to sit on. It should be quite safe if he drives slowly, which he will. I'm going to ask one of the parents to ride along in the back of the truck with the children. I'll take the first graders in my car with me and follow them. I'll probably take another parent along to help keep an eye on the children. That will be four adults, counting Davy. There should be no danger."

"Sounds like you got it all figgered out. I'm a goin' to let my girls go. They ain't ever been to a picture show before."

"Good. I know they'll love it."

She stepped a little closer to me and lowered her voice.

"While I'm here, there's somethin' I think I oughta tell you. I ain't one to go around stirrin' up trouble, but seems like this is somethin' you oughta know about."

"What is it Mrs. Miller?"

"Well, you know I was over to Miz Baxter's helpin' out with her young'un, who's been kinda puny. She said she saw your man this mornin'. He was in his truck with that Anderson woman, goin' down th' road toward town."

My heart jumped. I moved some papers around on my desk, then looked up at Mrs. Miller, hoping my expression didn't give away my inner agitation.

"Was he?" I asked, pleased that my voice was calm and cool.

"Miz Baxter said she was sittin' up real close to him. Looked like there wasn't no space at all between them."

"They would have had the younger children with them."

"Miz Baxter said wasn't no one in that truck but him an' her, far as she could see."

"She wouldn't see the children, of course, they're too small. Why are you telling me this?"

"Like I said, I don't want to cause no trouble, but you're a newcomer here an' likely you don't know that Anderson woman good as I do. She's th' kind of woman that'll jist wait for a chance like this, when you're big with th' baby an' can't be no proper wife to your man, if you know what I'm meanin'."

"I'm sure there's a perfectly understandable reason why they were together. He was probably taking her into town to get groceries or something, since she doesn't have a car. I trust my husband."

"S'cuse my sayin' this, but I ain't seen a man yet that can be trusted around a woman like that. They don't never see which way th' wind's a blowin' 'til it's too late, an' accordin' to some folks who've knowed them a long time, ain't a one of them Hilton men got in them to be beholden to jist one woman."

"You're mistaken, Mrs. Miller," I said coldly. "If you'll excuse me now, it's time for the children to come in. Thank you for stopping in."

"Wasn't aimin' to upset you, but to my way of thinkin', you got th' right to know."

"The right to know what?" I retorted, thoroughly angry now. "I don't believe a word of it, and I'm sick to death of all the gossip that goes on out here. Don't repeat what you've just said to me to anyone else. If you do, I'll be very angry. Now, good-bye."

I turned my back on her, took up the hand bell, and went out on the porch to ring it. Mrs. Miller followed me out and went off down the path toward the team of mules that was tied there. Furious with her and everyone else out here who so loved to indulge in gossip, I watched her climb into the wagon and drive off. At that moment, I felt that I hated them all and wished I'd never come out here.

I went back inside and tried to concentrate on the afternoon classes, but I found myself shaken and trembling. I loved Davy and I trusted him; hadn't he just reassured me a few days ago that he had absolutely no interest in Mrs. Anderson or anyone else? That he loved only me and would never be unfaithful? Nevertheless, I couldn't get what she had said out of my mind.

Davy must have taken Mrs. Anderson into town—surely they wouldn't make up something like that out of thin air—but there would be a perfectly legitimate reason for it. As for the two of them being alone and sitting close together, well, I just didn't believe it.

Deliberately, I willed myself to focus on my classes. It worked for awhile, then I would find insidious doubts creeping back into my mind. I kept remembering the old saying, "Where there's smoke, there's fire." It wasn't true in this case—I was sure of it—but a moment later, I would remember Mrs. Miller's words, which shook my conviction. Davy had just promised me he'd stay away from Mrs. Anderson, but evidently he hadn't kept that promise. Were there other promises he'd broken? Did these women know my husband better than I knew him? Was Mrs. Anderson the kind of woman they all seemed to think she was?

By the end of the day, I was a nervous wreck. I dismissed school a few minutes early because I couldn't endure it a moment longer. I had to hear from Davy what had actually happened.

"*I'll stay calm,*" I told myself as I walked home, Calvin skipping along ahead of me. "*I won't make accusations. I'll simply ask, quite reasonably, if he took Mrs. Anderson into town today and why. No, I'll say, 'I hear you took Jeanette Anderson into town today. Was something wrong?' No, I'll say, 'I hope nothing was wrong, was she sick or something?' Then he'll tell me, and I'm quite sure he'll tell me the truth. It will be some simple little thing, perfectly understandable. But he told me he would stay away from her. Why has he gone back on that promise?*"

When I came over the hill and looked down in the valley where our cabin was nestled, Davy's truck wasn't there. My heart sank. Surely he'd had plenty of time to get home if he'd only taken her into town. Of course, he could have taken the truck and gone somewhere else; he often did that. He'd be home soon and all would be well.

Of late when I came home from school, I lay down on the sofa for a half-hour rest before I got up to start supper. That afternoon I couldn't. I was restless, nervous. I kept going to the window and looking out. I picked up things and needlessly straightened magazines on the coffee table. I hadn't assigned any homework for the children that day, so Calvin had gone out to feed his rabbit and play with the dog. I was glad he wasn't there to witness my agitation.

An hour passed, then two. I prepared a light supper and called Calvin in. He ate heartily, but I was unable to do any more than pick at my own food. When he went outside again, I cleared the table and left the used dishes in the sink. I went back into the living room and plopped down in Davy's favorite rocker by the stove. I was fast losing any confidence I'd had. Davy was with Jeanette Anderson—had been all day—and he hadn't even bothered to leave me a note of explanation. One part of my mind kept telling me "I know he loves me. I know he wouldn't do this to me." A minute later, another part of my mind was crying out "How could he do this to me? How can he betray me like this, and just as I'm about to have his child?"

I was still sitting there, limp and drained, my hands crossed protectively across my swollen stomach, as if the child inside me was all I had left to hang on to. I heard the truck drive up and stop, but I just sat there. When Davy entered the room, I was suddenly filled with rage. I pushed myself up out of the chair, and my hand closed over a small glass figurine that lay on the shelf nearby. Without con-scious volition, I flung it as hard as I could at him. He dodged, a look of astonishment on his face. The figurine shattered against the wall and fell to the floor.

"Anne," Davy exclaimed. "What in th' world? ..."

"How could you?" I cried, reaching for something else

to throw. "How could you do this to me, after all we've meant to each other?"

My groping hand found the alarm clock. I threw it at him, but he deftly caught it, set it down, and came quickly toward me. He grasped my wrist before I could seize on anything else and held me in a viselike grip.

"What th' devil's goin' on here?" he demanded.

"How could you?" I cried again, tears beginning to pour from my eyes. "I've been absolutely faithful to you, I've never even looked at another man. I thought you loved me, you said you loved me. Why did you lie? How could you do this to me after you promised? ..."

"Hush," Davy said sharply. "Stop strugglin'. You'll hurt yourself."

"I don't care," I sobbed, the fight going out of me. I collapsed back into the rocker, hunched over in almost unbearable pain. I began to rock back and forth, my sobs breaking the silence. I couldn't see Davy for the tears, but I felt him kneel before me, his hands still tightly grasping my wrists. I knew in that moment that I loved him enough that I wouldn't let him go, even if he'd been unfaithful.

"How could you?" I repeated between sobs. "How could you do this to me?"

"How can I say why I done it if you don't tell me what I done?" Davy asked desperately. He had tried to talk to me before, but I was so intent on my pain that his words didn't register. He released my wrists and put his arms around me. My rage had abated enough to prevent me from struggling against him. My sobs began to subside; I felt utterly drained and almost limp.

"Sweetheart, what is it?" he asked. "What's wrong?"

"Don't you call me sweetheart," I said, my voice shaken. "Not after you've been with her."

"With who?"

"Her! That disreputable Jeanette Anderson."

He was silent for a long minute, then he removed his arms from around me and gently pushed me back in the chair.

"So that's what this is all about," he said grimly. "News sure does get around fast. Whose gossip have you been listening to this time?"

I slumped in the chair, not answering, knowing I must look a mess but not caring. It seemed as if my life was over.

"You promised me you'd stay away from her," I said, my voice dull and lifeless.

"I have stayed away from her, but today ..."

"Today you've been alone with her all day," I retorted, suddenly angry again. "You were seen with her practically sitting on your lap, going toward town in your truck."

"I wasn't alone with her, an' she wasn't practically sittin' on my lap!"

"Mrs. Baxter saw you."

"Of course Miz Baxter saw me, an' you'd take her word over mine—your own husband's—any day," he retorted, angry in his own turn. "Anne, for cryin' out loud, I thought you had better sense."

"Mrs. Miller came to school to tell me."

"I don't give a dang what Miz Miller told you or what Miz Baxter told her or what she thinks she saw! I did take Miz Anderson into town, but th' rest of it is a pack of lies!"

"You promised me you'd stay away from her."

"Sometimes promises can't be kept."

"Evidently."

"Are you gonna listen to me or am I gonna have to go out an' crack Miz Miller an' Miz Baxter's heads together?"

I turned my face away from him and didn't answer. He grasped my chin none too gently and turned me back to face him. His face was grim. I stared woodenly back at him.

"You're gonna look at me an' you're gonna listen to me," he said. "I did take her into town. Th' baby was sick an' ..."

"Why did it have to be you? Why couldn't someone else have taken her? And why couldn't you have left me a note or something?"

"I didn't leave a note because I didn't know I was goin'. I was drivin' by on my way to take them cabinets in to John, when she run out an' flagged me down. Th' baby was real sick an' she needed to get him to th' doctor. He was breathin' real funny an' runnin' a high fever. So I took her. What else could I do? Th' baby looked bad; I didn't even think about runnin' all over th' countryside lookin' for someone else to take her. I was goin' in anyhow, so what's th' big deal? We wasn't alone, either; we had to take th' other little ones along."

"Why was she sitting in the middle near you?" I asked, my voice still wooden. I was beginning to feel ashamed, but I wasn't going to be convinced so easily.

"She wasn't settin' in th' middle near me. Th' kids was in th' middle. She was settin' near th' door."

"Mrs. Miller said Mrs. Baxter said ..."

"Like I told you before, I don't give a good ..."

"Don't swear, Davy."

"I feel like swearin'. I feel like rippin' th' whole house apart. I feel like goin' out an' givin' Miz Baxter an' Miz Miller both a good cussin'."

I started to feel a whole lot better. I couldn't doubt my husband; he was wholly convincing and I wanted to be convinced. "Davy, I'm sorry, but ..." I started, but he interrupted me.

"But nothin'. You oughta have better sense than to listen to their gossip. Besides, I thought you trusted me."

"I do trust you."

"Like fun you do. If you wasn't so close to havin' that baby, I think I'd be tempted to beat you."

"I don't blame you. I don't know what got into me, but Mrs. Miller seemed so sure of her facts."

"Facts my foot! Facts don't enter into it when two women like that put their heads together an' start talkin'."

I leaned forward and put my arms around his neck. He removed my arms and pushed me back again.

"You're not gettin' by that easy," he warned. "You're goin' to sit there an' listen to ever' word I say, an' then you can start apologizin'. Then maybe I'll let you put your arms around me."

I pushed my hair back from my face. Davy leaned forward and gently dried my cheeks with his handkerchief. I knew then he was prepared to forgive me. I was also prepared to believe every word he said.

"Th' baby has pneumonia," he explained. I felt a fresh stab of remorse, but I let him continue. "Th' doctor put him in the hospital. I had to find her a doctor in th' first place, 'cause she hadn't been to one for so long. Then I had to make all the arrangements for the hospital. Once th' baby was settled in, th' doctor told Miz Anderson she could go on home, but she wouldn't. I had to talk to th' doctor an' convince him that she should stay, an' that took some time an' doin', I can tell you. She'll have to sleep in a chair tonight, but they finally said she could stay. Then I had to bring th' other little ones back home, but I couldn't leave them by theirselves. I went over to get Ellen an' bring her back to watch them 'til th' older ones got home from school, so she could explain to them where their mother was an' fix their supper. Then I had to go back into town an' take Miz Anderson some clothes an' things. I still had to go on an' deliver th' cabinets to John, like I was plannin' when I first started off to town. It's been 'bout th' most hectic, frustratin' day of my life, an' I was lookin' forward to a good hot supper an' a little peace an' quiet an' sympathy from my wife. Instead I come home to this."

"I'm sorry, Davy," I said contritely.

"I would hope so. Can't believe you'd throw a tantrum like that. You might've killed me, throwin' that glass thing at my head like that."

"I'm sorry," I repeated, hanging my head.

"But worse than that, Anne, you hurt my feelin's. How could you believe—even for a minute—that I'd do somethin' like that?"

"I don't know," I admitted lamely.

"That ain't good enough. I want to know why. I thought we understood each other better than that."

"I really don't know, Davy. I guess it's just that when someone who's older and more experienced tells you something like that and they say it's for your own good, and everyone keeps saying that Jeanette Anderson is not to be trusted around men ..."

"I ain't seen a bit of evidence to support that, an' what's more, I don't believe it. She's been a victim of gossip jist as much as you have here."

"Maybe, but Mrs. Miller said that ..."

"I don't want to hear another word of what Miz Miller or Miz Baxter said," he said, suppressing his anger. "I'm hopin' I don't run into either one of them before I have a chance to cool off. I might jist give them both a little piece of my mind."

We were both silent for a minute. I sat with my head bowed; Davy still knelt before me. He reached out and brushed a strand of hair away from my face.

"Okay then," he said gently. "If it's botherin' you, go ahead an' tell me what else Miz Miller said."

"She said that because of my condition ..."

"Yes?" he prompted.

"Well, she said that there are some women who will take advantage of that to get a man, and that men are more susceptible and more vulnerable then."

"You tell Miz Miller next time to mind her own business. She don't know what she's talkin' about, an' besides, I ain't most men. I'm me, an' I'll thank her an' you not to keep comparin' me to other men. I happen to be very much in love with my wife, an' I'd never be unfaithful to her. Tell her to put that in her pipe an' smoke it."

He reached for me and held me close. I put my arms around his neck and let my breath out in a long sigh.

"Davy, I am sorry," I said. "I promise I'll never doubt you again, no matter what anyone tells me."

"You better not. You got any questions about anything I supposedly done, you come to me with them first, 'fore you go flyin' off the handle like that again, you hear me?"

"Yes, Davy, I hear you. I'm sorry."

CHAPTER SIXTEEN

A Trip to the Movies

Sifting through the mail as he came in from outside, Davy pulled a lone envelope out of the stack. "You got a letter," he said, tossing it in my lap. He went over to his favorite rocker and sat down to look through his own mail. I opened the letter.

"My sister Mary wants to come out and spend a few days with us next week," I told Davy when I had read the brief message.

"Is her husband comin' too?"

"She doesn't say. She just says she's flying into St. Louis on Friday and will spend the weekend with Mom and Dad. Then on Monday, she wants to rent a car and drive on out here. She wants me to write or call Mom and let her know if it's all right for her to come. Any objections?"

"Nope, none from me. I like your sister."

"Good. Then I'll go into town Saturday and call Mom. It's not the best timing in the world, with Liz and me both working, and there's that trip into town to the movies I've planned next Friday. I know what, Mary can come along as one of the chaperones."

"Think that's a good idea? She ain't used to kids, is she?"

"As a nurse, she frequently works with children in the hospital. She'll manage. I'll have to let Liz know she's coming. Maybe we can all have dinner—I mean supper—together one evening while she's here."

I began to make preparations for her visit. Calvin would have to vacate his room again and sleep on the rollaway bed in the utility room. I washed all the bedding and hung it outside so my sister would have the chance to sleep under fresh, fragrant sun-drenched sheets, a luxury that I knew city dwellers seldom had the privilege of enjoying.

As I hung the clothes out on the lines that Saturday morning, the sun shone warmly on my back, and a gentle breeze blew my hair about my face. It was a gorgeous day, and I was once again filled with content for my home and the life I had chosen. For a few days after the encounter with Mrs. Miller, I had withdrawn into myself somewhat, feeling as if I disliked everything about these hills. Now I knew it wasn't true. This was home. It wasn't without its problems and shortcomings, but if I were given the choice I wouldn't trade it for any other life.

I turned back to the house, the empty clothesbasket in my hand. I waved at my mother-in-law, who was hanging out her own wash. I saw Davy in the garden hoeing and Calvin running over the hill, the dog at his heels. It was a restful scene, tranquil and peaceful. I hoped my sister would enjoy it as much as we did.

Later that morning I went into town to pick up a few groceries and to call my mother. Her voice was quiet and subdued when she answered the phone.

"Did Mary arrive all right?" I asked, after we had exchanged greetings.

"Yes, she's here, but she's taking a nap right now," Mom answered. "Do you want me to wake her?"

"No, that isn't necessary. Just tell her we'll be expecting her sometime Monday. I'll be at school, of course, but Davy will probably be around somewhere. If he isn't, just tell her to go on in and make herself at home. Calvin's room is ready for her, and we never lock the door. Does she need directions on how to get to our place?"

"Your dad can give her directions."

"If he will."

"Of course he will, Anne. He's not quite that bitter about your marriage."

"I'd hoped by this time he wouldn't be bitter at all, that he'd at least be resigned. Oh well, how is he, anyway?"

"He's all right, about the same as usual."

"How does he feel about becoming a grandfather twice over?"

"He doesn't say much. You know how your father is."

"Yes, Mom, I know how he is. How do you feel about it?"

"Anne, honey, you know I'm thrilled. I may not be there for the babies' births, but I intend to come out and spend at least a week with both you and Liz after the babies come. I wouldn't miss that for anything in the world. I've always wanted grandbabies."

"We'll love having you, Mom. Why don't you come on out with Mary now? Dad can get along without you for a week."

"I'd love to, but she hasn't suggested it. I was hoping she would, but I have the feeling she wants to be alone; she wants to talk to you privately or something. Mary is troubled, but she doesn't seem to want to talk to me about it, and I don't want to intrude."

"I had the feeling that something was wrong when they were here for Liz and Jim's wedding. Do you have any idea what it is?"

"No, unless it's trouble between them. I hope not, but I'm afraid of it."

"I had that feeling, too."

"Encourage her to talk, if she will, Anne. Maybe you or Davy will be able to help her."

"I'll try, Mom. Try not to worry, okay? I have to go now. Tell Daddy hello for us, and tell Mary we're looking forward to her visit."

I drove back home, pondering the situation with my sister. Was something really wrong with her marriage? How would my dad feel when he found out about that? Of his three daughters' marriages, hers was the only one of which he approved. In fact, he had introduced Mary to Kevin and had encouraged their relationship. I would be sorry to hear it if they were having marital problems, but perhaps it would help my father see that he was not infallible when it came to choosing husbands for his daughters.

On Sunday afternoon, I did some baking and advance preparations for the meal I would serve Monday evening. Liz and Jim were coming over, too, and I wanted the meal to be special; my sisters and I got together so seldom anymore. Mary was there when Calvin and I arrived home from school on Monday. Davy had made her welcome, directing her to Calvin's room and carrying her luggage in. The two of them were at the kitchen table having coffee. Mary rose and came forward to hug me.

"You're fat, girl," she said, as we stood apart.

"With good reason," I retorted. "Mary, it's so good to see you. I hope you can stay for several days."

"The rest of the week, unless you decide to kick me out. I don't have to be back to work until next Monday."

"Good. You remember Calvin?"

"Of course I remember him," she said warmly, holding her hand out to him. "How are you, Calvin?"

"I'm okay," he mumbled, his eyes downcast as he briefly took her hand. Calvin was still quite shy around strangers.

"Have you been here long?" I asked her, trying to break the awkward silence.

"Only about half an hour. I took my time, did a little sightseeing. I saw so many beautiful flowering trees. I recognized the pink-and-white dogwoods and the redbuds, but there were several others that I didn't recognize. Some kind of wild fruit trees, I imagine. And when I got out here, well, it's all just gorgeous, with the apple and pear trees in bloom and the lilac bushes in bud, and the forsythia and tulips. It's like having your own little corner of paradise. I envy you. I'm going to spend most of my time out here just soaking up the peace and quiet and sunshine. I'm tired."

I looked at my sister, thinking maybe that's all the problem was; she was just tired and needed a little rest and relaxation. I was glad we could provide it for her.

"I'm glad you've come," I said.

"I see you have some of your garden up, too."

"Yes, Davy gets most of the credit for that. I love getting out in the fresh air and sunshine and puttering around in the dirt, but I'm a little limited in what I can do right now."

"I imagine. Exactly when is the baby due?"

"About the first of July, just two months from now."

"You must really be excited. And Liz? Hers is due just about three months after yours, I understand."

"Yes. Hers is due the first of October. They'll be here for supper. They get home from work at about 6 o'clock, so we'll wait and eat then. Are you hungry now? Would you like a little snack to tide you over?"

"No thanks, I'm fine."

"Then we have time to sit and visit for awhile before it's time to start supper."

We had a pleasant visit, then she got up to help me with supper. Liz and Jim came and the meal was a success. We sat and talked until after dark, when Jim announced jokingly that he had to get his pregnant wife home and in bed. They had to get up early in the morning, and if she didn't get her eight hours, she was a bear to live with. We made arrangements to get together again at their house on Wednesday evening, then they left. Later, when I thought Mary would be in bed, I knocked on her door and went in to say goodnight to her.

"There's an old saying out here," I said, standing beside her bed. "If you sleep in the moonlight, you might go crazy."

She turned toward me. The moonlight, streaming in

through the open window, revealed the melancholy expression on her face. "Too late," she said. "I think I'm already crazy."

I sat down on the edge of the bed and put my hand briefly on her arm. "Mary, what's wrong?" I asked quietly.

"Oh, nothing and everything."

"What's that supposed to mean?"

"Oh nothing much. Just that there's nothing really wrong but there doesn't seem to be anything really right, either. I think I'm getting old."

"Old? You? Why, you've just turned thirty."

"Sometimes I feel a hundred."

"Can I help?"

She turned her face back toward the window and was silent for a long minute. Then she turned back to me.

"I don't know," she said. "Possibly. I at least wanted to come out and see how you and Davy were doing and how you felt about this baby coming. You and I are a lot alike, Anne. I wanted my career in nursing; you wanted your career in teaching. Kevin wanted children; I didn't. Davy wanted children; you didn't. But now you're going to have one. I just wanted to know how you feel about it, if you're prepared to give up your career for a family. Kevin is insisting that we have a child. I think he's even prepared to leave me if I don't agree, and I don't think I do. I've put too much into my career to give it up now."

"Mary, I didn't say I never wanted children, just that I didn't want to start a family right away. And I don't intend to give up teaching permanently, just while the child is small. I do want a family. I always have."

"But your situation is different. Davy is home, his work doesn't take him away for weeks at a time the way Kevin's does. What kind of life could we give a child, with my work, and him being away so much of the time? A child requires a lot of care, a lot of attention. I just don't think our situation would be fair to the child."

"Maybe some adjustments could be made. Maybe Kevin could take a different position so that he could be home more; after all, he has years of flying experience. He could teach and train younger pilots."

"Yes, he could do that."

"Then where is the problem? Having a child doesn't have to end your career in nursing. It might limit it temporarily, but I don't see why you would have to give it up entirely, any more than I intend to give up teaching entirely."

She was silent again. "I guess the truth of the matter is, I'm just plain scared," she admitted.

"Scared to have a child? But Mary ..."

"Not scared to have a child in that sense, just scared of what could happen to that child later. Anne, I've worked in pediatrics a lot. I'm good with children, but the things that can happen to them can be so heartbreaking. We lost a beautiful little seven-year-old boy just last week. I got too attached to him, and it just broke my heart, not to mention his parents. He was their youngest child, and they loved him dearly. They were just devastated. I looked at them and thought, 'I don't ever want to have to go through anything like this. It isn't worth the risk.'"

"I'm sorry. I know that has to be hard, all the suffering you have to see. What happened to the little boy?"

"Leukemia. It was hopeless from the beginning. You try to encourage the parents, try to stay positive and keep their spirits up, when all the time you know how it's going to end. Then when it does ... I've asked for a transfer from pediatrics when I get back home. I can't take it anymore."

"I do see what you mean, but that seems to be what life is all about these days, taking chances. You do have to remember, though, that you're constantly in a place where there's going to be a lot of pain and suffering. The average person probably doesn't see as much of that in a lifetime as you see in just a matter of weeks. Perhaps you're not getting a balanced perspective on things. Perhaps the risks are not as great as you think."

"Perhaps not. I guess I hadn't really thought of it that way." She sighed. "I wish now I'd gone ahead and had a child soon after we were married, the way Kevin wanted. I don't think I would have been nearly as apprehensive about it. Liz and Jim seem happy, don't you think?"

"Yes, I do."

"Neither of them seem to have any fears, as far as having children are concerned, but I hope Jim didn't mean it when he said he wanted ten. That would seem to me to be entirely too many for anyone."

"Davy's mother had nine and she seems to have done all right. Jim was an orphan, you know, and I think when he was growing up he always envied Davy's brothers and sisters. I wouldn't worry too much about it if I were you. Liz has a mind of her own. If she decides she doesn't want ten—after she has one or two—she'll stop."

"She seems to be enjoying married life. She was so full of talk about the way they're fixing up the house."

"Wait until you see it; it's darling. On the outside, it looks all run down, with this awful brown siding that is chipped and stained. The trim is peeling and the porch roof sags. It's a little comical, really, because when you step inside, it's like entering a whole different world. The walls are all papered, and the woodwork is painted in matching pastels. There's new linoleum on the floors and Liz has put up frilly curtains. The furniture is either new or freshly painted. You should see the room they're fixing up for the nursery. It's cute, but the baby had better be a boy: it's all blue and white. Liz has an unexpected knack for decorating—at least I never knew about it—and Jim is giving her free rein. It helps that he works in a lumber store. They've gotten a good discount on a lot of the materials and done all the work themselves. Jim promised her that they'll get the outside fixed up this summer so that it matches the inside."

"I'm looking forward to seeing it. I can't imagine our little sister so domestic."

She yawned suddenly, and I rose from where I had been sitting on the bed. "Good-night, Mary," I said. "Get a good night's sleep and forget about your worries while you're here. Maybe you're just overly tired. Shall I pull the window shade for you?"

"No. I like the moonlight and the fresh air. Thanks for coming in to talk to me."

She snuggled down under the sheet and closed her eyes. I went out of the room and softly closed the door, then went to my own bedroom.

The next morning Mary didn't want to go to school with me. She informed Davy and me that she'd just like to pretend she was alone on a deserted island during the day, with no responsibilities and no one to answer to or be responsible for. We gave her permission to make the place her own, so she proceeded to do just that. She explored the nearby woods and went for long walks along the banks of Willow Creek so she wouldn't get lost. She pulled her shoes off and went wading in the cold creek water, then spent hours sitting in the warm sunshine, doing nothing. By the end of the week, she had acquired an attractive tan and was looking much more rested and relaxed.

At the end of each day when Calvin and I came home from school, we were greeted by appetizing smells coming from the kitchen. Mary was an excellent cook, but she'd had little time for it with her demanding schedule and her husband so often away from home. Now she chased me out of the kitchen and took over. It was a pleasant change to come home from school and have nothing to do but sit and relax and be waited on by my sister.

Friday was the big day for the schoolchildren. We were

going to a movie in town. Afterward, we would stop at a drive-in for hamburgers and ice cream. Mary agreed to go with us and chaperone. Davy's nephew, Luther, would ride in the back of the truck with the older children to make sure everyone behaved themselves. That was a new role for him—and not one that I would have chosen. But he'd come home for a visit and Davy had asked him. I had to admit that he seemed older and more settled, not the troublemaker he'd been when I first came to the hills to teach school. He was working in town with his uncle, and it seemed to agree with him more than school ever had.

It promised to be an eventful day. The children were all so excited; it was touching to watch them and listen to their animated chatter. When I took the roll call, I was relieved to see that all the children were present. If any one of them had not been allowed to go on the trip, that child would have felt terribly deprived and disappointed.

Shortly before noon, Davy drove up in the truck with Mary and Luther. I lined the children up in the yard for last-minute instructions. They were an interesting, varied group. I smiled at them as I walked down the line. I was used to them, but I viewed them now through the eyes of my sister, who was standing aside, watching as if fascinated.

The boys all wore jeans: many of them too short in the legs, some of them torn and ragged, a few neatly patched. Most of them had seen a week's wear without being laundered. Their shirts were in much the same condition, hanging loosely out of their jeans. Without exception they were barefoot. I was glad I had the foresight to clear this with the theater manager; normally, the children would not be allowed in without shoes. I explained to him that many of the children didn't own a pair of shoes for the summer, and he agreed to make an exception.

The girls had made more of an effort to pretty themselves up for this special occasion. Unfortunately, it was evident that in most cases it had been done without the guidance of a more experienced person. Hair was inexpertly curled, with ribbons and bows indiscriminately added. No thought was given to matching colors or patterns. The little Baxter girl, who usually wore her brother's hand-me-downs, wore a dress today. It was an ugly brown and so badly wrinkled that it barely covered her underwear; no telling how long it had been stuffed at the back of a drawer and forgotten. I wondered if her mother had even seen her before she left for school. She would have been better off wearing her usual boy's clothes. I noticed as I paused beside her that there were signs of recent tears. I put my hand on her shoulder.

"I'm glad you could come with us today, Pearl," I said. I would have liked to add something such as, "You look nice today," but I couldn't in all honesty say it. I continued down the line.

Evidently, only the Proctor and the Miller girls had their mothers' help getting ready. They looked nice, but quite ordinary; they were the only ones who wore shoes. Mattie Anderson looked quite nice. Her mother was home, and the baby was recovering well from his illness. Her brothers were less presentable but reasonably clean. The Lovett girls had come to school as usual, uncombed and unwashed, looking as if they had slept in their clothes. Earlier in the morning I had sent them out to the pump to clean up, giving them each a comb and a toothbrush, but they still looked unkempt. Something needed to be done about that family, but with all my other responsibilities, I just hadn't had the time to look into it. Perhaps I could leave a suggestion for next year's teacher to take a special interest in them.

When I reached the end of the line, I couldn't help wondering what kind of reception we would receive at the movie theater. Not that it mattered that much. The children were all so excited that I believed they would be more-or-less oblivious to the impression they made.

"This is my sister Mary," I told them. "She is going along

with us. She'll ride with me in the car, along with the first graders. The rest of you can start climbing into the back of the truck. Davy and Luther will help you. Mary, if you'll go with the first graders to my car, I'll be with you in a minute."

We were soon on our way. Davy drove the truck slowly, and I followed close behind in the car. For a time, my sister and I were silent. The three first graders were in the back seat.

"Well, what do you think?" I asked finally.

"They're an interesting bunch. You love them, don't you?"

"There are a few that I have to work at liking, but for the most part, yes, I love them. I feel that they're, well, almost mine—that in a way, they belong to me."

"You're going to miss them next year, aren't you?"

"Perhaps not too much. I'm thinking of asking the superintendent if he'll let me go back next year, just part time, perhaps a couple of hours a day. I'd like to teach some classes in music and home economics, that sort of thing. I try to incorporate them into the classes now, but there are so many other subjects to teach that those things often get crowded out. I think Mr. Hooper will approve; he's very understanding and sympathetic toward my students. But if the school board doesn't approve, I'll do it without pay if necessary."

"Who'll take care of the baby?"

"Davy. His work schedule is flexible, and he's agreeable. He's very good with children."

"Yes, I've noticed that. You both are. You'll make good parents."

"Thanks. So would you and Kevin."

"Maybe."

"Well, we're almost there. This should be interesting."

CHAPTER SEVENTEEN

Mary's Decision

 M ary and I were sitting in the living room of our cabin. It was six o'clock, and we'd just arrived home from our trip to the movies. Davy and Calvin had gone out to do the chores.

"That was an enlivening experience," Mary said, her voice rich with amusement.

"I feel absolutely exhausted," I said. "but they had fun, don't you think?"

"Fun is much too mundane a word. The wonder in their eyes, the awe in their faces when we walked into that theater ... It's an experience they'll remember all their lives, and so will I. Isn't it funny, the things we take for granted? Had some of them never even been to town before?"

"It's possible. None of them have been there often, and when they do go, it's just to do some shopping. As far as I know, only the Proctor girls have ever been to see a movie."

"It was so real to them. Who was the little boy who stood up and cried out 'She's dead, they've kilt her!' when Lassie jumped out the window?"

"That was Timmy Hilton, Davy's sister's little boy. It was sweet of you to hold him on your lap and reassure him during the rest of the movie. Especially as he's one of the children who is ... well, never too clean."

"He quite won my heart, in spite of his rather ... er ... earthy aroma. He took it all so seriously; I felt as worn-out and drained as him when it was all over. Thank goodness for happy endings; otherwise, we'd have had them all in tears."

"Yes. I didn't quite realize the impact it would have on

them. I've read that same story to them at school, but I guess hearing it is quite different from actually seeing it. Well, it's an experience we'll all remember for a long time. But do you know what I think impressed them as much or more than anything?"

"What?"

"The rest rooms. Most of them had never used anything but an outdoor toilet or a chamber pot. I thought we'd never get them out of there and into their seats before the movie started."

Mary laughed. It was a light-hearted, bubbling laugh. "Did you see the expression on that other teacher's face? I guess she was a teacher, the one who was herding the ten prissy, frilly little girls around. She acted as if she thought her girls would catch something if they even got close to our kids."

"Our kids?" I challenged in a teasing voice.

"Well, your kids then. After today, I feel almost as if they're mine, too. No wonder you love them so. They're precious: original and spontaneous and so uninhibited."

"They got the uninhibited part from their parents," I said dryly. "They say what they think, nevermind how it might sound or who it might hurt. Do you know, this morning one of the mothers took it upon herself to warn me that she'd seen my husband with a good-looking city woman, 'a walkin' down by th' crick yesterday evenin', an' maybe I ort to spend more time at home where I belonged to keep a better eye on my man.'"

Mary sat up straight, a look of consternation on her face. "Why, Davy and I did go for a walk yesterday, but it was afternoon, not evening and I ..."

"Afternoon is always called evening out here, and no explanation is necessary. I agreed that you are indeed a very good-looking woman and thanked her for her concern. I also informed her that you are my sister, and you'd been visiting us this past week. She was somewhat mollified, but still thought it would be a good idea to keep closer tabs on Davy, 'cause when a woman's a carryin' a young'un, that's when a man's most likely to stray."

"She's got a nerve. I hope you told her to mind her own business."

"No. I've tried that before and it doesn't work. They all think it is their business. I just thanked her again for her concern and assured her that she needn't worry; everything was fine between Davy and me. I've learned that gossip is a favorite pastime around here, and there isn't much you can do about it. Are you hungry? Would you like something to eat?"

"Nothing for me. That hamburger, fries and malt I had are still sitting there, right smack in the middle of my stomach. The kids enjoyed it though, didn't they? Too bad that little girl got sick in the back of the truck coming home. I hope it didn't spoil the day for her or any of the others."

"I don't think so. They live closer to nature than most, and such things are taken very much for granted." I laughed. "I wondered why Davy put straw in the truck bed, as if it was a load of livestock he was going to be hauling around. I guess he knew what he was doing."

"Your husband is quite a guy."

"Oh?"

"That walk we took, down by the creek—I found myself telling him what I told you that first night I was here. He heard me out without a word. Then he just said, in that quiet way he has, that he figgered if a man wanted kids he oughta be able to, unless it would endanger his wife's health or something. It made sense, and it made me realize that I've been selfish: I've been thinking more of myself and my own feelings than I have about Kevin's. So in the morning, I'm heading home to give Kevin the good news. That is, unless he's decided to leave me in the meantime."

"He won't have done that."

"I hope not, but when I left to come out here, we weren't on the best of terms."

"I wish he could have come, too."

"He wanted to, but I wouldn't let him. I wanted some time alone. I guess I really have become selfish, haven't I? I'm going to have to rethink my whole attitude. It wouldn't have hurt a thing for him to have come, too; it might have been very good for the two of us."

"You can always come back later, perhaps in the summer or the fall. It's so beautiful here in the fall of the year."

"Yes. I remember from last year when we were here for Liz's wedding. We just might do that, have a second honeymoon or something. That's part of our problem. Because of my work schedule and him being gone so much, we've grown apart. It's time that was rectified."

"I'm glad to hear it, and I'm very glad you came for this visit. It's been wonderful having you, and the rest I've had has been very welcome. I feel ready to deal with the last two weeks of school now."

"It's been wonderful for me—just the break I was needing. Well, I'd better go and pack up my things. I want to get an early start so I can spend a little time with Mom and Dad before I fly home on Sunday. I think Mom would have liked to come with me, too, but I didn't encourage it. I hope she understood. I'll have to have a talk with her. I know she's been worried about me, but somehow I feel that everything is going to be fine with Kevin and me now. She'll be glad to hear that."

She went into her room, and I went into the kitchen to make the coffee for morning. Her visit had been a success. I felt closer to my older sister than I had for some time and hoped it was the beginning of a closer relationship between us. Now all that was left was to win my father over for our family circle to be complete.

CHAPTER EIGHTEEN

A Preacher of Sorts

Walking into the room, I let my books drop to the coffee table with a bang. "That time you went out with Goldie Sutton, did you take her to a movie?" I demanded of Davy.

He looked up at me warily. He was sitting in his rocker, the newspaper on his lap. He didn't immediately answer. I stood with my hands on my hips, glaring at him.

"What's that got to do with anything?" he asked quietly. "That was a long time before we got together."

"That's not the point. Did you or didn't you take her to a movie?"

"I did, but I don't see why ..."

"Her father was waiting for me when I got to school this morning. He read me the riot act for taking his boys to the movie Friday. He said 'them pitcher shows are agents of the devil' and that I'm liable to the fiery hell for taking the kids there. You'd think he was a preacher or something, the way he was carrying on, screaming at me and quoting scripture, and right in front of all the children, too."

Davy tried to hide a little grin. "He is a preacher, of sorts," he said.

I gaped at him. "He is? Why, the man is totally ignorant; his grammar is atrocious."

"He don't have a church or anything like that, jist goes around preachin' at get-togethers an' things like that."

"Self-appointed, I suppose?"

"Naturally. I doubt th' man can even read or write."

"That would explain why he didn't know the boys were

going to the movie. I sent a note home with all of them and told them what was in it. I also told them they had to have permission from their parents. Alan Ray looked me in the eye and told me that his parents said he could go."

"I'm jist surprised he waited until today to talk to you. What'd he say when you told him th' boys had lied to you?"

"That it was my fault, of course. I put temptation before them and caused them to fall into sin. I ain't fittin' to be no teacher, an' he aims to see to it that I don't come back next year."

"Oh well, you don't have to worry about that, seein' you ain't gonna be teachin' next year anyhow."

"I am too going to be teaching—at least part time—and if he thinks he can stop me ..."

"He'll forget all about it by then, an' even if he don't, he ain't got that much influence around here. He's about as popular around here as ol' Ned Reynolds. Remember him?"

I shuddered. "Yes, I do remember him. You're right, that's exactly who he made me think of. Is he still around? I haven't seen him since that night at the pie supper."

"When I rescued you an' got myself properly slapped for my efforts," Davy joked. "Yes, he's still around, far as I know. He keeps to hisself a lot."

"I'm glad to hear it. Well, I've had my excitement for the day. I've never liked those Suttons, and I like them even less now. What is Mrs. Sutton like?"

"Real quiet. Hardly ever says a word. There's some folks who think he mistreats her."

"I don't doubt it. Those self-righteous kind often do. He said something about hanging a millstone around my neck and casting me into the sea where the worms would eat me up. But he finally forgave me because I'm untaught and know not what I do."

Davy chuckled. "Uh," he stammered, "I'm almost afraid to ask what you said to all that."

"I stayed calm, but it wasn't easy. The man has the right to his opinions, of course, and he certainly had the right to keep his boys home from the movie Friday. But as I told him, I thought they had permission to go. I also told him that the rest of us had the right to go, if we choose. He said something about me leading them into a pit. Oh well, I'm not sorry I took them, and I certainly can't see the harm in watching a movie about a dog, but to each his own." I sighed and sank down onto the sofa. "I could have done without the public spectacle, though."

"Th' kids won't think any less of you for it."

"I was sorely tempted to give him a few home truths about the conduct of his boys and his daughter, but I didn't. Did he know you took her to the movies?"

"Dunno. Meant to tell you, Sue was by. She wants us to come over for supper Friday evenin'."

I smiled at him. "Trying to change the subject?" I asked.

"Course not. Why would I want to do a thing like that?" he retorted with an answering grin. "Well, want to go for supper?"

"That would be nice. Be sure and remind me this time. It would be unforgivable to forget again."

"You feelin' all right?"

"I'm fine, Davy, just tired. There's been so much going on lately that I can't keep up with it all. I'm looking forward to a quiet summer."

"Might not be so quiet, with a new baby an' all."

"After dealing with some thirty children for nearly a year, one small baby will be a refreshing change. As soon as school is out, Davy, we've got to start making some plans."

"What sort of plans?"

"For the baby, of course. Names, where he or she is going to sleep, whether I'll have the baby in the hospital."

"I thought that was already decided," he said sharply.

"Well, I've been thinking, since I'm a permanent resident

here now, and everyone else has their babies at home ..."

"No."

"No?"

"No. I ain't willin' to risk it, I already told you that. 'Specially after I saw what your friend Jane went through."

"But Davy, she didn't go to the doctor. I've been going all along. If there was going to be a problem similar to Jane's, he'd be able to tell me."

"No."

"You're rather arbitrary, aren't you?"

"Maybe, but I don't want to take any chances with you or the baby. You both mean too much to me."

"All right, Davy," I relented. "this time. But next time, if all goes well, it may be a different story."

"There's goin' to be a next time, then?"

"Three, I think. That's a nice-sized family, don't you think? Two boys and a girl."

"Why not two boys and two girls?"

"We'll see."

"Have you seen your friend Jane lately?"

"No. Why?"

"Jist wondered. I was out that way this mornin' an' there wasn't any sign of life atall. Jist wondered if ever'thin' was all right."

"As far as I know it is. The boys were at school today. Maybe they went into town or something."

"Maybe."

"I do need to get out and see her, though. Maybe when school is out I'll have more time for visiting. Well, I'd better get up and start supper. Anything in particular you'd like?"

CHAPTER NINETEEN

Play Day

*I*t was the last day of school, and I had just finished the book we had started some weeks earlier. I laid it aside and looked out across the roomful of children with affection and the beginnings of nostalgia. There had been problems during the school year, of course, but I had thoroughly enjoyed it and would miss them all.

"I would like for all of you to do something for me if you will, please," I said. "I have a small autograph book here that I would like for all of you to sign for me. If you would like to write a little something in it, you may; if not, just your name will be fine. I want to keep the book to remember all of you by and to remember the year we've had together. I'll give the book to Andrew first. He can pass it on to Chad, and then on down the row. While we're doing that, the rest of you can study for the spelling bee we'll have later this morning."

When the book was returned to me, I laid it aside to look at later. We had the spelling bee, which occupied the next hour, then we spent the rest of the morning clearing out the desks and straightening the schoolroom. At noon, the parents and anyone who wanted to come would bring picnic lunches, and we would all eat together. After that would come what we called "play day." There would be baseball and volleyball and basketball for those who wanted to play. There would be sack races, broad jumping, high jumping and other games of competition, with blue, red or white ribbons given to first-, second- and third-place winners. Since I was almost eight months pregnant I had assigned several of the parents to be in charge this year. Davy was going to come early to set up tables for the food, then he would be in charge of the baseball game. Play day would be over at 4 o'clock, our usual time of dismissal. I had a small gift for each child that I would pass out with their final grade cards, then school would be over for another term.

I saw Davy arrive in the truck. When he had the tables set up, I dismissed the children. It was a little early, but they were too excited to concentrate on anything else. I followed them outside and went to talk to Davy for a few minutes.

"How goes it?" he asked me.

"All right. I'm a little tired. I'll be glad when the day is over, and I won't be glad. Did you bring the potato salad I made?"

"It's in th' cab of th' truck."

"Thank you, Davy. I don't know what I'd do without you. Well, here come the Wilsons. The fun begins."

After that, everyone seemed to arrive at once. The tables were soon filled with food: good substantial home-cooked food, with plenty of pies and cakes and cookies. They all brought their own plates, cups and spoons, and soon everyone was lining up before the table. I was surprised to see a last-minute arrival: Mr. Sutton and his quiet, almost shrinking, wife. I went forward to greet them, since no one else moved. I held out my hand, first to her, then to him, hiding my dislike for him as best I could.

"You're just in time," I said, smiling. "We were just getting ready to eat. Come and join us."

"I'd be right willin' to call on th' Lord for his blessin' on all these good folks before we begin," he said pompously. I hesitated a moment, my heart beginning to beat more rapidly in my breast. It had been just a short time ago that he railed at me for my so-called sin of taking the children to a movie. I wouldn't be at all surprised if he took this opportunity to implore the Lord's forgiveness on my behalf in front of all these people, but what could I do?

"All right, Mr. Sutton, that will be fine," I said, bowing my head. I still watched him out of the corner of my eye. He spread his legs slightly, clasped his hands behind his back, and lifted his face heavenward, his eyes closed. I cringed as he began to call the Lord in sonorous tones. I had no idea what he was going to say, and I feared the worst.

It was not a long prayer. He asked the Lord to bless the food and all the people assembled, and to make all of us willing to be used in his work. Then it was over. Dazed, I lifted my head and met Davy's amused eyes. I smiled in return, knowing that he'd been aware of what I was thinking.

The women stepped behind the table to begin serving the food. If it had been left up to me, everyone would just serve themselves, but I knew the women thought it was their duty to see that the men and children were served first. I didn't offer to help, because I knew they didn't expect me to. Being the teacher, I was exempt. However, I chose to wait and eat when the rest of the women did. Meantime, I circulated among the people, trying to be sure I greeted everyone and exchanged a few words with them.

"Well, Tom." I said to my brother-in-law. "We haven't seen much of you lately. How are you?"

He glanced at me, then averted his eyes. I was getting used to that from the men. For some reason my pregnancy seemed to embarrass them. Perhaps they thought a schoolteacher shouldn't have babies. I didn't know, but it didn't matter that much to me anymore. The women seemed to welcome it because it made me one of them. The children accepted it because it had grown on them gradually.

"I'm fine," Tom said briefly.

"I just wanted to let you know your children have all done quite well in school this year. Ruth is a bright girl. You can be proud of her; I know she'll do well in high school. I'm so glad you're sending her."

"Still ain't so sure it's a good idea to send a girl on to get more schoolin', but she's a wantin' to go an' her mama is backin' her up, so ..." He shrugged and left it at that.

"Times are changing, Tom, and high school is somewhat of a necessity nowadays for both boys and girls," I said, much less forcefully than I would have a year ago. "Ruth will make something of herself, you'll see. As I said, you'll be proud of her."

"Was a time no one thought Luther there would ever amount to a hill of beans, but looks like we was all wrong," he said, nodding toward his nephew. "He's doin' real good at block layin' now, John says, an' he didn't even finish grade school."

"I know and I'm glad for him, but not everyone gets the kind of help Luther got from his family. Most of the children here will have to make their own opportunities, but they can do that with the proper education."

I moved on, glancing around the crowd. Jane Decker, her husband and younger boys were not there. I knew she seldom went to social functions but I had hoped she would make an exception this time. I was apprehensive about how things were going for her and her family. I must go out and check on them soon.

"How's Jim an' that sister of yours gettin' along?" one man asked me when I paused to speak to him. "Usta always see Jim at these kind of doin's, but ain't seen hide ner hair of him for months now."

"He's fine, and so is my sister," I replied. "They couldn't come because they both work in town all week."

"If he's a workin' steady, reckon your sister's been th' makin's of him. Usta think that boy wasn't worth knockin' in th' head, always galavantin' around an' jist workin' when he had a mind to. Reckon he'll be able to keep it up?"

"He seems to be doing fine." I moved on. "How are you, Mr. Baxter? And how is Billy these days? I haven't seen him since he finished school last year."

His head down, he mumbled something about his son living in town now. I'd heard that Billy had been in trouble with the law and hoped it wasn't true, but it wouldn't have surprised me if it were. However, I had no wish to embarrass his father. "Tell him hello for me when you see him," I said.

Davy paused beside me, a full plate in his hand. "Ain't you eatin'?" he asked.

"I will in a little bit."

"Noticed our latest romance?"

"Who?"

"Over there by the pump."

"Todd and Evelyn?" I asked incredulously. "Your imagination is running away with you, Davy. They've known each other all their lives. Just because they've been thrown together so much, going back and forth to high school, doesn't mean they're anything other than friends."

"Uh-huh. You jist watch," he said, moving on.

I looked again. The two young people were walking together toward the tables. As I watched, Evelyn gave Todd a sweet, shy smile. It gave my heart a jolt. They were so young, but not too young to fall in love. I wondered if their parents were aware of the obvious attraction between them. According to rumor, Evelyn's mother didn't intend for her daughter to get involved with any of the hillbillies out here; she had more important things in mind for Evelyn. I told myself they were still very young, and it wasn't any of my concern. How often was it that first love endured? They would grow up, likely grow apart and go their separate ways, but what kind of heartache lie in store for them in the meantime? I felt a pang of pity for them, as well as sweet nostalgia, remembering my own first love. Funny, though, at the moment I couldn't remember his name. I looked at Davy and we exchanged a smile. I walked on.

My sister-in-law Ellen, Tom's wife, stopped in front of me. She had a plate in either hand: one full to the brim, the other with only a small piece of corn bread and a pickle on it. She handed the full plate to me.

"I fixed you somethin' to eat," she said. "I put a little of ever'thing on th' plate. I hope that's all right."

"That's very much all right, Ellen. Thank you. But what about yourself? Only a pickle and a piece of corn bread? Surely you aren't dieting."

She wrinkled her nose in distaste as we turned away to find a place to stand apart from the crowd. "Not hungry," she said.

"Oh, I see. Well, I'm starved, and this all looks so good. Better have some of this ham at least. It's delicious."

She made a sound of revulsion, and I looked at her in surprise. Her face had turned an odd shade of green; she looked as if she was going to be sick.

"Why, Ellen, what is it? Are you ill?"

It took her a moment to answer. She was obviously fighting back a surge of nausea. She put her plate down on the tailgate of Davy's truck and looked at me, her face stricken.

"I can't stand th' smell of meat. I can't hardly even stand to look at it," she moaned.

"Ellen, are you?"

"Yes, I think so."

"How far along?"

"I don't know, not far. I've just started getting sick the past week or so. I haven't even told Tom yet. He thinks I've had the flu. He don't want any more kids."

"He'll get used to the idea," I said. "But you shouldn't have fixed this plate for me. You've been standing over that table for the last half hour. You should have made some kind of excuse, Ellen."

"That's what did it. I thought I'd be all right, but that ham ..."

"I'm sorry. I won't eat it in front of you."

"It's all right, I'm over it now, I think. Just don't make me have to smell it."

"I'll turn my back and eat it. There, it's all gone. But I'm sorry you have to be so sick. Is it always this way for you?"

"Always. Night and day, every day, for three whole months," she said with a moan.

"I seldom was really sick, just a little queasy, mostly in the afternoons. But of course, I'm well over that now. If there's anything I can do to help ..."

"Th' kids can manage. Ruthie's awful good."

"I know she is. I was just telling Tom how proud he can be of her. This won't have any effect on her going to high school next term, will it?"

"Oh no. All my kids are goin', whether they want to or not, an' Ruthie wants to. Do you think there'll be a bus to come out and pick them up?"

"I rather doubt it this next term, but we'll arrange something. The following year, however, there should be bus service. They're putting in a new county road, and it is supposed to be done by then. In fact, they're talking about closing down all the small country schools such as ours and sending the children to school in town."

"I heard about that, an' I don't like it. I don't like th' little ones havin' to get up that early and ride all that way on a bus an' bein' so far away from home. What if one of them was to get sick or somethin'? I don't mind Ruthie goin', she's older, but I don't like it for th' little ones. Why can't they jist leave things like they are?"

"It's progress, so they say. I have mixed emotions about it myself. I've come to love this little school. I'd like for my own children to be able to attend here."

"Can't you do somethin'? I mean, you're th' teacher, you ought to have some say-so."

"They asked my opinion, and I told them I was in favor of retaining the one-room country school, at least in these out-of-the-way areas. They asked my reasons and I gave them. They listened attentively, but I don't think it will make any difference. They won't consolidate next term, though, unless they're unable to find a teacher."

"Couldn't you?... No, I guess not."

"I want to be home with my baby, at least for the first year. I do intend to teach a few classes, though, such as home economics and music. They've agreed to let me do that, and Davy and Clemmy have agreed to baby-sit. I can't see myself giving up teaching entirely, not even for a year."

"That's good. I'm glad. Th' kids all love you. You've done so much for them; you've made learnin' fun an' interestin'. Since you been teachin' here, I don't have to do no proddin' to get them out th' door in th' mornin's."

"I'm glad to hear it. Thank you, Ellen. I think Mrs. Miller is trying to get my attention. Come visit me now that school is out, and if you need any help let me know."

"I'm okay, but maybe I will drop in to visit one of these days when I'm feelin' a little better."

I moved on to Mrs. Miller, and we talked about her two girls. The rest of the afternoon passed swiftly. Soon I was passing out grade cards and gifts and saying a warm farewell to each of my students. Some of the girls shed a few tears. I hugged and reassured them, inviting them to come visit me anytime they could. By 4:30 the schoolyard was empty, and my family and I could go home.

CHAPTER TWENTY

A Surprise Shower

Coming into the house in mid-afternoon, Davy said, "It's a real scorcher out there. How you doin' in here?"

"It's not bad with the fans on."

"You been cryin'?" He came to where I was sitting in the rocker and put his hand under my chin, lifting my face. I smiled at him but knew my eyes were damp with tears.

"I'm not crying," I said. "I was just reading what the children wrote in my autograph book on the last day of school. I haven't had an opportunity to look at it before now."

He took the book from me and opened it. His eyebrows lifted.

"'I love you little, I love you big, I love you like a little pig?' That made you cry? Or was it th' next one? 'Roses are red, violets are pink, someone in this room sure does stink?'"

I laughed. "No, it wasn't any particular one. It's just that so many of them begged me to come back and teach again next year. They told me that I'm the best teacher they ever had, or, as little Andrew put it, I'm the 'bester' teacher he ever had. Several of the older girls even said I could bring the baby to school with me and they'd take turns baby-sitting. It's quite touching. It makes me feel as if I really did make a difference in their lives."

"Course you did. I don't think there's anyone out here who would deny that." He scanned the book, then handed it back to me.

"Me an' Cal come to take you for a walk down by th' crick," he said. I noticed Calvin hovering in the kitchen doorway.

"That's nice of both of you, but I think I'd rather just sit. I may even take a little nap. I'm tired today. I think the heat is getting to me."

"That's why we come to take you for a walk. It's at least ten degrees cooler down by th' crick, an' if you sit on a rock an' put your feet in th' water, you'll soon be feelin' like you're in one of them air-conditioned buildin's like they got in th' city."

"Davy, we're going to have to do something about that grammar of yours," I said sternly.

"Uh-oh. You're through teachin' th' kids an' now you're ready to start on me, huh? You can give me a lesson down by th' crick."

He took the autograph book from me and put it on the shelf. Taking both my hands, he pulled me up out of the chair. "Come on, lazy bones. It'll do you good to get out of th' house. 'Sides, Cal's got somethin' he wants to show you, ain't you, Cal?"

Calvin looked surprised and somewhat alarmed. He shifted from one bare foot to the other, looking at Davy, then at me. He nodded.

"Can it wait? I really would like to take a nap. I didn't sleep well last night."

"You can take a nap later. You'll sleep better for havin' a little exercise an' coolin' off down by th' crick."

"You're very persistent," I said in slight exasperation as he drew me toward the door. "Seems to me I should know best whether I need a walk or a nap."

"You haven't been for a good walk since school was out. You got to keep in shape for when th' baby comes. I been kinda concerned 'bout you jist settin' there this last week."

"I was tired. School was pretty hectic those last few weeks, you know."

"I know, but now it's time you started walkin' again."

"Perhaps you're right," I conceded. We went out

through the back door and across the backyard. Brownie joined us, tongue hanging out and panting. For a short distance we were out in the bright, hot sunshine, and I felt beads of perspiration form on my upper lip and forehead. It really was a hot day. Davy took my arm.

"It'll be cooler once we get in th' trees," he said.

"I'm all right. What is it you wanted to show me, Calvin?"

Again Calvin's eyes flew to Davy, then to me, and back to Davy. He seemed at a loss for words.

"Better hang onto Brownie or there might not be no surprise to show her," Davy said casually. Calvin's face seemed to clear. Before he could speak up, however, I spoke.

"The lessons start right now," I said crisply. "Rephrase that last statement."

"What last statement, an' what's rephrase mean, anyway?"

"You know very well what it means, and the last statement was 'There might not be no surprise.' That's a double negative: unnecessary, and very bad grammar."

His brows wrinkled in pretended puzzlement. "There mightn't be nary surprise?" he asked.

"Oh Davy, honestly."

He grinned at me. "You tell me how to say it," he said.

"You know how to say it."

"No, I don't, so tell me, Teacher."

"You could say, 'There might be no surprise,' or, 'There might not be a surprise.'"

"Ain't that what I said?"

"No, that ain't what you said," I mocked. "Seriously now, Davy."

"I don't want to be serious right now. I want to go for a walk by th' crick with my wife, not th' local schoolteacher."

"I'm afraid the two are inseparable. If not now, when?"

"Maybe startin' next week, in th' evenin's."

"You mean it?"

"Yes, I mean it. Got to keep you happy, at least until th' baby comes."

"We'll start Monday evening, then, and I'm going to hold you to it. Maybe you can be included, too, Calvin. That will give you a head start on the next school term and maybe then ..."

Davy and Calvin groaned together.

"Not that again," Davy said, "I thought we had that all settled."

"I don't know what you're talking about. I just said ..."

"We heard what you said. Let's just forget it for now, okay? Feel how much cooler th' air is down here?"

"Yes. It is much cooler. It feels good."

"See? Ain't you glad you come now? Aren't you glad you come," he amended quickly.

"Came," I automatically corrected. "Yes, I am glad. Thank you for making me come. It's beautiful and so peaceful. Why has no one thought of building a house down here by the creek?"

"Don't know. Might be pretty cold in wintertime."

"It might. What did you want to show me, Calvin?"

"It's down th' crick bed here, jist a little ways. Come on," he answered. I silently resolved to include him in the lessons, whether he liked it or not. If I could make it interesting, as my pupils seemed to think I could, maybe he'd even want to be included. He and Davy were both avid readers. Maybe I could use their love for reading to spark their interest.

"You comin'?" Davy asked. Calvin had gone on ahead, leaping from rock to rock, following the bend of the creek. Davy took my arm, and we followed more slowly. When we reached Calvin, he was squatting down before a small cave in the rocks, restraining Brownie, who was struggling to get closer.

"It's a cave, see?" Calvin said excitedly, squinting up at us. "Couple days ago, I seen a mama coon come out of there with her babies. There was three of them. I thought maybe when they was older I could make pets of them. I been comin' down here ever' day, so's they'll get used to me, but I gotta train Brownie not to bother them. No, Brownie, you can't go in there, you hear me? You leave this here pertickeler hole in th' rocks alone, you hear me? Sit, Boy."

Brownie whined but obediently sat, panting, his tongue lolling, his tail thumping the rocks while he eyed the cave.

"They're afraid to come out when Brownie's here, so you won't likely see them today," Calvin explained.

"Maybe you ought to take Brownie on home an' shut him up in his pen," Davy suggested. "Maybe then th' coons would come out an' Anne could see them. Ain't nothin' much cuter than a baby coon. Awful pests when they grow up, though."

"If I was to make pets of them, I'd train them not to get in th' garden or th' cornfield," Calvin promised.

"We'll see. But right now, why don't you run on home with Brownie?" Davy suggested.

"Okay. Come on, Boy."

He was off down the path at a run, the dog right behind him. Davy helped me back the way we had come.

"Do you think he will be able to make pets of them?"

"No, not unless he was to trap one an' pen it up, an' I won't let him do that. He's got enough pets, with th' rabbit an' th' dog. Wild things should be let be. Won't hurt him none to try, though. Might succeed to a certain extent."

"Won't they bite?"

"They will if he tries to catch one of them."

"Maybe you should warn him."

"No need. They won't let him get that close. Besides, if he gets bit once, he'll learn wild things like that are not to be messed with."

"The hard school of experience, right?"

"Best way in th' world to learn."

"I'm not sure I agree with you."

"Didn't figger you would. Here, come over an' sit on this big rock. Take your shoes off an' put your feet in th' water, an' forget for a minute that you're a teacher."

"All right."

He helped me onto the rock and removed my shoes for me. I gasped as I put my feet in the cold, swift water.

"Very refreshing," I said after I had sat there a few minutes. "It makes me feel quite cool all over."

"Told you."

"Come join me."

He took his shoes off and rolled his pant legs up, then sat down beside me. I sighed contentedly and looked up at the green of the trees overhead. There were no sounds except the rushing water, the chirping birds and the stirring of the leaves blown by the gentle breeze.

"It's heavenly," I said.

"Bet you never had anything like this in that big city you come from," he said complacently.

"You're right. I love it."

"If you really want to cool off good, put your hands down in th' water an' let it flow over your wrists. That's what I do when I'm workin' close by an' I get all hot an' sweaty. Cools you off quicker'n anythin'."

I leaned forward, then sat back again. "I can't," I said. "Not unless I lean sideways. If I do I'm afraid I'll lose my balance and fall in, and I don't want to cool off that much."

"Here, I'll hold onto you. Forgot about your big belly."

"Davy!"

"What? Go ahead an' lean over, I got you."

"Nevermind. I'm cool enough, thank you, and you can just let go of me anytime."

He chuckled and put his arm around me. He placed his other hand on my stomach. "Big belly or not, you ain't ever been prettier."

"Thanks a lot. Who gave me this big belly, I'd like to know."

"Me," he crowed, "an' boy, am I ever proud of myself."

"Davy, we should be thinking about names," I said dreamily, leaning against him. "Do you have any ideas?"

"Ain't thought much about it. Have you?"

"Yes. If it's a girl, what would you think of Annabel Lee?"

"It's an old-fashioned name," I continued, while he thought about it. "It would also mean the baby was named after both of us, the Anna part for me and the Lee for you, since it's your middle name."

"I like it. Where'd you come up with it?"

"It's the name of one of Edgar Allan Poe's poems, one of my favorites. 'It was many and many a year ago, in a kingdom by the sea, that a maiden there lived whom you may know by the name of Annabel Lee; and this maiden she lived with no other thought than to love and be loved by me,'" I quoted dreamily, kicking my feet gently in the water.

"I remember readin' that now. But she died, didn't she?"

"Yes. Does it matter? You aren't superstitious, are you, Davy?"

"Don't think so, but that don't seem to set too good with me. I'll have to think about it."

"All right. It was just an idea. If you don't like it, we can think of something else. How about Pliny Jane?"

"Pliny Jane!"

I laughed. "There's a song about a Pliny Jane. I rather like it."

"Well, I don't. What if it's a boy?"

"How about David?"

"Th' Proctors already got a David, an' since we're friends with them an' th' boys would be pretty close in age, wouldn't that be awful confusin'?"

"Probably. We could just reverse your name and call him Lee David."

"Dunno. I'll have to think about that one, too."

"If you can come up with something else ..."

Calvin came running up then, minus the dog, his hair in his eyes, his breath coming fast.

"They're there," he panted.

"The raccoons have come out?" I exclaimed. "Oh good. I want to see them. Help me with my shoes, Davy, before they go back in."

"I don't think he was talkin' about th' coons," Davy said easily, taking his handkerchief out to dry my feet.

"What was he talking about then?" I asked, puzzled.

"Nothin' important. Here, hold still if you want me to get this shoe on you."

"If you weren't talking about the raccoons, Calvin, what were you talking about? Who's where?"

"Jist someone." Calvin muttered, his head down, kicking at the dirt.

"Quit kickin' dirt all over us an' run on back to th' house," Davy said casually. "We'll be there in a minute."

Calvin turned and fled back up the path. I looked at Davy in puzzlement.

"What's going on here?" I asked. "Are you two up to something you don't want me to know about?"

"Don't you women have secrets you don't let us men in on sometimes? Well, us men do, too. It's a secret between me an' Cal. Come on, up with you. It's time I was gettin' back to work."

"I'd like to stay here awhile. It's so peaceful and cool."

"It's been nice, but I can't give up my whole afternoon to you, you know. I got things to do."

"Then do them. You don't have to stay with me. In spite of the big belly, I can still get around by myself, you know."

"Yeah, but I don't like to leave you down here, so far from th' house. You might slip an' fall or somethin'."

"That's sweet of you, but I'm not going to slip and fall."

"How do you know? It ain't exactly somethin' a person plans to do, you know. Come on."

I sighed and shook my head, but allowed him to take my hand and lead me down the path toward home.

"Surprise! Surprise!"

The shouts came from everywhere as we stepped through the utility room door into the living room. I stopped—startled—then gasped, covering my mouth. The surprise was complete.

"W-what is this?" I stammered in bewilderment.

The girls were jumping up and down with excitement, laughing because they had taken me so completely by surprise.

"Did we skeer you?" they asked. "We brung you presents for th' baby. We brung supper, too, so's you don't have to cook for all of us. You wasn't expectin' anything like this, was you?"

"It's a surprise baby shower," Sue Proctor explained, taking pity on my confusion. "We all know how busy you've been teaching our children, and we know that you've had no time to get ready for your baby, so we wanted to help."

"Thank you. That's very sweet of you, but ..." I paused and looked reproachfully at Davy. He was grinning at me. In the kitchen doorway, Calvin was giggling at my evident confusion. "You were both in on this, I suppose," I chided. "That's what that little excursion down to the creek was all about, was it? To get me out of the house?"

"It worked, didn't it?"

"You could have given me a little hint or something so I could have at least combed my hair and put on something more appropriate," I said, glancing down at the shorts and suntop I wore. I was afraid some of the women would think my dress was indecent. The children wore shorts and brief tops, but all the women except one were in dresses, and she wore slacks.

"You look just fine," Sue said. "That's a cute outfit. Come over here and sit in the place of honor."

She led me to the rocker that had been placed in the middle

of the room. Beside it, the coffee table was piled high with gifts: some wrapped, some not. Davy and Calvin had disappeared. Evidently this was an occasion for women only. There were a few very young boys present; the rest were women and girls.

"This is so sweet of all of you," I said helplessly. "Thank you very much."

"Open your presents, open them!" the girls urged as they gathered around my chair, as excited as if they were receiving the gifts themselves. I smiled at them and took the gift one of the girls handed me.

"This one's from me," she said shyly. "I made it all by myself. I hope you like it."

"Why, thank you, Mary. I wonder what it could be?"

"You girls back up a little there an' give th' teacher some room," one of the mothers said. "You can all sit here on th' floor. That way th' rest of us can see what she's gettin', too."

The girls backed off and sat cross-legged on the floor in front of me. Still feeling slightly overwhelmed, I was grateful for the space. I opened the gift Mary had given me. It was a baby blanket made from a piece of flannel, with rickrack sewn unevenly around the edges. I held it up for all to see.

"It's beautiful, Mary, and very useful. Thank you." I leaned forward, and she rose to meet me. We exchanged a hug, and she sat back down, beaming.

I folded the blanket, then laid it aside. Another girl bounced up and took a package from the pile. "Open this one next," she said. "It's from me."

It was a small pillow with a lace-edged pillowcase, also homemade. I held it up.

"It's beautiful, Carrie. Did you make it?"

"Yes, but Mama helped me some."

"It's very nice, thank you. The baby will be able to use that for a long time."

I took up the next gift. Before me, Nonie Johnson

clasped her hands tightly in front of her and bit her lip. This gift was from her. She was a quiet, shy girl from a large, needy family. She was nervous, afraid that her gift might not meet with my approval. I then realized what a responsibility I had not to hurt anyone's feelings. Some of them had little to give, but what they had, they were willing to share with me. I was touched.

"Oh, how pretty!" I exclaimed, lifting it up. It was a small nightgown made of light cotton material and embroidered down the front with multi-colored flowers. "This will be perfect for the baby to wear right away, it's so lightweight and cool. Who is it from? Oh, here's a card. It's from Nonie. Thank you, Nonie. You embroider beautifully."

Nonie smiled and visibly relaxed. I carefully folded the gown and laid it aside, taking up the next gift.

"I didn't have no money to go into town an' no time to do no sewin'. I got all them things left over from my last young'un, an' since it 'pears like I won't be havin' no more of my own, I thought maybe you could use them," one woman said. "Young'uns grow so fast, don't have no chance to wear things out, so most of them are in right good shape. I washed them up an' aired them good on th' clothesline for one whole day, so they should be all right for a brand-new baby."

"Thank you, Mrs. Adams. All the little undershirts and gowns and bibs will come in handy. I'm sure I can use them all."

"Them flour sacks make mighty good diapers," another woman said. "Didn't have no time to hem them, but they work jist as good without hems."

"They're nice; I'll need all the diapers I can get. Thank you."

There were more hand-me-downs, and some new things, too. Clemmy had made a beautiful patchwork quilt. Ellen had been to town and bought me a gift package of powder, lotion and baby soap, along with safety pins and rubber pants. Sue gave me a big, roomy diaper bag. Hers was the last gift I opened.

"That's for when you have to take the baby with you when you go to teach school," she said slyly.

"Thank you, Sue, but I won't be teaching school next year, remember?"

There was a chorus of protests from the children. I smiled at them, touched.

"I am planning on coming back for a couple of hours every afternoon, but Davy has agreed to keep the baby for me. Thank you again, all of you, so much. I have everything I need for the baby now; I won't have to buy a thing, at least for awhile. I really do appreciate it."

"Davy and Calvin have set up a table under the shade tree in the backyard and taken the food out there," Sue said. "So, if you'd like, we can all go out there and have something to eat before we go home. It will be closer if we all go out the back door, if that's all right. Anne?"

"Not th' back door." Mrs. Wilson spoke up quickly before I could answer. "We all come in th' front door an' it's bad luck if you leave by a different door when you go a visitin'. It'll cause trouble between these folks an' us."

"Oh," Sue said blankly. She looked at me, then shrugged. "All right. We can all go out the front door, if you prefer."

"I never heard anything so silly," she whispered to me as we followed the others out. "Cause trouble, just because you happen to leave by a different door?"

"You can't fight superstition," I whispered back. "You don't have to agree with it, but it's useless to say so. You'll get absolutely nowhere."

"No, I suppose not."

We all filled our plates and stood around under the shade tree, eating and talking. It was getting toward evening, and a soft breeze had come up, making it pleasantly cool.

"This is so nice," I said. "All those gifts and supper, too. Do you mind if I fill a plate for Davy and Calvin, so I don't have to cook for them? I don't know where they've disappeared to."

"I'll do it," Ellen said. "There's food a plenty here."

"Are you feeling any better?" I asked, stepping aside with her.

"I'm better, jist have to be careful what I eat," she said.

"You're definitely expecting then?"

"Yes, but I'd jist as soon ever'one didn't know about it yet, it's early days. Want me to put jist a little of ever'thing on these plates?"

"That will be fine. Thank you, Ellen. You and Sue planned this, I suppose?"

"Yes. Your sister wanted to be in on it, but she couldn't come durin' th' week. Weekends an' evenin's ain't good for most of th' rest of us, so she said to go ahead. She said she'll jist wait 'til th' baby comes, then get you a present."

"It was very nice of you. I just wondered, was Jane invited?"

"Yes. Sue made a point of goin' over an' invitin' her, but she said she wasn't able to come 'cause of th' baby an' all. Sue was a little worried about her, said she seemed awful low in spirit."

"You talkin' about that Decker woman?" one of the women asked. "'Hear tell her ol' man's up an' left her again."

"Oh no. You don't mean it."

"That's what I heard. Been gone pert near two weeks now, or so they say."

"Should of knowed he would," another woman said, " a no-account man like that. Shoulda knowed he'd jist stay long enough to get her in th' family way again, like he done last time."

"Is she—is she expecting again?" I asked. Little Jacob is only a few months old."

"I don't know it for a fact. Jist sayin' it's what's likely to be. That man jist ain't no good, no matter which way you look at it."

"Ain't worth knockin' in th' head, accordin' to my ol' man," another woman spoke up. "From what I been told he's involved in shady dealin's in town. Likely got th' law after him an' that's why he took off."

"Hear tell he took ever'thing she had. Ain't got a thing left in th' house, 'ceptin' what was too big for him to carry off. Even took her milk goat, or so I heard."

"Oh no, not her milk goat. That's the only source of milk she had for those boys," I exclaimed.

They nodded their heads. "He don't keer. Man like that don't keer about nothin' or no one ceptin' hisself."

"Poor Jane. We'll have to all pitch in and help her as much as we can."

There was silence. I looked around at all of them.

"You've all been so kind to me and so generous," I said. "Please, let's all extend some of that generosity to Jane. I know none of you know her well, but she really is a fine person. She's a good friend of mine."

There was a slight murmur, whether of assent of dissent, I didn't know. I happened to glance at Jeanette Anderson just then. A look—almost of contempt—passed over her face and was gone. The look seemed meant for the other women, not me. It made me wonder, but there was no one to ask what it meant.

The party broke up soon after that. I thanked them all again, and they gathered up their dishes and children and were gone. I went back into the house, my head full of thoughts about Jane.

That night I lay in bed, unable to sleep. Beside me, Davy snored gently. I tossed and turned, unable to relax for thinking of Jane. Finally, I moved over against Davy, accidentally waking him.

"What is it?" he mumbled sleepily. "You feelin' okay?"

"I'm all right, but I'm worried about Jane. Davy, we have to help her."

"Okay," he mumbled. He would have turned over and gone back to sleep but I persisted.

"We have to do something right away. Those women said Jesse has been gone a couple of weeks, and he took everything, even her goat. She relied on that goat for milk for the boys."

"I'll go in to th' sale barn Friday an' get her another goat. Get her two goats, or three. Now go to sleep."

"I'm so worried about her. I should have kept in closer contact. Goodness knows how she's managing."

"Can't do nothin' about it tonight. Go see her tomorrow."

"I'm sorry I woke you, Davy. Good-night."

"Night."

He was asleep again in a matter of minutes, but I lay there for what seemed like hours before I finally dozed off.

CHAPTER TWENTY-ONE

Clemmy Gets Angry

*I*t was breakfast time. I called Calvin to eat, but there was no response. "Calvin, didn't you hear me call you?"

I opened his bedroom door and stuck my head in. He was still lying in bed, the covers pulled up to his chin, although the temperature was already in the eighties. He opened his bleary eyes and looked at me, but didn't move.

"Why, Calvin, what is it? Are you sick?" His face was flushed. I went over to his bed and put my hand on his forehead.

"You have a fever. What is it, Calvin? Where do you hurt?"

"Sore throat," he croaked.

"Why didn't you tell me? Let's get some of these covers off you to cool you down. What's this around your neck? Phew! Calvin, why do you have one of Davy's dirty socks tied around your neck?"

"Granny always had me do it. She said if you put a dirty sock around your neck when you go to bed, it'll cure a sore throat."

"Well, obviously it didn't," I said, removing the sock. "I can see how it might clear your sinuses, though. How in the world did you stand this so close to your face all night? Nevermind. I want to take your temperature, then I'll get you some aspirin. I'm sorry you're sick. I wish you'd told me last night. I could have given you something to relieve the pain."

I left his room and went to the bathroom to toss the dirty

sock into the clotheshamper and wash my hands. I took down the bottle of aspirin and went to the kitchen for a glass of water. Davy had already eaten and gone out. My breakfast and Calvin's were sitting on the table getting cold.

I gave Calvin two aspirin and washed his face with a cool washcloth, then laid it across his forehead. His temperature was one hundred and two. I looked down his throat with the aid of a flashlight and saw that his tonsils were red and swollen, but there were no white spots. I sat on the edge of the bed and watched him while he drifted off to sleep again. He was obviously quite ill, but what to do? Should I take him to the doctor or wait it out and hope he'd get over it on his own? People out here didn't run to the doctor for every little thing the way people in the city did, but was this a little thing? Then I remembered Clemmy's sore-throat remedy from the time I'd had tonsillitis while I was still living with her. I decided to walk over and talk to her.

She was canning peaches. The kitchen was sweet-smelling and steamy with heat. Her face was flushed and perspiring, but she greeted me with her usual placid smile.

"Clemmy, why won't you come over to our house to do your canning?" I chided, not for the first time. "Then you wouldn't have to stand over this hot wood stove all day."

"I ain't used to no kind of stove but a wood stove," she answered.

"But you could get used to it. You got used to my washing machine, didn't you?"

"It ain't so bad, as long as I get started early enough, before th' heat of th' day sets in. This'll be my last batch this mornin'."

"Think about it at least, Clemmy."

I knew the real reason she didn't take me up on my offer: Mr. Hilton had essentially forbidden it. He didn't approve of "new-fangled" things, as he put it. Clemmy still did the majority of her wash on the washboard. Only when her husband was away on one of his hunting trips did she come over and do her wash in my machine.

I picked up a peach, halved it and took a bite. I wiped away the juice that ran down my chin.

"These peaches are so good, Clemmy. I'd like to can some of them myself, if there's enough."

"There's a plenty. Tell Davy to get you some anytime you want them. There's a plenty tomatoes, cucumbers, beans an' squash a comin', too. You jist help yourself to anything you're a wantin'."

"We've already been doing that. Clemmy, Calvin is sick. He has a sore throat and he's running a fever."

She paused from ladling peaches into a jar and looked at me. "I thought he looked kinda peaked when I saw him yesterday," she said.

"Well, I didn't notice. I wish I had. He's feeling pretty bad. I gave him some aspirin, but I don't know what else to do. I was wondering if you have any of that salve you put on me that time I had a sore throat, and if you think it will help Calvin."

"In that lard bucket right up there. Put yourself some in one of them little jars."

I reached up and got the bucket. When I removed the lid, I took an involuntary step backward.

"I made it jist a couple weeks ago," she said. "It should be plenty strong still."

"It is. What shall I dip it with?"

"Use one of them ol' bent spoons in that drawer there. You got any outing flannel to put around his throat? You got to keep his neck warm after you put th' salve on. Is he hurtin' any in his chest?"

"I don't think so. It just seems to be his throat."

"Make sure he drinks water a plenty."

"I remember that part, but he's finding it rather difficult to swallow."

"This'll take th' swellin' down. Jist make sure you keep his neck covered up an' warm, or he might take cold."

"You don't think I should take him to the doctor?"

"He'll be better tomorrow, more'n likely. Soon as I finish this batch of peaches, I'll come over an' take a look at him."

"Thank you, Clemmy. What would we all do without you?"

I took the jar of salve and went home. Calvin was still asleep. I found a soft cloth and went back to his room. I put my hand on his forehead; he seemed a little cooler.

"I have some of Clemmy's salve here," I said when he opened his eyes. "I'm going to put some on your neck. It may burn a little and it smells awful, but after that dirty sock last night you probably won't mind it. First, though, I want you to drink a glass of water. Yes, I know it hurts, but drink it anyway. It will help you get well sooner."

He drank half a glass, then lay back down. I rubbed the salve on his throat, then wrapped the soft cloth around his neck. I replaced the cool, wet cloth on his forehead and left him. He was already half asleep again, which I knew was the best thing for him.

In the kitchen, I nibbled on a piece of bacon and threw the cold scrambled eggs and toast in the covered bowl I kept near the sink for table scraps. We'd use them later to feed Brownie. I peeled a small cucumber and put the peelings in another bowl for the pigs, then I buttered a slice of bread, wrapped it around the cucumber, and sat down at the table to eat my breakfast. I had developed a craving for cucumber sandwiches and had one at almost every meal. I finished off my breakfast with another fresh peach, thinking all the while about Jane. I had intended to go see her right after breakfast, but now I couldn't. I didn't feel comfortable about leaving Calvin.

I cleaned up the kitchen, then moved through the rest of the house, straightening, picking up and plumping pillows, being as quiet as possible so I didn't disturb Calvin. In an hour, the house was in order. I was left with time on my hands and nothing to do. I wasn't in the mood to sit and read, and I didn't want to do any baking because turning on the oven heated the kitchen up so. Nothing like Clemmy's kitchen, of course, but since I was eight months pregnant, the heat was affecting me more than it normally would. I decided to do my laundry. That would leave me free to visit Jane tomorrow, if Calvin was better.

I was filling the washer out on the back porch when Brownie began barking excitedly in the side yard, right under Calvin's window. I hurried over to the edge of the porch to quiet him.

"Brownie, hush," I ordered. He ignored me, lunging at something in the grass then jumping back. When I saw the snake strike at him and barely miss, I gasped and shouted urgently: "Brownie, get back! Come here, Boy."

It was as if I hadn't spoken. He lunged at the snake again, and again jumped back. He was young and inexperienced with snakes, and I was afraid he was going to get bitten, as the other Brownie had. I had to kill the snake, and quick. Davy always used a hoe, but I didn't know where one was, and I was afraid to get that close to the snake. Perhaps I could shoot it. I went inside and got the rifle.

"Brownie, get back!" I ordered again, afraid I would shoot him instead of the snake. Calvin woke and called to him from the window, but he was oblivious. The snake struck again and again, Brownie springing back just in time.

"What's all th' fuss?" Davy asked, coming around the corner of the house.

"Davy, watch out! There's a snake."

Davy paused, then approached Brownie from behind, grasping his hair and pulling him back.

"Okay, go ahead an' see if you can hit him. It's a copperhead."

"I don't think I can. You kill him."

"Can't. Got to hold onto Brownie. Go ahead an' try, at least."

"Get back a little more, then."

The snake's last strike had brought it closer; I could see it well. I raised the rifle, aimed and pulled the trigger. A spot of blood appeared on the snake's back. He writhed, then started to slither away.

"Try again," Davy said calmly. "Aim for th' head this time."

I aimed and shot again. This time a spot of blood appeared on the snake's head.

"Got him!" Davy exclaimed, grinning. "I'll make a crack shot of you yet."

He brought the heel of his boot down on the snake's head, then released the dog. Brownie rushed at the snake and grabbed it, violently shaking it. I rested the butt of the rifle on the porch floor, feeling rather smug and satisfied with myself.

"What are you doin'?" Clemmy exclaimed from behind me.

She was as perturbed as I had ever seen her, and she almost snatched the rifle from me.

"Why, Clemmy, what's wrong?" I asked in surprise.

"You ain't got no business shootin' no snake in your condition," she almost snapped. "You'll mark that baby you're a carryin'. Davy, what was you thinkin' about anyway? You know better'n to let her do somethin' like that."

"Sorry, Mom. Guess I forgot."

"Forgot! You ain't forgot what that Phillips boy looked like, have you?"

"No, Mom, I ain't forgot that."

I looked from one to the other of them. There was no doubt that Clemmy was genuinely disturbed. Davy looked shamefaced as he eyed his mother. She thrust the rifle at him.

"Now you take this here gun an' put it away. An' don't go puttin' her up to shootin' no more snakes ner nothin' else 'til after that baby comes."

"Yes, Mom." He took the gun, while Clemmy turned and marched into the house, the picture of righteous indignation. I looked at my husband, puzzled.

"What was that all about?" I asked.

"Folks around here think you can mark a baby by doin' somethin' like you jist done while you're carryin' it."

"That's ridiculous. I never heard of such a thing."

He shrugged. "You won't convince her of that."

"No, I suppose not. What's this about a Phillips boy?"

"His mama was out milkin' when she was carryin' him. Th' cow kicked her an' bruised up th' left side of her face. When th' baby was born, th' whole left side of his face was covered with a big, ugly purple birthmark."

"But that wouldn't have had anything to do with the cow kicking her. It was just coincidence."

"Like I said, you won't convince her of that, nor anyone else out here, either. Well, I better get this gun cleaned an' put away. You better not touch it again 'til after th' baby comes, unless it's some kind of emergency. Good shot, though."

I followed him into the house. Calvin's door was open, and I could see her leaning over his bed.

"What's goin' on? Cal sick?" Davy asked.

"Yes. He has a sore throat. Otherwise, I'd be at Jane's right now."

"I can stick around th' house an' keep a eye on him for a couple hours if you want to go ahead an' go."

"Would you, Davy? I'd appreciate it. You don't have to stay with him every minute. Just check on him once in awhile and make sure he drinks plenty of water and keeps his neck covered."

"Okay. I can do that."

"I put some of your mother's salve on his throat. Remember when I had tonsillitis the first winter I was here, and your mother put that salve on me? You checked on me in the middle of the night and brought me that whiskey with honey and lemon to drink?"

"I remember. Had a real hard time leavin' you that night. I was already head-over-heels in love with you by then."

"Were you? You were very sweet and kind. Do you think I should give Calvin some honey and lemon with whiskey to sip?"

"If you do, go easy on th' whiskey. Might jist give him th' lemon an' honey with a little hot water, 'stead of th' whiskey. Might soothe his throat some."

"That's a good idea. I'll fix some, then I'll go to Jane's. I'll try not to stay too long."

"Okay."

When I went into Calvin's room, he was wide awake because of all the commotion over the snake. Clemmy had rubbed more salve on his neck and was replacing the flannel cloth. His cheeks were still flushed with fever.

"What do you think, Clemmy?" I asked.

"He'll be all right, jist keep him in bed a couple three days 'til he's over it."

"What about the fever?"

"Fever won't hurt him none, long as you keep plenty of water down him. Likely it'll go up tonight, it always does in th' evenin', but it'll be down in th' mornin'."

"Thank you, Clemmy, for coming over and for the salve."

"You better get some rest yourself," she said, turning to leave. "An' you leave that gun alone, long as you're carryin' that young'un."

"Yes, Clemmy. I'm sorry. I didn't know." I stopped, feeling like a hypocrite but wanting to appease her.

"Didn't figger you did, but Davy knowed. I ain't mad at you none, but if that baby comes out all marked up 'cause of this, I'll be tempted to take a willer switch to him, way I used to do when he was a boy."

With that, she left. I couldn't help smirking at Davy. He grinned in return and shook his head.

"I'll be in her black book now, 'til after th' baby comes an' she sees for herself that it's all right. Mom don't get mad easy, but when she does, she simmers awhile."

"I'm sorry, Davy, It's my fault. I had no idea."

"Forget it. Get yourself off to Jane's. I got things to do after dinner."

"I'm on my way. Thanks."

CHAPTER TWENTY-TWO

Superstitions

Davy was full of questions when I returned from Jane's.

"How is she? Is it true her ol' man's left her again?"

"It's true," I said flatly. "He didn't exactly take everything like those women said, but he took all the money she'd been saving for winter. It wasn't much, but it was all she had. He took her goat, just like he took Rosy that last time, only this is more serious. She needs that goat for the baby's milk."

"She was givin' th' baby goat's milk?"

"Yes. She started him out on the formula that the welfare people gave her but she said it didn't agree with him. He was always fussy and colicky and didn't act as if he was satisfied. She switched him to goat's milk and she said he did fine on it; he started sleeping better and gaining weight. Now she's had to put him back on formula, and she says he isn't doing well again. She's worried about him. Davy, we have to get her another goat."

"What's she goin' to say about that?"

"She won't like it, but there won't be much she can do about it if we just go ahead without telling her. This is one time when she's just going to have to swallow her pride and accept help."

"Maybe we could work out somethin'."

"Like what?"

"Have them two biggest boys come over an' stack wood or somethin'. They could pay us back that way."

"Good idea. I'm sure that will make her feel better.

Let's go ahead and get the goat and tell her about the arrangements later."

"Okay. I'll go to the sale barn tomorrow, see what they got."

"Thank you. How is Calvin?"

"Mostly been sleepin'."

"Is he still feverish?"

"Some."

"All right. Davy, why doesn't anyone out here breast feed their babies? I know it isn't the 'in' thing to do anymore, but out here, with people closer to nature as they are, you'd think they would. It's so much better for the baby, and it's cheaper and easier, too."

"Dunno."

"Did your mother?"

"Dunno. Don't think so."

"Why not?"

"Dunno."

"Davy, am I embarrassing you?"

He scratched his head. "Little bit, maybe," he admitted.

"Why? And don't say 'dunno' again."

"Well, I don't know. Guess maybe it don't seem decent or somethin'."

I frowned at him in exasperation. "Is it indecent for a calf or a baby pig to nurse?" I asked.

"Course not. It's nature."

"Exactly. It's nature for a mother to nurse her baby, too. I'm going to, so get used to the idea."

"You won't."

"I won't what?"

He swallowed. "I seen a woman in town doin' that a couple weeks ago. She was sittin' in th' grocery store, right there in front where that bench is. It was embarrassin'."

"Didn't she cover herself?"

"No. Ever'body was starin'."

"I promise I won't embarrass you like that," I said with a laugh. "There's a time and a place, you know, and a way to do it discreetly. Now, what would you like for lunch?"

"Whatever you got."

"I can fix tuna salad sandwiches or bacon and tomato."

"Tuna will be all right."

He came into the kitchen with me and sat down at the table. I took a can of tuna down and opened it.

"Davy, Jane needs some wood. Can you take her some?"

"Yep."

"How is Jeanette Anderson doing in that department? Are you still keeping her supplied with wood?"

"I ain't been near her place since you laid down th' law. Scared to."

"Sure you are. Who's helping her out now, if you're not?"

"Lewis."

"And Sue is allowing that?"

"She goes with him."

"Oh. Well, she said she was going to, and perhaps she's wise." I set the plate of sandwiches on the table and Davy helped himself. I poured two glasses of milk, then sat down across from him, taking up half a sandwich. "Who can we get her married off to," I mused.

"Who?" he asked, startled.

I smiled. "Jeanette, of course. She's young still, and attractive when she tries. All those kids need a father. And she needs a husband so she'll leave ours alone. Now let me see."

"Better forget it. Ain't no man in his right mind gonna marry a woman with eight kids, 'less she's got a million dollars or somethin', an' she ain't."

"You never know. There might be somebody."

"Not around here."

"There does seem to be a shortage of good men around here. I wonder who you would have married, if I hadn't come along."

"Nobody."

"Like fun," I said. "Goldie Sutton would probably have you."

"Not on your life."

"Well, then, Mrs. Anderson."

"You got rocks in your head."

I laughed. "It was just a thought. Then there's Jane."

"Whoa there, woman. She's still married."

"Yes, but to what? She deserves better. She's so down and discouraged because of what that husband of hers has done. I feel so sorry for her."

"We'll do what we can, but forget the matchmakin'. That's a good way to get yourself in a whole passel of trouble."

"I suppose so. I wish every woman could be as fortunate as I am, though. Some women are such bad judges of character."

"An' you're not?"

"No. I'm a very good judge of character. Just look at who I got."

"If you're tryin' to flatter me, you're succeeding. What do you want?"

"Well, I just thought, when you go to the sale barn tomorrow, besides the goats—and I do think you should get two—if there's a special sale on pigs or ducks and chickens or anything like that ..."

"Thought she had chickens."

"She only has one hen left. A fox got into her chicken house. They've been eating some of them, too."

"I see. Anything else?"

"Nothing I can think of at the moment. Just keep an eye open for bargains."

"I'll see what I can do."

"Thank you, Davy, you're sweet."

"Sure I am. That's why you married me. See you later," he said, pushing his chair back and bending to kiss me. "I've got to go to the back forty this afternoon, but I'll be home in time for supper."

"All right, Davy. Don't work too hard."

I cleared the table, checked on Calvin, then went out to finish my laundry.

Calvin woke in mid-afternoon, feeling somewhat better. His fever was down, and he ate some chicken soup. He sat up in bed and read awhile, then started to complain of a headache. I gave him two more aspirin and rubbed some more salve on him. He lay down and went back to sleep.

He slept through supper. Davy went out to do the chores and I was washing dishes when I heard Calvin call me. When I went into his room, his face was wet with tears and screwed-up in pain.

"What is it, Calvin? Are you feeling worse?"

"My ear," he sobbed. "It's killin' me."

"Oh dear. I'm sorry. I probably should have taken you to the doctor. I'll get some more aspirin and the heating pad, maybe that will help."

When Davy came in, I was sitting on the edge of Calvin's bed, holding the heating pad against his ear and trying to comfort him. He was crying with pain.

"He has a bad earache," I told Davy. "Can you go ask your mother if she knows of anything that will help?"

"I'll go get Dad," Davy answered, leaving the room.

Dad? I wondered why he said he was going to get his dad, when I had asked for his mother. His dad didn't have anything to do with Calvin. I wondered if Davy had somehow misunderstood what I said, but when he returned a short time later, it was his dad who was with him and not his mother. I was too surprised to say a word when Mr. Hilton came to the side of the bed and indicated that I was to vacate my position.

"Hush up that bawlin'," he said to Calvin. "You ain't no baby."

I opened my mouth in indignant protest, but when Davy shook his head at me, I closed it again. Mr. Hilton pulled up a chair and sat down by the bed.

"Turn over on your side so's your bad ear is up," he ordered. Calvin obeyed, stifling his sobs. Mr. Hilton put his pipe in his mouth and drew on it. Then he leaned close to Calvin and carefully blew the pipe smoke into Calvin's left ear. Davy and I stood and watched while he repeated this action several times. I saw Calvin's eyes close and his breath gradually deepen; he was soon asleep. I stood and watched in amazement.

"Ya'll go on," Mr. Hilton said then, glancing up at me and Davy. "Ain't doin' nobody no good jist standin' there gawkin'."

We left the room, but he remained at Calvin's side. I looked at Davy.

"I've never heard of anything like that," I said slowly. "Is it the warmth of the smoke that did it, or is it some narcotic in the smoke itself?"

"Dunno, but it works. 'Bout th' only time I remember Dad doin' anything for any of us kids was when we had a earache."

"I'm surprised that he would do it for Calvin. Will wonders never cease? I'm learning new things every day. If you'd told me pipe smoke could relieve earaches and I hadn't actually seen it for myself, I would have classed it right along with the dirty sock theory."

"Th' what?"

"The dirty sock theory. Calvin had one of your dirty socks tied around his neck when I went in this morning. He said Granny told him it cures sore throats."

"Oh yeah, I've heard of that. They say tyin' nine knots in a black thread an' wearin' it around th' neck for nine days will prevent a sore throat, too."

"You're kidding."

"Nope. An' did you know tellin' lies causes sties?"

"It does not."

"An' to keep mumps from goin' down on a boy, you jist tie a red cloth around his waist."

"That's ridiculous."

"An' warts are caused by handlin' toads."

"I've heard that one but it's not true, either. Warts are caused by a virus."

"Not around here. An' they say if you get blisters on your tongue, it's 'cause you been tellin' lies."

"What else?" I asked, beginning to be amused.

"If a woman's second toe is longer than her big toe, it means she'll henpeck her husband. Let me see your toes."

"I will not."

"If you happen to have a problem with pimples, all you have to do is wash your face with a wet diaper. That one ought to come in handy after you have th' baby."

"Not on your life."

"One of my sisters tried it."

"Did it help?"

"I don't know. She used to mash strawberries an' put them on her face, too, an' sometimes she'd beat up th' white of a egg an' smear it all over her face. Sure did look funny when it dried."

"I've heard of those last two. Which sister was this?"

"Ruth Ann. You ain't met her yet. She was th' prettiest one. Don't know why she had to go to all that trouble. Well, why don't you go on to bed an' get some sleep. You may have to get up later if Cal gets bad again. I don't know how long Dad'll stay; I'll jist lay here on the sofa in case anyone needs me. I'll call you if you're needed."

"Thank you, Davy, I think I will. I'm tired. It's been a full day, and I missed my nap."

"Sleep tight."

"Good-night, Davy."

193

CHAPTER TWENTY-THREE

Jane's Hero

I didn't wake up the next morning until Davy came in with a cup of coffee. I sat up.

"Calvin?" I asked.

"Better. Dad stayed with him 'til about midnight. He only woke up once after that. I gave him a drink and some more aspirin an' he went back to sleep. Still want me to go in to the sale barn?"

"Yes, please. I have the car. If I need to, I can take Calvin to the doctor."

"Okay. I better get goin' then, if I want to get in on th' good sales. Don't know when I'll be back."

"I'll get up and fix your breakfast."

"I already had breakfast."

"What did you have?"

"Cornflakes an' a couple peaches."

"Will that be enough?"

"It'll hold me. I may get me a few doughnuts when I get into town; ain't had one for a long time. See you later. Why don't you stay in bed? If Cal needs you, he can holler."

"I think I will."

I drank my coffee, then slid back down in the bed. I heard the truck start up and drive off, then drifted back to sleep. When I woke at midmorning, it was getting hot. I threw the sheet aside and got up to check on Calvin. He was sitting up in bed, reading a book.

"How are you, Calvin?" I asked, putting my hand on his forehead. He was warm, but that might be because of the heat of the day. I took up the thermometer and shook it down.

"I'm better," he said.

"Good. How's the earache?"

"Still hurts a little once in awhile."

"And your throat?"

"Better."

"Good. Open up."

I placed the thermometer under his tongue and went to the kitchen for a glass of orange juice. When I came back and removed the thermometer, his temperature was right at one hundred.

"You're much better," I said. "Your temperature is almost normal. Drink the orange juice. Are you hungry? Do you want something to eat?"

"No."

"All right. You can eat later. I'll rub some more of the salve on you."

"Do you got to?"

"Yes, Calvin, I have to. I know it smells awful, but if it does the job, it's worth it. You must stay in bed all day today. You can get up to go to the bathroom, but that's all. Okay?"

"Okay."

"If you need anything, I'll be in the kitchen."

He stayed in bed, alternately reading and sleeping. His temperature stayed down, and he was able to eat a light lunch. Clemmy came over to check on him, then she and I sat in the kitchen and talked awhile. I desperately wanted to ask her about her husband's feelings toward Calvin now, but I didn't know how to frame the question. From Calvin's birth, he had refused to have anything to do with the boy— refused even to acknowledge him—because he was one of his daughter's illegitimate son. Since Calvin had come to live with us, Mr. Hilton's attitude seemed to be softening. Now he had stayed up with Calvin for close to five hours. What did it mean? Had he finally accepted Calvin as his grandson, or would he have done the same for anyone else?

I wished I knew, but Mr. Hilton was an enigma. No one, not even his family, really knew him.

Davy came home in the middle of the afternoon. He stopped at the house and I saw that he had a couple of animals in the back of the truck. I assumed they were the goats for Jane.

"You got the goats?" was the first thing I asked him as he came through the door.

"Yep. Got a couple of runt pigs, too, for next to nothin', don't know if they'll even live. Got half a dozen chickens and two ducks."

"Thank you. Jane will be so happy."

"You got to come out with me so she can be happy at you an' not at me."

"Why Davy!"

"You know how she scares me. I don't want her feelin' beholden to me. You got to tell her it was your idea to do this, not mine."

"Well, all right, if it will make you feel better."

"It will. How's Cal?"

"He's better."

"Okay to leave him for awhile?"

"Yes. Are you going out to Jane's now? I'll just tell him where we're going."

"You better follow me in your car. Road's pretty rough, an' I don't want to bounce you around too much in th' truck. I got to come straight back anyhow, an' you'll prob'ly want to stay and visit awhile."

"All right."

When I told him where we were going, Calvin wanted to go along, which was a sign he was feeling much better. I refused, leaving him in something of a huff. Davy called me over to the truck.

"Oh, there's a baby with one of the goats," I exclaimed. "How sweet."

"Think you'd recognize Jane's goat?" Davy asked.

"What do you mean?"

"I mean I'd almost swear that one is Jane's goat. Didn't notice until I started tryin' to get her in th' truck; goats all look pretty much th' same to me. But I spent close to an hour that last time we was out there, draggin' her home from the Miller's pasture. I'd almost swear that's th' same goat. If it ain't, it's her twin sister."

"You don't suppose?"

"Well, we'll soon see."

"But you didn't ... no, of course you wouldn't have bought her from Jesse Decker."

"Bought her from a man named Smith. Well, let's get this over with."

He started the truck, and I followed in my car. When we got to Jane's house, I parked the car near the house and got out. Davy drove on down to the shed Jane used to house her animals and backed up to the gate. By that time, Jane and the older boys had come out into the yard.

"What's he doin'?" Jane asked as I joined them.

"Come and see."

"It's Dinah! Mama, he's brought Dinah back!" one of the boys cried. They all converged on Davy as he led the larger goats towards the pen. It was obvious that their goat was more than just a source of milk; she was a great pet. Jane cried out and covered her mouth. Tears welled in her eyes.

"Lord love th' man," she said when she could speak. "He's gone an' got Dinah back for us."

Jane and I joined Davy and the boys, who were joyously cavorting around the goat.

"How did you find her?" Jane asked. "How'd you get her away from Jesse? Did he give you any trouble?"

Davy gave me a quick, furtive glance and looked away. "No trouble atall," he answered briefly.

"No, a course he wouldn't. Jesse's always been a coward

when he comes up again' a man who's bigger'n him," Jane said with a malicious touch of satisfaction. "She's needin' to be milked, too. If you folks'll excuse me, I'll jist run an' get th' milk bucket an' check on Jake. He's been awful fussy all day, an' I want to get some of Dinah's milk down him. Don't run off, I'll be right back."

"Here, you boys, come on an' help me," Davy urged, as soon as Jane was out of hearing distance. "Make it snappy. I'm in a hurry."

He leaped into the back of the truck and untied the other goat. Leading her to the back, he forced her to jump down. He gave the rope to Johnny.

"Take her in with th' other goat an' tie her to a fence post," he said. Here, Jimmie, you carry her kid. You there, can you carry a pig?"

He gave the third boy one of the small pigs. The youngest boy waited expectantly, so Davy put the other pig in his arms.

"Take 'em to the pen, quick, an' don't drop 'em," Davy said, leaping down from the truck. He slid a large crate to the ground, then carried it inside the fence and set it down. I saw that it contained the chickens and the ducks.

"See you later," he said to me. He got in the truck and drove away just as Jane came back down the path with the milk pail. When she saw the collection of animals, she stopped. Steadying herself on the gate, she stared, seemingly oblivious to the boy's excited clamor. Slow tears slid down her face.

"What's he gone an' done?" she asked, sounding almost dazed.

"It was my idea, not his. He went to the sale barn today. Things were going cheap so he picked up a few animals for you."

"But I can't pay for all this stuff. Jesse took all my money."

"Don't worry about paying for it, Jane. Davy wants

Johnny and Jimmie to come over later this summer and help stack firewood and do a few other things around the house. There's a lot to do, and I can't help this year. You won't mind the boys doing that, will you?"

"You mean it?"

"Yes, I mean it. Davy said to tell you the pigs went for next to nothing; he says he doesn't even know if you can keep them alive. The chickens and ducks didn't cost much, either."

"I never even thanked him," she said slowly. "You tell him how much I 'preciate gettin' Dinah back an' all them other animals, too. My goodness, with two goats we'll have enough milk for ever'one to have a little an' maybe still have some left over for th' pigs. You folks are mighty generous. You jist let me know when you want help with that wood, an' we'll all come over an' pitch in."

"*Uh-oh*," I thought. "*What have I gotten us into? Davy isn't going to like that.*" Aloud I said, "We'll let you know. I'll give Davy your message. Bye, Jane. Bye, boys, be good."

I started home feeling mixed emotions. The most important thing was that Jane had her goat back and there would be milk for the baby again. I wondered if she would ever find out that Davy hadn't gone out searching for her goat, or wrestled her away from Jesse. I grinned to myself. It seemed Davy was destined to be Jane's hero, whether he wanted to be or not.

CHAPTER TWENTY-FOUR

A Lesson in Grammar

I went to my rocker and sat down, a book in my hands. Davy was sitting in his rocker reading the newspaper. Calvin was curled up in a corner of the sofa reading a book. The supper dishes were done, and Davy had finished the chores. "It's Monday," I said.

"Yeah?" he said, barely glancing up from the paper.

"You said we could start the grammar lessons on Monday," I reminded.

"I'm readin' th' paper right now."

"The paper can wait. Calvin, put your book down for a few minutes, please."

Davy laid the paper on the floor beside his chair with a sigh. Calvin looked up from his book but didn't close it.

"I thought we could begin by doing some reading aloud. The more we read good grammar, especially if we read it aloud, the easier it becomes to speak well. I have a book here that I thought we'd all enjoy, so Davy, I'd like you to begin." I leaned forward and held the book out to him, opened to the page where I wanted him to begin.

"I got somethin' I'd rather read from a different book," he said. He leaned over and took the Bible from the shelf. He grinned at me and opened it.

"Well, all right," I said, surprised. "The Bible contains some of the greatest prose and poetry ever written. Perhaps something from the book of Psalms or Proverbs."

"I had somethin' in mind from th' book of Timothy. First Timothy, chapter two, verse twelve. 'But I suffer not a woman to teach, nor to usurp authority over the man, but to be in silence.'" He looked up with a quirky grin and flipped over a few pages. "Th' book of Ephesians, chapter five, verses twenty-two, twenty-three and twenty-four."

"Have you been talking to Mr. Sutton?" I interrupted suspiciously.

He ignored me and began to read.

"Wives, submit yourselves unto your own husbands, as unto the Lord. For the husband is the head of the wife, even as Christ is the head of the church; and he is the savior of the body. Therefore as the church is subject unto Christ, so let the wives be to their own husbands in every thing."

He slowed, putting special emphasis on the last three words, then closed the Bible and sat back with a smug smile. In his corner of the sofa, Calvin put his hand over his mouth and giggled. I was momentarily silenced.

"Let me see that," I said curtly. He opened the Bible again and handed it to me.

"Ephesians, chapter five, verses twenty-two through twenty-four."

"Not that one, the first one you read."

"Second Timothy, chapter two, verse twelve. It's over jist a few pages."

"I can find it," I retorted. "Since when did you get to be such an authority on the Bible? Have you been talking to Mr. Sutton?"

"Not a bit. I kinda got away from it lately but I used to read th' Bible all th' time. Lots of times that's all there was around to read. It's got some real hair-raisin' stories in it."

I found the scripture he had read and read it for myself, as well as the verses surrounding it.

"I think you have been talking to Mr. Sutton, and I think you're twisting the scriptures to suit your own purposes just as he did. This is obviously talking about teaching in the church, not teaching proper grammar."

I found the other scripture and read it, too. Then I

looked up at Davy with a smirk of my own. He was watching me with a mischievous twinkle in his eyes.

"Why didn't you read on?" I asked. "The next part seems to be directed toward husbands. Is there perhaps something there that you didn't want me to hear?" I began to read it aloud, being careful to enunciate properly, as I wanted them to learn to do.

"Husbands, love your wives, even as Christ also loved the church, and gave himself for it; that he might sanctify and cleanse it with the washing of water by the word, that he might present it to himself a glorious church, not having spot or wrinkle or any such thing; but that it should be holy and without blemish. So ought men to love their wives as their own bodies. He that loveth his wife, loveth himself. For no man ever yet hated his own flesh; but nourisheth and cherisheth it, even as the Lord the church; for we are members of his body, of his flesh, and of his bones. For this cause shall a man leave his father and mother and shall be joined unto his wife, and they two shall be one flesh. This is a great mystery but I speak concerning Christ and the church. Nevertheless, let every one of you in particular so love his wife even as himself; and the wife see that she reverence her husband."

I sat silently for a moment then looked up, meeting Davy's eyes. He looked as touched as I felt.

"That's beautiful," I said, almost in awe. "That portion of the scriptures should be used in every wedding ceremony. Why don't I remember ever reading that before?" With a little effort, I brought my mind back to the issue at hand. "So," I said to Davy, "Are you saying that I'm not a properly submissive wife, just because I want to teach you good grammar?"

"Jist teasin'. I know it ain't talkin' about that."

"Seriously, Davy, I'm not trying to force you. I thought you wanted to learn."

"I do, it's jist a little hard to get started, I guess. What was it you was wantin' me to read?"

"It wasn't anything special, at least it doesn't seem so special after reading that," I said, indicating the Bible that still lay open on my lap. "I notice the next chapter here seems to be directed toward children. Calvin, perhaps you could read that aloud to us."

He took the Bible from me and began to read.

"Children, obey your parents in th' Lord; for this is right. Honour—they spelled that wrong. Honor ain't got a 'u' in it."

"It's Old English, Calvin; this was published back in the 1600s. They spelled their words a little differently then. Go on."

"Honour thy father and mother; which is the first commandment with promise; that it may be well with thee, and thou mayest live long on the earth." He paused again and looked up at me. "God sure does talk funny. What's mayest?"

"It means may. It's English as it was spoken years ago, rather like Shakespeare's writings. Remember when we read that play by Shakespeare?"

"Oh yeah. He talked funny, too." He began reading again.

"And ye fathers, provoke not your children to wrath;" He paused and looked up at Davy, grinning. "I know what that means. It's like that time you wouldn't let me go over to Chad's house."

"Keep readin', brat," Davy said mildly.

"But bring them up in the nurture and admonition of the Lord. What's nurture?"

"It has a meaning similar to nourish, Calvin."

"What's admonition?"

"It means we should be makin' you learn what th' Bible says," Davy spoke up.

"No, it don't," Calvin crowed triumphantly. "It means you got to teach me th' Bible. It says fathers, don't it?"

"He's right," I said. "It does say fathers."

Davy looked a little uneasy. "Never pictured myself as a teacher," he said. "Don't think I'd know how to go about it."

"The best way in the world is probably just to read the Bible aloud as we've been doing this evening," I said. "People always used to do that, didn't they? Did your parents do it, Davy?"

"No. My parents couldn't read, remember? Mom learned to read a little with us kids, but not enough to do any reading in the Bible that I know of."

"It might be a good idea for us to do it. I think I'd like that. What do the two of you think?"

"Guess it'd be all right."

"All right with me," Calvin said. "You want me to read some now?"

"I think that's enough for tonight, Calvin. Perhaps we can read some more tomorrow night. Now, shall we have that lesson on proper grammar?"

CHAPTER TWENTY-FIVE

Davy's Accident

Davy rose early the next morning to get a jump on the day's work.

"I'm goin' out to th' back forty to cut wood," he said, sitting beside me on the edge of the bed. "Want to come along?"

"I don't think so, Davy. I think I'd just rather stay here. I'm tired today."

"I was afraid you might be overdoin' it yesterday."

"I had all that energy yesterday but I seem to have used it up. Have you had any breakfast?"

"I had some of that zucchini bread you made yesterday with peach jam. It sure was good. Sure you're all right? I can stay closer to home if you want me to."

No, I'm all right. The doctor says the baby won't be putting in an appearance for a couple of weeks yet. I just want to go back to sleep."

"Okay. I'll see you at noon then."

He leaned over and kissed me on the forehead, then left. I turned on my side and went back to sleep.

About an hour later, something woke me. I opened my eyes and lay there for a moment, wondering what it was. I knew it wasn't Calvin, because I'd taken him in to stay with Granny for a few days when I went to see the doctor. There were only the usual sounds: a dog barking in the distance and a rooster crowing. I felt a slow tightening sensation in my lower back that gradually spread to and across my stomach. I put my hand on my stomach, wondering what it meant. I glanced at the clock. It was a few minutes after seven.

I lay there, beginning to doze off again, but I became wide awake when the tightening sensation began again, a little stronger this time. I glanced again at the clock. It was 7:30. Was I in labor?

I lay there, feeling elated, but a little frightened, too. The doctor had said I wasn't ready to deliver yet, but could he be wrong? It was the last day of June. Was this the day my baby would be born?

Twenty minutes passed and nothing happened. I was disappointed. Perhaps I was experiencing false labor; I'd heard that some women did. I threw the sheet aside and was preparing to get up when the tightening began again. It had been half an hour this time. I'd read that it wasn't unusual for labor pains to be irregular right at first. It looked as if this might be it. I began to wish I had taken Davy up on his offer to stay close to home, but there was probably plenty of time. I could tell him when he came in for lunch.

I drank a cup of coffee and ate a peach; didn't the book say to eat lightly during the initial stages of labor? I kept my eye on the clock. The contractions were coming twenty to thirty minutes apart. I took a bath and dressed carefully, willing myself to stay calm. All my brave words about having this baby at home were forgotten. I wanted to get to the hospital, where my doctor and the nurses would be around me because I was feeling quite nervous and scared. Perhaps if I had Davy with me, I would feel a little more confident. I glanced at the clock again. It was 10:30; the contractions were getting closer and coming stronger. Perhaps I shouldn't wait until Davy came in at noon. Perhaps, just to be on the safe side, I should go out and find him now. He'd need a little time to clean up and change his clothes, and while he was doing that, I could pack my bag. I picked up my keys and went out to my car.

Clemmy was in the garden, bent over, probably picking green beans. She straightened when she saw me.

"How you feelin' this mornin'?" she asked me.

"I think I may be in labor," I answered. "I'm going out to find Davy now."

"Thought you might have that young'un today. A woman always seems to have a lot of energy th' day before th' baby comes, an' you was doin' all that cannin' yesterday. You wantin' me to come with you?"

"I don't think it's necessary, Clemmy, I know where he is. But thank you anyhow."

When I stopped my car at the edge of the clearing near Davy's truck, I could hear the sound of the chain saw a short distance inside the woods. The sound stopped, followed by the crash of a tree coming down. I waited for a minute, then decided to honk the horn instead of walking into the woods to find him.

I waited awhile longer, leaning against the side of the car as another contraction began. It passed, but Davy had not yet put in an appearance. Perhaps he hadn't heard the horn. I honked again, longer this time. I waited, but he didn't come. Puzzled, I walked to the edge of the woods and called his name. There was no answer. Perhaps he was farther back in the woods than I thought. I honked the horn several more times. When he still didn't come, I began to be alarmed. Had the tree fallen on him?

I went into the woods, picking my way through the underbrush toward where I thought the sound of the chain saw had come. I hadn't gone far when I saw a pile of freshly cut wood. I kept going until I saw the fallen tree, but there was no sign of Davy.

"Davy?" I called. "Davy, where are you?"

There was no answer. Fearfully, ignoring the contraction that was starting, I stepped forward and pulled a limb aside and looked under the tree. Davy was lying there in a pool of blood. I cried out, pushing more branches aside to try to get to him. I finally had to get down on my knees and crawl.

When I reached him, I saw that he was unconscious but breathing. The trunk of the tree was not on him, but a smaller branch was pinning him down. The blood was coming from a deep, wide gash on his shoulder. There was a raised purple bruise on his forehead. I leaned over him and pressed hard on either side of the wound, knowing that the most urgent thing was to stop the bleeding.

"Davy! Davy, can you hear me?" I called. "Davy, wake up, please. Oh God, what am I going to do?"

I couldn't leave him. The pressure I was putting on either side of the wound had slowed the bleeding, but he had already lost a lot of blood. I couldn't risk him losing any more, but I needed to go for help, too. What was I to do?

I tried desperately to think. A tourniquet would work, but I had only my dress to make one of, and how to apply it to a shoulder so that it would be effective, I didn't know. If only he would regain consciousness, perhaps he could put pressure on the wound himself while I went for help.

"Davy, Davy, can you hear me? Davy, darling, please wake up."

There was no response. Despite my efforts, it seemed possible that he might lay there and die. I started to cry.

"Oh God, why doesn't someone come?" I sobbed aloud. "News travels so fast around here, why can't someone know about this and come help us? If these hills or trees really do talk, why don't they talk now?"

I knew that I was becoming hysterical, so I got a grip on myself. No one was going to come; the hills didn't actually talk and I knew that. Perhaps Clemmy would notice that I hadn't come back and send someone to look for me, but that might not be for some time. It was up to me. I would have to think of something. Davy's life depended on it.

A strong contraction hit me and I doubled over. I moaned but did not loosen my hands. Perhaps it was the cramped position I was in that made my contraction so strong. I moved carefully until I was sitting beside Davy.

I called as loudly as I could, hoping someone might be in the area and hear me. The woods remained silent. I started to feel light-headed. Surely I wasn't going to faint. I couldn't: Davy might bleed to death.

Something came crashing through the woods. My first thought was that it sounded like a bear, which would be drawn to Davy's blood on the ground. But a minute later someone was calling my name.

"In here," I cried, my heart thumping with relief. "I'm in here, under the tree. Please hurry. Davy's badly hurt."

The limbs parted, and Lewis Proctor's head appeared. He was beside me in a minute.

"He's lost so much blood," I sobbed, "and I can't rouse him. I'm afraid he's going to die."

Lewis felt Davy's pulse. "He's not going to die," he said calmly. "He's tough, he'll be all right, but we've got to get him out of here and to a doctor. Can you keep up the pressure while I clear away some of these limbs? Where's the chain saw? There it is. The noise will be bad, but it will only be for a few minutes. Hang on."

He started the chain saw and quickly cut off the limbs that surrounded Davy and me, holding onto each limb as he cut so it wouldn't fall on us. Once Davy roused and groaned. I spoke soothingly to him and he lapsed back into unconsciousness.

Lewis threw the chain saw aside, and suddenly Tom was beside us. He lifted me to my feet and put me aside, then knelt by his brother. I noticed that my hands were covered with blood. There was blood on my dress, too, but it didn't matter. However it had come, help had arrived. With both Tom and Lewis there, they would know what to do. I went over to a tree and leaned against it while another contraction washed over my body. Despite my labor, I had no time now to think of the baby.

Tom took his shirt off and bound it around Davy's shoulder, then he and Lewis lifted Davy and carried him out of the woods. I followed.

"Let's put him in th' back of th' truck," Tom said to Lewis. "That way we can lay him flat; we don't know what might be broke. You drive; I'll stay with him. Take it as easy as possible an' stop at Mom's. We'll get a mattress to lay him on, then you can hit th' gas when we get on th' highway."

Lewis jumped down from the back of the truck and went around to the driver's side. Tom, kneeling beside Davy, looked up at me.

"That ain't any of your blood, is it?"

"No, I'm not hurt. Take good care of him, Tom. I'll follow in my car."

"If you'll jist take th' time to unhitch th' mules there an' tie the reins up, they'll go home on their own."

The truck started up, and I was left standing there alone. I looked at the mules and wagon and almost decided to leave them as they were, but perhaps I had better do as Tom said. I put a hand on the rump of the nearest mule as Davy had instructed me, said "whoa" and reached for the reins. I had to stop for another contraction, but I succeeded in unhitching the mules from the wagon and starting them on their way. Then I got into my car and drove toward home.

When I got to the house, there was no one in sight, but I knew from the pall of dust on the road that the truck was not far ahead of me. I didn't stop, hoping to catch up with them.

I never did. The strength of the contractions slowed me down. Once I had to pull over to the side of the road and stop until it passed, then drive slowly on.

When I reached the hospital the truck was in the emergency room parking lot, but there was no one in sight. The lot was full so I had to drive to the visitor's lot to park, then walk back to the emergency room entrance. As I walked in, a nurse bustling around a corner stopped short at the sight of me, then came toward me. When she reached me, I was leaning against the wall, gasping and holding my stomach.

"Here, let me help you," she said, taking hold of my arm. "Have you been in an accident? Where are you hurt?"

"I'm not hurt. It was my husband. They've just brought him in."

"The concussion and shoulder wound? That's your husband? The doctor is with him now. Is it his blood you've got all over you?"

"Yes."

"Were you with him in the accident?"

"No. Is he all right?"

"We'll know something soon. How long have you been in labor?"

"Since about seven this morning."

"How far apart are the contractions?"

"I don't know, not far," I groaned, bending over again in pain.

"Hmm. About five minutes, I'd say. Who is your doctor?"

"Dr. Rommel."

"You're fortunate. He's on the staff here. Let's get you down to admitting."

"But my husband."

"Your husband is in good hands. He doesn't need you now but your baby does. Here, Nurse Johnson, put ..." she paused to look at the chart in her hand. "Mrs. Hilton, is it?"

"Anne Hilton," I said.

"Put Mrs. Hilton in a wheelchair and get her down to admitting. Have them call Dr. Rommel, right away."

She bustled off. I allowed the younger nurse to help me into a wheelchair and push me down the hall to the elevators. Tears were streaming down my cheeks. Davy was lying in a room somewhere, and I didn't even know if he was going to live or die. I couldn't be with him because I had to go have this baby, and he didn't even know about it. Another strong contraction hit me and I cried out, more from grief than pain. Tears poured down my face and I sobbed aloud. The young nurse panicked and took me straight down to obstetrics.

"What happened to her?" someone asked, as nurses gathered around me. "Was she in an accident?"

"I don't know," the young nurse said, sounding scared. "Nurse Owens just said ..."

"I wasn't in an accident," I interrupted tearfully. "It was my husband, it's his blood. He's seriously injured and I have to know how he is. He may be dying for all I know."

"Calm yourself," an older nurse pacified. "You have to think of your baby now."

"I can't think of my baby until I find out how my husband is," I said, still crying.

"Where is he? In emergency?"

"Yes."

"Nurse Johnson, go back down and find out how her husband is. Let us know as soon as possible. Nurse Dalton, help me get her stripped and cleaned up. What is your name and who is your doctor?"

"Dr. Rommel, and my name is Mrs. David Hilton," I replied morosely.

"Go call Dr. Rommel."

"He's out of town."

"Dr. Rommel is out of town?" I wailed. "Am I going to have this baby completely alone?"

"Dr. Rommel's partner, Dr. Caldwell, is a fine doctor, too. He'll take good care of you. You won't be alone."

That wasn't what I meant, but I didn't bother to explain. I let them clean me up and put me in a hospital gown, and then into a bed. By that time the young nurse was back.

"Your husband is going to be okay," she said. "They're getting ready to sew up his shoulder. He has a concussion, but the doctor says he's going to be fine. He's regained consciousness and is perfectly coherent. The doctor says he'll have no permanent damage."

"Thank you," I said. I laid back and tried to relax as another contraction started.

Less than an hour later I heard the words I'd been waiting nine months to hear.

"You have a baby girl."

I closed my eyes in exhaustion but opened them again when they laid the baby on my chest. I put my hand on her and raised my head to look. She was red and wrinkled, her face screwed up in what looked like rage, crying lustily. She had a thatch of dark hair, and she was so tiny. I started to laugh and cry at the same time.

"She's all right?" I asked anxiously.

"One hundred percent all right, I'd say, from the sound of her," the nurse replied.

"But she's so tiny. She's not premature?"

"Not at all. She's not so tiny for a first baby. She's all of six pounds, I'd say."

I put my head back on the pillow, feeling completely drained, but I kept my hand on the baby until the nurse lifted her and wrapped her in a blanket.

"Time to get this little lady down to the nursery and cleaned up," she said.

"I wish my husband could have been here," I said, fresh tears spilling down my cheeks.

"We don't allow husbands in the delivery room, you know."

"I know, but he was planning on being with me until I went to the delivery room. As it is, he doesn't even know I've had her."

"He'll know soon enough. First things first, you know."

"Do you know how he is?"

"No, but I'll find out for you. You just relax now and let

the doctor finish with you. By the time we get you to your room, I should have some information."

"Thank you. Take good care of her," I said, as she carried my baby from the room, still crying.

When they got me to my room I was very drowsy, but I wouldn't let myself go to sleep until the nurse who had promised to get news of Davy came back.

She returned with good news. "He's got a concussion and something like thirty stitches in his shoulder, but nothing is broken. The doctor says he'll be up and around in a few days."

"Does he know about the baby?"

"I'm sorry, I don't know. They gave him a painkiller, and he was asleep when I was down there."

"It doesn't matter, as long as he's all right. Thank you, you've been very kind."

I went to sleep then. They woke me a short time later when they brought the baby to me. I sat up and held out my arms. I held her against me and gazed down into her sleeping face. She was a little less red, and they had brushed her hair and put a tiny pink bow in it. She was adorable. I was thrilled to be holding her at last, all the pain of having her forgotten. The only disappointing thing about it was that Davy couldn't be there to share this experience with me.

That night, just before I went to sleep, I had a moment to ponder what had happened to Tom and Lewis. Had they just gone home and totally forgotten about me? It seemed strangely unlike Lewis; he had always been so considerate. Their disappearance puzzled me, but the question soon faded from my mind as I quickly drifted off to sleep.

CHAPTER TWENTY-SIX

Lewis's Confession

*I*n the morning I was eager to see Davy.

"I want to see my husband," I said petulantly when the nurse came in to check on me.

"You'll have to wait and see the doctor about that," she replied.

"When will he be in?"

"He's here now. He'll be in to see you soon."

She took my breakfast tray and left the room. I waited impatiently, watching every person who went by my open door. They'd brought my baby in earlier, only to take her away too soon. I wanted to keep her with me for awhile, but they wouldn't hear of it. It was against policy, they said. It was also against policy for me to go down to the nursery to see her or to go downstairs to see my husband. I felt fine except for a little soreness, and I wanted to be up. I was concerned about Davy, but no one seemed to know how he was or be willing to take the time to find out. The nurse who had been so helpful the night before was off duty.

At last the doctor came in. I hardly recognized him; I'd seen so little of his face the day before. He was very complimentary about the baby, having checked her over before he came to see me.

"I want to know how my husband is and no one will tell me," I said as he was checking me over. "I want to go to his room and see him for myself, and if he's able, I want him to see the baby."

"Perhaps we can arrange for you to be taken down in a wheelchair to see him this afternoon," he offered, "but as far as him seeing the baby, I'm afraid that will be impossible until he's able to come to the nursery himself. We can't allow the baby to be taken from this area. You're doing just fine, Mrs. Hilton. Just stay in bed and do as the nurses tell you. You'll be up and ready to go home in six days."

"Six days! But I feel fine. Why do I have to stay here for six days?"

"It's policy. We find that if we let new mothers go home too soon, they tend to overdo it. That could have some serious, lasting aftereffects."

I was silenced. I looked over at the woman in the bed next to me. "Then could I possibly have my husband in the room with me?"

"I'm afraid not. We don't allow male patients in the maternity ward."

"Then could I be put in a room with him?"

He shook his head. "It's against policy."

I sighed. "I might have known."

"You want to be near your baby, don't you?"

"Yes."

"Relax, Mrs. Hilton. Six days is not forever. You'll soon be back in your own home with your family around you. I'll see you again this evening."

"Dr. Caldwell?"

"Yes?"

"I must see my husband as soon as possible."

"I'll see what I can do."

It wasn't until after lunch that a nurse came for me and took me down in a wheelchair to the second floor where Davy was. He was lying in bed, a dark bruise on his forehead, his shoulder heavily bandaged. He looked pale and exhausted, but when they wheeled me in, his face lit up. He raised his head, then winced and put it back on the pillow.

"Davy, are you all right?" I asked, almost crying. He reached for my hand, closing his over mine, his head turned toward me. I leaned forward and kissed him.

"Just fifteen minutes," the nurse said as she left us.

"A fine husband I am, sawing a tree down on myself just as my wife's about to have our baby," he said. "Are you okay?"

"I'm just fine, Davy. So they told you about the baby?"

"Yes. How is she? Wisht I could see her."

"I tried to arrange it but they say it's against policy. When you're able to be up in a wheelchair, they said you can come to the nursery and see her."

"What's she look like? Does she look like you?"

"I don't think so. I don't think she looks like anyone but herself. She has dark hair and dark eyes, but all the nurses say that will probably change. She's beautiful, Davy, so perfectly formed, every tiny finger and toe in place."

"Where'd you expect her fingers an' toes to be?"

"Well, sometimes you worry about those things, you know. But she's perfect. I can't wait for you to see her. They won't let me have her for very long at a time. I can't wait until we can all go home and be together, and I can hold her whenever I want to. Davy, it's so wonderful, actually holding her in my arms after all this time."

"Bet it is. Did you have a hard time havin' her?"

"Not too bad. It was well worth it. I was just sorry that you couldn't experience it with me."

"I'm sorry, too, real sorry."

"It's all right, Davy, you'll be there next time. How did the accident happen?"

"Ain't real sure. Think I tripped over a root or somethin'. Th' chain saw come up an' cut my shoulder, then I saw th' tree comin' down on me. That's about all I remember."

"What happened to Lewis and Tom? Did they go on home after they saw you were going to be all right?"

"Don't know. Didn't see them after they brought me in to stitch me up. You didn't see them?"

"Not a sign of them."

"You mean you was totally alone when you had th' baby?"

"Yes, if you mean as far as having anyone I knew there. Even Dr. Rommel was out of town; a Dr. Caldwell delivered the baby. But it's all right, Davy," I added quickly when he started looking disturbed. "I hardly had time to think about it. The baby came just an hour after I got here."

"Time's up," the nurse said, bustling in and taking hold of my wheelchair. I barely had time to kiss Davy again before she wheeled me out.

I had visitors that evening. Jim and Liz stopped by the hospital on their way home. I got up and went to the nursery with them, and no one tried to stop me. The nurse moved my baby closer to the window, while Liz and I cooed and admired her. Jim was strangely silent.

"Well, Jim, what do you think of her?" I asked. "Isn't she beautiful?"

He scratched his head while he studied the baby. "Well," he said, "'pears to me she's th' spittin' image of ol' Grandpa Hilton. You didn't never see him, a course, but he was all red-faced and shriveled an' didn't have no teeth, either. Course she's got a sight more hair than he had."

"Jim!" Liz protested, hitting him on the arm. "What an awful thing to say!"

Jim grinned, and I laughed. "It's all right, Liz. I guess no newborn baby is actually beautiful except to its own mother. Just you wait, though, until your own baby comes in a couple of months. Then we'll see how beautiful she is."

"We're gonna have a boy, an' boys don't have to be beautiful."

"Think so?"

"Yep. I done put in my order."

"Well, Davy requested a girl and got her, so perhaps you will have your boy."

"How's ol' Davy doin'? Hear you guys had quite a lot of excitement out your way yesterday."

"You should have called me," Liz said reproachfully. "I was right here in town. I would have come so you didn't have to be all alone."

"I'm sorry, Liz, I didn't even think about it; it all happened so fast and I was so worried about Davy. They pretty well took me into the delivery room as soon as I got here, and no one is allowed in there."

"Just the same ..."

"I'm sorry. There was no time, but it turned out all right."

"What if it hadn't?"

"I don't know. I didn't even think about that. All I could think about was whether Davy would be all right."

"How's he doin' now?"

"He's better. Of course his shoulder is painful, and he's still weak from losing all that blood. He had a headache, too, when they let me see him earlier this afternoon."

"Has he seen the baby yet?"

"No. They won't let him up, and they won't take her to him. I'm hoping he'll get to see her tomorrow."

"That's a shame. Have you named her yet?"

"Not officially. I haven't had a chance to talk to Davy about it; they only let me stay with him for a few minutes at a time. But we'll probably name her Annabel Lee."

"That's pretty. Mom wanted to know. I called her this morning, as soon as I found out myself."

"None of this has gone as planned, Liz. I haven't done anything except have the baby and worry about Davy. I'll call Mom this afternoon."

"Do you think they'd let us see Davy, if we promised to stay just a few minutes?"

"Maybe. Try anyhow. I know he'd be glad to see you."

"We'd better be going then. Is there anything you need?

We can stop by again tomorrow evening."

"No, nothing. Oh, yes there is. Can you stop by the house and pack a suitcase for me? Just bring a change of clothes for all of us, if you will, including the baby."

"What specifically shall I bring?"

I told her what to bring, then walked with them down the hallway for a short distance. It felt good to be up and around. "Bye, Jim. Bye, Liz. Thanks so much for coming."

"The baby is darling," Liz said.

"You take care of yourself," Jim said. "An' I'm sorry I said th' baby looks like Grampa Hilton, even if she does."

"See you tomorrow."

When they were gone I went back to the nursery and stood before the wide window that separated me from my baby. I was still standing there gazing at her when someone put their hand on my arm. I turned. It was Sue and Lewis.

"Hello," I said, surprised and pleased. I returned Sue's hug and took the hand Lewis held out to me. "How nice to see you. Look what I did," I said proudly, indicating the baby. Just then she stretched and yawned widely before settling back to sleep.

"Oh, she's adorable," Sue said. "I'm so happy for you."

"I'm surprised you're even speaking to me," Lewis said glumly.

"Why Lewis, why?"

"For running off and leaving you to have your baby all alone like that," Sue broke in indignantly. "I couldn't believe it when he told me."

"I forgot," he said simply. "We were so worried about getting Davy to the doctor that I completely forgot Clemmy told me you were in labor."

"Oh, it was Clemmy who told you. I wondered how it was that you happened to come. But she didn't know Davy had been hurt, did she?"

"No. It was you she was worried about. I came to bring

the mules back, and she asked me to go make sure you'd found Davy all right. When I heard you calling for help and saw Davy lying there unconscious and bleeding, I forgot everything else. I'm sorry."

"It's all right, Lewis. You and Tom rescued Davy and got him here in time, that's all that matters. But how did Tom know about it?"

"He'd been out hunting and heard you honking the car horn—thought he'd better investigate. When he came closer, he heard you calling for help, too. In all fairness, he didn't know you were in labor until we were almost home."

"Almost home?"

"Yes. After the doctor had stitched Davy up, he told us we could go on home because they'd given Davy something to make him sleep and he wouldn't be awake until morning. So we got in the truck and started home. About halfway there, I remembered you. I slammed on the brakes so hard I almost threw Tom through the windshield. He asked what was wrong, and I told him. I asked him if he'd seen you follow us into town. He said you'd said you were going to, but he didn't see you. Then he said, 'Oh Lord, I told her to unhitch the mules from the wagon. You don't s'pose she got kicked or somethin'?' I didn't know what to do, go back to the hospital to see if you were there or go home and look for you. We decided we'd better go on home, because if you'd come on into the hospital, you'd be all right, but if you'd been kicked by the mules ... Talk about burning up the road. We were scared to death, both of us. When we got to Davy's folks, Tom and I both piled out of that truck and ran up to the house so fast we scared Clemmy half to death. We both asked 'Where's Anne?' She said she'd gone back into the house after we left with Davy, because she was going to change her clothes and come in with you, but you didn't stop, you just drove on by. We still didn't know what had happened to you, whether you'd had an accident or what.

So I drove back to the hospital, and they said you'd had the baby and you were both fine. I couldn't see you because it was after visiting hours and you were asleep. So I drove back to Clemmy's and told her everything was all right, then went home and collapsed. Can you ever forgive me?"

"Lewis, there's nothing at all to forgive. You saved Davy and that's all that matters. I was never so thankful to see anyone in my whole life. I was afraid Davy was going to bleed to death before I could get help. I didn't even think of stopping at Clemmy's. All I thought about was catching up to the truck so I could be with Davy when you got him to the hospital. I never did catch up with you, and when I got here, they took me straight down to obstetrics. The baby was born just an hour later. I did wonder what had become of you and Tom, but not to any great extent. The baby was okay, and they told me Davy was going to be all right, so I forgot about anything else and went to sleep. Anyway, I bet I got a much better night's sleep than you did," I ended, laughing.

"I didn't get any sleep at all," he admitted. "Especially after Sue lit into me."

"Oh, Sue, you shouldn't have. I was all right."

"But to have to go through that all alone, especially after the way you stood by me when I had little David."

"The circumstances were entirely different. I was at a hospital, I had a good doctor—even though he wasn't mine."

"You didn't even get to have your own doctor?"

"No, he was out of town," I said, laughing. "Nothing went as planned, but it really wasn't that bad. I had a much shorter and easier labor than most women have with their first baby, or so the nurses tell me. And look who I have to show for it."

"She's beautiful. It's a shame Davy hasn't had a chance to see her. He must feel awful about that."

"He does, but he'll get to see her tomorrow. Meanwhile, I'm enjoying her enough for both of us. I never knew babies were so wonderful. I may decide to have a dozen."

"There you are!" a nurse exclaimed, coming toward me. "We've been looking all over for you. You've been gone from your room almost an hour. Time you were getting back to your bed. Visiting hours are over for this section, folks."

"Bye, Sue. Bye, Lewis. Thanks for coming, and do run by to see Davy for just a minute. Tell Clemmy we're all fine."

"We will, and congratulations again, Anne, she's adorable."

CHAPTER TWENTY-SEVEN

Annabel Lee

*D*espite the hospital's policy, the next morning I sneaked down to the nursery to peek at my little girl.

"There you are," a nurse said. "I might have known I'd find you here."

I turned from the nursery window. "She's crying," I said. "It breaks my heart that I can't pick her up and hold her."

"It doesn't hurt a baby to cry a little, it's good for them. I came to tell you a nurse is bringing your husband down to see the baby. They should be here any minute."

"Oh good, but I wish he didn't have to see her for the first time when she's crying."

"He'd better get used to it."

She hurried off and I turned back to the window. Soon Davy was beside me in a wheelchair, looking pale and shaky, his arm in a sling. The purple bruise on his forehead was turning a sickly yellow.

"Which one is her?" he asked.

"The one who's crying. I wish they'd come pick her up. Oh good, here comes the nurse now."

The nurse did pick her up, putting her over her shoulder to pat and soothe her. She stopped crying and held her head up. It bobbed unsteadily, but she kept it up while she looked around with bright, inquisitive eyes, her mouth in a round, concentrated 'o'.

"Oh Davy, look how bright and alert she is," I said. "Isn't she beautiful?"

He didn't say anything, but his eyes were glued to his

daughter. The nurse smiled at us and brought her closer, turning her face to the window. She seemed to be squinting to see us.

Davy held out his arms and mouthed the words "Can I hold her?" I was sorry for him, feeling that the answer would be "It's against policy." But the nurse spoke to another nurse, who soon came out to where we were with a white gown and a mask. She proceeded to put them on Davy. Then the first nurse came out with the baby and laid her in his good arm.

"We couldn't do this, you understand, if anyone else was out here with you," she said, "and it can only be for a minute."

"Thank you."

Davy held his daughter, who lay staring up at him, as if she were trying to figure out who he was. He put his finger near her hand; she grasped it and held on. I couldn't see much of Davy's face—just his eyes, which never left the baby—but I saw him swallow and knew how moved he was. The baby was bright and alert. When I spoke to her, she turned her face toward the sound. A moment later the nurse was taking her from us.

"Feeding time in half an hour, Mama," she reminded me as she took the baby back to the nursery.

"Well, what do you think?" I asked Davy, when I had helped him remove the mask and gown.

"She's somethin' else," he said, his voice subdued.

"They're asking me for a name for her records. Annabel Lee?"

He nodded.

"Good. I'm glad you like the name, too; it fits her somehow. I've been calling her that already."

"She's somethin' else," he repeated, shaking his head in wonder.

"Isn't she? I can't wait to get her home so I can hold her

more, and you can, too. Davy, how are you feeling?"

"Kinda weak in th' knees, but otherwise, not too bad."

"Your headache is better?"

"Yes. How about you?"

"I feel fine. I wish I could go home sooner, but the doctor said not for three more days. Davy, did you notice that little red place on the side of Annabel's nose?"

"Yes. Looked like a little broken blood vessel to me. Why?"

"I asked the doctor about it, and he said it's a small birthmark, not at all unusual in newborns. It will fade and probably go away entirely in a few weeks."

"Okay. Is it worryin' you or somethin'?"

I swallowed. "There's another one exactly like it in the middle of her back, only it's a little larger."

"It won't show if it's on her back."

"No, I know."

"What's botherin' you?"

"Do you remember what your mother said when I shot that snake?"

"Yes, I remember. What about it?"

"I shot that snake in the head and in the middle of the back. Now Annabel has birthmarks in exactly those same places."

He looked surprised, then grinned. "You're not gettin' superstitious in your old age, are you?"

"No, but you'll have to admit, it's a very strange coincidence. It's no wonder some people think ..." I paused and shook my head. "No, it can't be. It's impossible."

"If th' doctor says it's common in babies, then that's why she's got them. Don't have nothin' to do with you shootin' th' snake. If that was true, what would you findin' me under the tree like that have done to her?"

"Yes, that's true. I know it's just a coincidence, but it does seem strange. I can see why people might believe it."

"Doctor says I might be able to go home tomorrow."

"No, Davy, you can't!"

"Why can't I?"

"You can't go home without Annabel and me. We want to go home, too."

"Didn't you say th' doctor said you had to stay six days?"

"Yes, but there's no reason for it, it's just policy. I'm in better shape than you are, and the baby is fine. Please don't go home without us."

"You'll have to ask your doctor. If you can get him to agree to it, it's fine with me."

"I'll talk to him when he comes in tonight. I'm sure he'll agree. You just wait, Davy, so we can all go home together."

The doctor didn't come that evening, so I had to wait until morning to talk to him. He was late, perhaps because it was Saturday morning. I had almost given up on him when my own doctor walked through the door.

"Well, young lady, decided not to wait for me, did you?" was his greeting.

"Dr. Rommel, it's good to see you. Can I go home today?"

"Why today? Aren't they treating you right?"

"They've been very good, but my husband is going home today and I want to go, too."

"Your husband?"

"Oh, you haven't heard about the accident?"

I was explaining it to him when my parents walked in. I was surprised and overjoyed to see them. I had just talked to my mother on the telephone the day before. I knew she wanted to come but didn't think it would be this soon.

"Now you have to let me go home, Dr. Rommel," I said. "Mom will take real good care of me and the baby, won't you, Mom? I won't have to do a thing but lie around and take it easy. Please, Dr. Rommel."

"I'm staying a week," Mama stated. "I'll see that she takes it easy."

"All right," Dr. Rommel said. "On those conditions, I'll let you go. You're young and healthy and you shouldn't have any problems, just don't be on your feet too much, and don't do any lifting. Don't lift anything heavier than the baby."

"All right, Dr. Rommel, I won't, and thank you very much."

"And now I want to see my granddaughter," Mama said when he was gone. "Where is the nursery?"

"I'll show you. I want the nurse to let Davy know we're going home, too. I'm so glad you came, especially when you did. They were going to make me stay until Monday."

An hour later we were ready to leave the hospital. They made me get into a wheelchair, though I was perfectly capable of walking. While one nurse pushed me down the hall, another followed, carrying Annabel. Mama and Daddy followed them, carrying my things and those the hospital was sending home for Annabel. We met Davy in another wheelchair with another nurse at the front entrance of the hospital. We made quite a group as we went out the door and across the parking lot to my parent's car.

"Oh, I forgot," I said. "My car is still here, too."

"Your mother can drive you home," Daddy said. "I'll follow in your car."

"Thank you, Daddy."

I got into the front seat of my parent's car, and the nurse put Annabel in my arms. Daddy took Davy's arm and helped him into the back seat. They piled the suitcase and the packages in with him, then the nurses went away. I gave Daddy my car keys, while Mama got into the driver's seat.

"We'll have to make a stop on the way home to pick up Calvin," I told Daddy as he turned away.

"All right," he said affably. "He can ride with me."

"What's gotten into Daddy?" I asked as we drove away.

"How do you mean?"

"Bringing you here without a fuss—I assume it was without a fuss. You told me on the phone you thought you might have to take the bus. Then being so helpful to Davy and so ... well, so agreeable about everything—even volunteering to let Calvin ride with him. Has something happened?"

"Not that I know of. You'll have to tell me where to go."

"Left at the next corner," I said, my mind still on my father. "I don't know. He seems different somehow. Maybe I'm just comparing his manner now to the last couple of times I saw him. Well, whatever is responsible for the change, I'm thankful for it."

CHAPTER TWENTY-EIGHT

A Happy Ending

*I*t was early Sunday afternoon. We were all sitting around the living room: Mama and Daddy, Liz and Jim, Davy and I, Calvin, and of course, the new addition to our family and the center of attention, little Annabel.

"It's so good to be home," I said with a sigh. "That was a delicious meal, Mama, thank you."

"With all that good home-grown food Clemmy sent over, how could it help but be good?" Mama replied. She was sitting in the rocker with the baby in her arms, rocking gently. She wanted to invite Jim and Liz over for a meal before Daddy had to leave for St. Louis, but it hadn't been necessary. They came over in the middle of the morning, and so far it had been a pleasant, relaxing day. I was feeling quite affectionate toward my father. He hadn't joined in the conversation a lot, but he had done nothing to distract from the harmony of the day. Both Davy and Jim were making an effort to be deferential toward him. Calvin had been very quiet since we got home, but that was not unusual for him when there were other people around. There would be plenty of time for him to get acquainted with the baby when our company left.

"I thought some of your neighbors or Davy's relatives would be dropping in to see the baby today," Mama said. "But perhaps they don't know you're home yet."

"They know," Jim said. "But they know you folks are here, too, an' they wouldn't be wantin' to intrude. They'll come after you leave an' th' teacher an' Davy get back on their feet."

"Oh I see. That's wise. Too often, people are not that considerate. But how do they know Davy and Anne and the baby are home and we're here, since there are no telephones?"

Jim shrugged. "Word gets around," he said.

"It surely does," I added. "I've sworn more than once that these hills talk. Everyone always seems to know what everybody else is doing, sometimes almost before they know it themselves. I even thought ..." I stopped. Embarrassed, I looked at Davy.

"You thought what?" Liz asked.

I laughed. "I guess I was getting hysterical or something, but when I found Davy hurt and bleeding so badly, I didn't know what to do. I had to stay with him to put pressure on the wound to slow the bleeding, and I didn't know how in the world I was going to let anyone know we needed help. I knew it would be some time before anyone missed us, and by then it might be too late. So when Lewis came so soon, I thought, well, I thought maybe the hills really did talk and they'd told Lewis. I know how silly that sounds; it wasn't the hills talking at all. It was just Clemmy being her usual sweet, concerned self. She was afraid I might not be able to find Davy right away and sent Lewis after me. I've never been so glad to see anyone in my life."

I glanced apprehensively at my father. He probably thought I'd lost my mind, but he was looking at me thoughtfully.

"Speaking of telephones," he said, "Where is the nearest one?"

"You know that nice brick farmhouse at the end of the dirt road—where it joins the highway? That's the Owen Miller home. They let us use their telephone whenever we want."

"Do you suppose they'd let me use it?"

"I don't know why not, they're very hospitable people. Just tell them you're my father."

"I believe I'll go call my boss and tell him I've decided to take a week of my vacation. That is, if the two of you don't mind my staying here with your mother?"

"We'd love to have you, Daddy, wouldn't we, Davy?"

"Sure would, sir," Davy said. Though he tried to hide it, I could see that he was as surprised as me.

"Coming here yesterday, Calvin mentioned something about a good fishing hole nearby," Daddy continued, looking at Davy. "I haven't been fishing for a good long while. Any chance of doing some while I'm here?"

"Any time, sir. Cal can show you where the good fishing holes are, an' maybe I can join you in a couple days. I haven't been fishin' myself for months."

"Evenin's th' time to go fishin'," Jim spoke up, trying to hide the eagerness in his voice. "I get home by 6:00. If you go some evenin', I'd sure like to go along."

"Sounds good," Daddy said. "Well, I'll go on in and make that call. I'll be back in a little while."

He rose from his chair and went out. We all sat in dead silence for a long moment, looking at each other. Liz was the first to break the silence.

"Will wonders never cease?" she asked. "What's going on, Mama? And don't tell me it's his first grandchild who has softened him because I won't believe it. He's never paid the least bit of attention to babies."

"Anne asked me almost the same question yesterday," Mama replied. "I've been thinking about it, and I guess it must be what Mary said when she came back from visiting here. She sat up late and talked to both of us the night before she went home. She told us a little about the problems she and Kevin were having and how much you helped her, Davy."

Looking surprised, Davy glanced quickly at me. I thought I had been able to help her some, too, but perhaps Mary had a reason for mentioning only Davy's help. Daddy was very proud to have Kevin for a son-in-law: he was an airplane pilot, a prestigious job in Daddy's opinion. Daddy had introduced Mary to Kevin and encouraged their marriage. Perhaps the fact that their marriage was in trouble and Davy had been able to help had affected him. I could see Mary deliberately using that reasoning to help our cause.

"Mary talked a lot about the peace and quiet out here," Mama continued as she rocked gently, her eyes on Annabel. "She told us about that school trip she took with the two of you and how good both of you were with the children. She also mentioned how much you loved teaching out here, Anne. She said that she thought the way you and Davy live is so much more natural and healthy than the way she and Kevin do. She told us about your house, too, Liz—the way you and Jim were working together to fix it up and how happy you both were. She was even thinking of asking Kevin if he might consider the two of them moving out here to join you. Your dad didn't say much, but I could see he was impressed. Since then, he hasn't said anything. ..." Mama stopped and looked at us apprehensively.

"Go ahead and finish, Mama," Liz said dryly. "We all know how Daddy feels about Davy and Jim. You were going to say he hasn't said anything especially derogatory about them since then, weren't you?"

"Well, yes," she said apologetically.

"Dear Mary," I said. "Always the peacemaker. It was sweet of her to do that for us. It may very well be what has softened him. Mary always was his favorite."

"Not his favorite, Anne, but she is the oldest, and he has always been closer to her than the two of you. You'll find out; there's always a special bond with your oldest child."

"It's all right, Mama. We don't mind, do we, Liz? Now if you and Jim can just take him where he can catch a few big fish, Davy, we're home and dry."

"I know jist th' place," Davy said. "Remember where we

used to go fishin' all th' time when we was growin' up?" he asked Jim. "Haven't been there for years, but I know it's still there, an' not fished out. It's too far back in th' woods."

"Don't take him there 'til I can come along," Jim said.

"Can I go, too?" Calvin asked.

"Sure you can, kid. All th' menfolk will go an' leave th' womenfolk home to tend to th' cookin' an' th' baby."

"Suits me," I said.

"If the two of you can contrive a way to let Daddy catch everything," Liz said, "you might really get somewhere with him."

"We can at least let him catch th' most," Jim said.

"This calls for a celebration," I said. "Let's make some ice cream."

"You sit still, Anne," Mama said. "If there's ice cream to be made, I'll make it. And how about a big chocolate cake to go with it? Your dad loves chocolate cake."

"Sounds great to me," Jim said. "Me an' Cal'll take turns turnin' th' handle for you when you get th' ice cream made. That way you can get at th' cake."

Mama rose and started to give Annabel to me, but Davy held out his arms.

"Let me have her," he said. Mama laid her in his arms.

"You're all going to spoil that baby rotten, holding her all the time," Liz said.

"Probably," I said, " but it's such fun. Just wait until you have your own."

"Do you think your mother and father would come over later for cake and ice cream if we invited them?" Mama asked Davy.

"Mom might. Don't know about Dad."

"We'll invite them anyway. Where's the ice cream freezer, Anne? Do you have enough ice? We should have had your dad drive to town and get some."

"We've got some at the house," Liz said. "Jim can go get it."

"I'll do 'er," Jim said agreeably. "Want to ride along, Cal? I'll let you have a try at drivin' th' truck."

Calvin's whole face lit up as he went out the door with Jim. Mama went to the kitchen, and Liz rose to join her. I got up and went to stand beside my husband and child.

I stood with my hand on Davy's shoulder, looking down at the baby in his arms. I put my other hand on Annabel's soft hair and stroked it gently.

"It's all so wonderful, isn't it, Davy?" I asked softly. "She is so precious."

"She's a miracle," Davy said.

"In spite of the accident and everything else that has happened lately, everything worked out so well. I feel as if I could almost burst with happiness. Are you as happy as I am, Davy?"

"You jist bet I am," he said, reaching up to pull me down so he could kiss me.

"When you two lovebirds are through billing and cooing in there," Liz said from the kitchen doorway, "come on in the kitchen, Anne, and show us where the ice cream freezer is. Otherwise, you're not going to have any ice cream to go with the cake."

"Coming," I said.

The End

Don't miss these other great "Hills" titles by Letha Boyer...

These Lonesome Hills

Anne Davis is full of youthful optimism when she leaves St. Louis for the Ozark hills to teach in a one-room, eight-grade schoolhouse. Eager to broaden her rural students' horizons, she finds her efforts thwarted by the overpowering forces of tradition, ignorance and poverty. How can she gain the support of a hostile community? Will Anne follow her heart and find happiness in these lonesome hills? *Quality Soft Cover*, **0017**, **$6.95.**

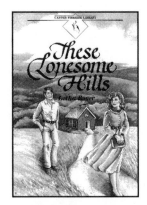

Home in the Hills

Newlyweds Anne and Davy Hilton begin their marriage living with his parents, while Davy builds their home. Anne continues her crusade to improve her students' lives, only to find herself drawn into family dilemmas in the poor Missouri Ozarks community. How can she help Calvin, her special student, escape the clutches of Granny Eldridge? Can Anne and Davy make a home in the hills? *Quality Soft Cover*, **0006**, **$6.95.**

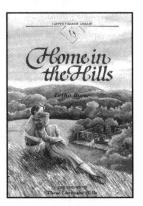

Of These Contented Hills

Anne and Davy's whirlwind first year of marriage includes raising a 12-year-old, planning Anne's sister's country wedding and contending with the volatile family situation of one of Anne's most promising students. Anne is caught off guard by her father's firm disapproval of Davy and her sister's new husband—will the family be reunited? Will they find contentment in these Ozark hills? *Quality Soft Cover*, **0033**, **$6.95.**

To Order: Call toll-free, 1-800-678-5779, ext. 4316, and charge to MasterCard, VISA or Discover. Or send check or money order to Capper Press, 1503 S.W. 42nd St.,Topeka, KS 66609.